PETALS OF A ROSE

Written by Lydia Trent

www.hermitmedia.co.uk

Published by Hermit Media

England 2014

Published June 2014 by Hermit Media Ltd. PO Box 804,Haywards Heath, England, RH16 9LB

Printed by T J International Ltd. Trecerus Industrial Estate, Padstow, England, PL28 8RW

ISBN : 978-0-9927180-2-2

This book is dedicated to my dad, my sister and my brother

Chapter One

'How do you plead, guilty or not guilty?'

Rose stared blankly at the man in the wig, following the sound, her head juggling with a million scattered bits of thought but none of them making any sense. A pretty one floated past, a pink thought. She put her hands up and grabbed it. She was laughing and jumping up and down, the sun shining down on her. In her hand she held the letter which would change her life, the letter of admission to the University. Josie and her mum and dad were there too. Everyone was happy. Rose's face turned and smiled at her, getting bigger and bigger in the pink thought, so close that she didn't like it.

'Again, how do you plead, guilty or not guilty?'

The pink thought went away. A man took her hand and called her name from somewhere far away. She turned her head to follow the voice but it was all too foggy, making her dizzy, so she closed her eyes.

'Your Honour, she pleads not guilty on the grounds of diminished responsibility.'

Chapter Two

The light of day slipped quietly by as evening fell on the tiny room. The bright, yellow flowers which busied themselves on the wall slithered and merged into one, mimicking the colour of the wet patches which hid beneath the window and escaped into the corners. The ghost of dampness clung silently as the coldness grew. The once–pink candlewick bedspread, plucked into smoothness, knew the cold and damp as old friends, adding to the chill which filled Rose as she shivered upon its edge.

Her head hung limply in her cold hands. A dark stain seeped through her skirt, soaked by the tears which slid unnoticed from her face. Time sneaked by as she huddled in the grip of damp twilight. She would have to move soon before her mother came to see where she was, what was wrong. She didn't want to explain yet. She didn't want to explain ever.

The metal–springed bed sighed with relief as she got up, her tiny frame sending small shudders through its aged spine. Drawn to the window despite its whispering draught, she leant her head against it. She often stood there lost in the darkness to look out, not think, her head becoming colder and colder as the night fought to force its way in. She needed to feel part of her small bit of the world, to make sure that it hadn't changed. All was as it should be, as it always was, but it held no reassurances tonight.

The yard below was smothered in darkness, hiding its secrets till morning, just like all of the other yards filed like dominoes, silently giving cover to tykes prowling the alleys, looking for mischief. She hated the yard with its high walls and stale smells, its uneven paving which wriggled to trick you in the dark. She raised her head heavenwards, eagerly searching the sky, her imagination straining to follow the twinkling, guiding lights to some faraway place filled with new people, new sights, new adventures; places where she was someone. But the sky wasn't playing tonight. It hid its stars from her, veiled behind a white mist and denying her comfort.

The loud click of a latch broke the silence and the yard glowed with light. The privy door opened wide and with another click the light was gone. The hunched figure scuttled into the house. Her mother would deny ever going there if she could, but instead she crept in and out like the mice which scurried through the rubbish piles in the alleys. Rose would smile, amused by such prudishness, wondering not for the first time how she could be the product of such a woman; but not tonight. She slid to the side of the window, hiding in the shadows of the curtains. She didn't want anyone to see her yet. She had to prepare herself to seem normal but hadn't yet figured out what normal must now become.

'Tea's ready, Rose.'

Rose swallowed and heaved a sigh. She must concentrate on anything except what governed her thoughts. She mustn't give herself away. Her mother would take some shaking if she sensed that there was anything wrong, like a dog with a gnarled bone scraping every last morsel. Rose straightened her skirt, hoping that the damp patch would go unnoticed. Brushing her short, black hair, she winced at the redness of her eyes. Oh well, nothing she could do about it.

The neatness of the small, square room focused Rose as she struggled to imitate the neat control over her thoughts. A small kitchen was attached at the back, not quite big enough to eat in. They were the envy of the street having a kitchen, however small, since the other houses had only a cellar–head. The magnolia which streaked across the walls was painted thickly in an effort to make the whole place look bright and big. It did the trick much more efficiently than the other houses with their gaudy, multi–coloured wallpapers. Whilst time took its toll and the wallpapers became dingy and discoloured from the fire smoke, Alice would be busy once again with her paintbrush and paint. She was always one step ahead in her strive for perfection.

The fold-down dining table was opened up against the back wall, tucked in a corner. Alice and Bert had already begun eating. A smile passed between father and daughter which said everything that needed to be said.

"ad a good day, luv,' he asked.

'Yes, ta, dad. 'Ow 'bout you?'

'Fine ta. Liverpool today it wer.'

'Never mind all that,' interrupted her mother, 'haven't you got something to tell me?'

Rose froze. Ice raced through her blood, starting at the back of her neck. Her thoughts ran aimlessly, bumping into each other, confusing. What did her mother ask? What was the answer?

Rose hated going to Doctor Pearce. He reminded her of a priest waiting for a confession, eager to deliver his penance. She didn't know why but he always made her feel guilty. His eyes — small, black holes buried in his ruddy face — would peer accusingly at her over his half-glasses, waiting for the confession of her sins. He smelt too. Perhaps he was the one with the guilty conscience, with his smell and his lecherous glare. Or maybe she just imagined it. Anyway, she didn't like him. But she had to see him, so she sat there in his waiting room full of coughing, sneezing, pale people and waited.

Winter was a silly time to come and see a doctor. You were more likely to come out with something nasty after having sat in that room full of sickies. She hoped that nobody would notice that she wasn't coughing and sneezing. They might have asked what was wrong with her. No, they would have asked. People could be so nosy. It gave them something to talk to their friends about.

'I saw Ethel in the docs.'

'What wer wrong wi' 'er?'

'I dunno. She wouldn't tell me, but she didn't look very ill. Mebbe she's bin playing t' field again 'n' caught summat nasty.'

'Well, I did see 'er t' other night....'

and so it goes.

The rickety, wooden chairs huddled against the walls of the waiting-room, forcing their occupants to huddle too. Its white paint had stood the test of time and had stayed white despite the sticky fingers and muddy boots which passed through the room. The doctor's inner sanctum was gently but efficiently guarded by Miss Booth. Rose made her the object of her concentration as she busied herself, tidying the depleted magazines on the scratched coffee-table, magazines which disappeared as the day went on but would reappear a few days later.

Rose had never been such a victim of dread; a villain in the dock waiting for a verdict, waiting to see if she had got away with it. She wanted to go in quickly before anyone saw her, yet scared of what she might find out once in there. She kept her head bent, avoiding the nervous smiles, fixated on her worn, brown, sensible, flat shoes which had walked forever. She hated having to wear them, but her mother insisted that no daughter of hers was going to walk around like a tart in high heels during the day.

'Rose Gallagher, please.'

Her turn had come. She felt sick. As she picked up one foot after the other towards the door she felt every eye following her, their stares reaching out to question her as she hastened to be free of them. She went through the door to be assailed by Doctor Pearce's glare.

'Sit down please, Rose.'

She sat obediently, her dark eyes pleading. She had

prayed that he would have good news of a serious medical problem; cysts, tumours, anything that could be removed. Looking at his grim face, she knew that he was going to tell her what her body had told her a long time ago.

'You know what I am going to tell you, young lady. You're pregnant.'

The silence hung in the air. What did he expect her to say? Sorry?

'What will your mother have to say about this?'

'You won't tell 'er, will you?'

'I'll leave that to you, but you'd better make it sharpish or she'll guess for herself. The only other thing that we need to find out is how pregnant you are, so if you'd like to get on the..'

There was no way on this earth that she was letting his clammy, greasy hands anywhere near her. Doctor he may be, but her dislike of him made her stomach wretch at the thought of him touching her. And he was particularly smelly that day.

'I know that already. Twelve weeks.'

'Then there's not much more I can do. I'll pass the information to the hospital and they'll be in touch.'

The sneer threatened to engulf his face, the sneer that said that he always knew that she'd end up like this. She was the type. Big boobs and short skirts.

'What d' you mean?' Rose asked innocently.

'I saw Mrs Emmett today and she was telling me about her visit to the doctors this morning and just happened to mention that she'd seen you there. What's the matter? Are you ill?' Alice quizzed.

'It's jus' those 'eadaches I keep gettin'. I went to see if 'e could gi' me summat a bit stronger like. That's all.'

The defiance in Rose's glare dared Alice to disagree; her head prayed that she wouldn't.

'Why didn't you tell me?' Alice was not yet ready to let

go of the bone.

'I jus' didn't think it important. I've 'ad 'em for so long now, 'aven't I? There wer no need to mek a fuss, was there?'

Rose knew that her mother didn't believe her, but there was nothing that Alice could do, at least for now.

The interrogation over, they both returned in silence to eating their meal; Rose relieved that she had put the matter off for now, Alice frustrated and determined to find out why her daughter was lying. Rose aimed a pleading glance at her father. He continued to eat, head down, and said nothing.

Chapter Three

Rose struggled with numb fingers to pull on her familiar black slacks. The frozen chill now owned her room. The light in the hallway cast its faint beam over her dressing–table and its mirror. Rose caressed its soft wood, so proud to have it share her room. It was one of the perks of being an only child, having her own space, cold comfort though it was.

Rose was pleased with the reflection which looked back at her. Her legs were long for the small amount of height which she had and were slender, as were her hips. She knew that the slacks that she wore did nothing to hide this. She swivelled her tiny waist, proud as her full breasts jiggled in time to the movement. She had been embarrassed by them when growing up, as most girls were, but soon overcame the embarrassment once she realised the fascination which these biological features held for the opposite sex. She dressed to make the most of what she had, wearing tight–fitting jumpers, but why shouldn't she? Coupled with the allure of a perfectly structured face, she knew that she was attractive, even pretty. Her deep brown eyes were like pieces of coal when set against her pale complexion. She let her eyes continue their journey over the person in the mirror, lost in vanity. Turning sideways she let her hand run down over her stomach. It felt the same. It looked the same, firm and flat, but she knew that slowly it would become alien to her. She knew that she would no longer look like this; she would no longer be Rose.

She would no longer be Rose. The solid punch of realisation hit her. It had been a distant nightmare until today and now there was no escaping it. What had she done? She was supposed to be clever, she was going to university and now she had thrown it all away. What would her dad say? She could already see the sad disappointment in his eyes. They'd huddled together, planning, preparing so that she wouldn't be left with the only option of keeping house and having children. She wanted time to enjoy herself, to explore what life had to offer. She wanted the challenge of working hard to achieve her goals, of getting out of her home town and seeing something more. She had put such effort into doing well at school, even forfeiting dates and having fun, and now, just as she was reaching her dream, it floated away like ash from a fire, so close yet forever gone. Who was she going to be now? Somebody's mother? Now what did she have? An alien growing inside her. Surely there must be something that she could do? Surely her young life could not be destroyed so easily? She wasn't pretending to be the Virgin Mary, but she didn't deserve this, she was sure. She went to church with her mother and prayed to a God who had been good to her up until now.

The feeling of hatred at that moment laid its seeds within her along with the unborn thing. She didn't want it. She didn't want to be its mother.

She snatched her hands away from the creature, not wanting to feel any part of it. The chill, forgotten during her daydreams, grabbed her in its arms and shook her harshly, causing her teeth to chatter. She hastily finished dressing and fled from the house. Her parents exchanged a silent question which neither of them wanted answering.

Josie and Rose linked arms in silence, picking their way across the weather-worn cobbles to the red-brick, frost-licked, giant wall at the far end of the alley, deserted by all but lovers and spiders since the old brick-works had closed down. They snuggled against the wall, huddled together to whisper and warm themselves with their breath.

'Well then, did you go?' A nod was the only response.

'You wer right, then?' Another nod.

'Well what yer gonna do?'

Josie recoiled from the look in the eyes that met hers. Expecting her to be distraught, upset, regretful, only resentfulness, anger, hatred shone there. This wasn't Rose. Josie didn't like it.

"Ow could 'e do this to me?' she spit, "ow could 'e let this 'appen? I thought 'e knew what 'e wer doin."

'Let's be fair, Rose. 'e didn't do it all by hissen now, did 'e? Anyroad, you're not that naive, are you?' Josie teased uneasily.

'Yes, Josie, I am. I know I flirt with t' lads an' tease 'em an' everyone thinks I could lay lads for England, but that's really all I've done til now, just tease. I only mess wi' 'em, nowt serious, 'cos believe it or not I'm not stupid. I've alas been too interested in gettin' where I want to go in life to saddle missen wi' a bloke. I didn't want a proper boyfriend. I jus' let missen get carried away. It just 'appened. You know 'ow it is.'

Josie didn't but said nothing. All that she ever got were the ones who couldn't have Rose, who went out with Josie to be part of 'that' group, but Josie didn't mind. She accepted it, just as she accepted that Rose was the pretty one, Rose was the popular one. But she was Rose's best friend and no-one else could claim that so she was happy.

'Are you goin' to tell 'im, Rose?'

'Not yet. I don't want it, Josie. There are things you can do, places you can go to get rid of 'em, I know there are. I'm off to Maddy's. She'll know what to do. You comin'?'

'Course I am, if that's what you want.'

'I only know one thing. I didn't ask for this. I don't want it. I don't want to settle down 'n' end up like mi mum. I've got chance to mek summat o' missen. I'm too young to 'ave to do this. I might as well be dead if I 'ave to do it. I want rid.'

As Maddy opened the door to the two girls, their breath spontaneously abandoned them, both from the overpowering pungence of the expensive perfume and in awe at the vision before them, this enchantress of men. Her bleached, blonde hair sat neatly on top of her head in a silk pink ribbon like a poodle. Her lipstick shone bright red and perfect.

'Sorry Maddy. You off out?' asked Josie.

'No. Why do you ask?'

'Well, you're all med up.'

'Did you ever see the Pope without His cap? Well then.' She purred as a smirk sneaked across her face.

Rose felt silly — silly to be there, silly bothering this girl/woman that she barely knew. Why should she want to help Rose? Maybe she should forget it — but she didn't have a choice.

Maddy held her hand out to steer them in, her manicured nails glinting in the light, standing like red talons on the end of her hands.

'Now girls, what can I do for you, because I'm sure that it's not a social visit at this time of night.'

She sat them down in the kitchen around the blue Formica table where the remains of egg and bacon were sticking to the plates. Her trim thighs strained against the tightness of the silk material which passed for a skirt as she crossed them neatly.

'Anyone like a cigarette?'

Josie and Rose shook their heads, entranced as Maddy daintily let the cigarette hang limply between two fingers, put it to her mouth and lit it. Her arm swooped in a wide, exaggerated arc away from her body, carrying the small red–tipped stick which hung like a broken twig, dangling limply, now forgotten, the motion theatrical but effective. It would seem to be Maddy's role in life; to have an effect on people.

'Rose has a problem, a big problem,' confided Josie.

'I gathered that. How can I help?' asked Maddy, eyeing the opposition with interest.

'I'm pregnant,' confessed Rose.

'Now why doesn't that surprise me. You should be more careful with your teasing lass. Got you into trouble this time, eh?' Though Maddy's words were harsh, her tone teased and there was sympathy and warmth in her deep–blue eyes.

Rose could only stare at her lap where her hands sat twisting and turning anxiously around each other, fighting for composure in her position of subservience, uncomfortable not to be in charge.

'Now what do you suppose that I can do to help? Why did you come to me?' Maddy continued soothingly.

'I know a girl at school once bein' in t' same boat 'n' she told us you 'elped 'er,' blurted out Josie.

'I don't mek 'abit o' this sort o' thing,' Rose snarled, struggling to contain her anguish, desperate to scream, hit something, tear at her hair. She felt the stickiness of blood on her palm, painlessly clawed unseen. 'I've just bin unlucky, that's all. This boy was t' first un I've done owt wi', 'onest.'

Maddy took a long drag on her cigarette, saying nothing, her eyes never leaving Rose's distorted face, pondering. After an eternity she spoke.

'Does he know about this, the lad?' quizzed Maddy.

Something in Maddy's voice gave the question weight and Rose sensed that the answer which she gave could sway Maddy one way or the other.

'Yes, 'n' 'e wants nowt to do wi' it, or me for that matter. 'e denies everythin' 'n' says 'e can't be sure as it's 'is. I don't know what to do. My parents 'll kill me if they find out.'

Maddy knew Rose's parents, especially her mother, and she knew that she was right. She wanted to help Rose. She liked her, felt that they were alike in lots of ways, yet she seemed so pathetic as she sat tearing at her hands, staring blankly into space.

'I don't know who else to turn to. I don't want this baby. I can't 'ave it. Surely there must be summat I can do to get rid of it. Please 'elp me, Maddy. If I 'ave this baby, me life may as well be over. I've so much to do 'n' I can't do it wi' a baby, or even worse an 'usband. Can't you suggest owt?' Rose pleaded.

'What about an abortion? Have you thought of that?'

What was she asking? Had she thought of the backstreet abortionists who butchered and damaged you for life, still with the shame of having slept with a boy because you ended up in hospital so everyone knew anyway?

'That'd be a last resort. I'd 'oped there might be some other way, but if not then that's what I'll do.'

Maddy sucked noiselessly again and frowned. Rose and Josie joined her in her silence. They were fearful of stopping a train of thought which may lead to her helping them. Without a word, Maddy stretched her long legs, smoothed down her skirt and teetered from the room. The two girls didn't dare to move or speak, afraid to voice their questions. The left–overs on the table became the distraction, adding to Rose's nausea, stifling the tiny kitchen with their smell and in league with the heat from the back boiler.

Maddy stood before Rose and held out her hand. In it lay ten white tablets. They sat huddled, small and innocent, in a cluster on her palm.

'What are they?'

'You don't need to know that. I've got a friend who works at the Infirmary and every now and then he gets hold of these on the quiet. I can't guarantee they'll do the job, but I've had friends who've used them before and they've worked. Then again, I've had friends who've used them and they haven't worked. But apart from getting an abortion, they're the only remedy that I know of that can solve your problem. If you take them, you must never tell anyone where you got them. You must promise that, or else it will ruin the chances of some other poor sod in future if I lose my supply. Now do you want to take them or not?'

'What 'll 'appen to me if I tek 'em?' Rose asked.

'Take them before you go to bed. You'll know straight away by the morning if they're working because you'll start to lose the baby. If they don't work, then nothing will happen. I don't really know how it all works, must be something in them that triggers a reaction, but I do know that they can work. It won't be nice for you, but it's better than having a baby.'

'Okay, I'll tek 'em. 'Ow much will you want, Maddy?'

'I don't want your money, lass. I'm only glad if they happen to work for you. I get these tablets for nothing, as I said from a friend, and I was once in the same boat. Luckily for me they worked. I'm only glad if I can help. But please remember what I said. You mustn't tell a soul, either of you.'

Josie and Rose shared a silence, sensing that words could solve nothing, the strength of their bond enough. Josie was the sister that Rose didn't have and she had longed to share the long, dark winter evenings in the cold bedroom with somebody, to share her secrets late into the night under the covers, to laugh and giggle at a joke which no–one else would understand. Josie filled this gap for Rose. Josie never had chance to get close to her sisters. There never seemed to be a chance to talk to any of them as the house was always so alive and noisy, hectic with the comings and goings of one or other of the family. This meant that Josie was lonely, too, so she lavished the love which should have been given to her sisters on Rose.

Now they were sharing yet another secret. They were both filled with fear — fear of the unknown, fear that things could go wrong, fear of getting caught — but for Rose the fear of going through with having a baby was greater by far.

They reached Rose's house. Josie's house and its cheery warmth beckoned across the street.

'Are you gonna tek 'em tonight?'

'Yep. If I don't, old hawkeye 'll find 'em 'n' then it'll all be over. The sooner it's done the better. Don't worry. I'll be alright. See you tomorrow.'

'Good luck.'

Rose crept silently up the stairs to her room, relieved that her parents were already in bed. She couldn't have faced them, to be further questioned about her visit to the doctor. Rose tugged her curtains sharply together, closing out the world. She turned on her bedside light and dropped the tablets beneath it. She snuggled deep under the covers, pulling them over her head, pulling her knees up to her chest and breathing quickly and heavily, heating the closed space.

As the cold bit her nose, she cautiously peered out at the tiny tablets, sitting there so innocently, waiting to enter her body and put her life back into order, waiting to rid her of this thing which grew inside her. The glass of water was there as usual, ready to assist, the unsuspecting accomplice given ironically by her mother.

What would happen? Would it hurt? She didn't really care. She didn't care because she just needed to get it done. With her small, cold hands quivering, she raised the tablets and the glass of water towards her. She threw the two tablets into her mouth and drank. There was no turning back now. She had started, and now it needed finishing.

Two at a time she took the tablets, forcing herself to swallow, willing them to destroy what was inside her body.

Finally, they were all inside her. She felt no different, nothing. How long would they take to work? It didn't matter. It was done. Now she could go to sleep.

Chapter Four

The Jojoba Club was the undisputed King of the Red Light district. It was housed in a building which belied its existence. The façade gave the impression that within thrived a nest of grim, low-budget offices, occupied by questionable solicitors whose clients ranged from pimps to prostitutes, undoubtedly shared by sleazy loan sharks. This initial notion was accurate, for the second and third floors were, indeed, occupied by such tenants, operating almost legitimate businesses.

There was a large, solid-oak door guarding the building at the front, the same large, oak door which fronted hundreds of similar-looking office buildings in the city. Nothing to take notice of, nothing special.

A high-walled, well-lit alley circled the whole of the building. The alley was narrow and the wall which protected it crumbled with age. It led to nowhere except the rear of the building and once in it there was no way out, nowhere to hide. At the back of the building was another large, oak, non-descript door giving no indication as to what lay beyond. Nobody passed down the alley without being scrutinised, checked — the two Jamaican Goliaths on the back door made sure of that.

The door hid a secret world far removed from the cold, dark, depressing streets outside with the desperate prostitutes flashing their pieces of flesh, vying for the punters who crawled their cars along the kerbs, hoping that their enticements would lure some money for their next meal for them, or their children, or — more likely — their next fix.

Soft lighting bathed the relaxed sophistication of the room in an amber hue. The gentle calm of a faraway melody lulled, unobtrusively swirling around, artfully casting its spell on the unsuspecting victim, soothing the body, preparing it for an evening of enjoyment and fulfilment.

The thick, dark–peach carpet cradled each step, giving in and then springing back, like a wave rising and falling, floating feet along, only acknowledged somewhere deep inside where the floating took place, further soothing the guest into a sense of safe security within this haven.

Low couches lay at strategic angles to one another, upholstered in soft peach, the sides and back high to provide a degree of intimacy and privacy to the occupants. Each couch had its own low, glass table standing guard against intrusion.

Stark, three-dimensional shapes hung randomly on the walls — no pictures, just the shapes. After long concentration the images representing naked figures became recognisable, silver or black, some alone, some part of a couple or group, erotic in their static poses.

Otherwise the room stood bare, no clutter to distract, only the deliberate achievement of a cultured retreat from all that may offend one's desire for peace and calm tranquillity.

Inside the door stood two clean–shaven reincarnations of Adonis dressed immaculately in dinner suits. They didn't speak, other than to wish the visitor a good evening. Patrons of the establishment knew what was expected of them. The first Adonis received a sum of money, placed into a large, black pouch. It wasn't counted. It wasn't required as no-one would dare to risk being caught short–changing the owner. The second tipped his head in greeting and offered a tray of champagne–filled glasses, an offer which was rarely refused. The guest would then be greeted by one of three 'hostesses': Christine, Isabelle or Louise.

The hostesses were extremely important employees, and were rewarded as such. Their job was to know the regular guests who attended and to quickly and efficiently transfer them to their usual and preferred entertainment area, for the greeting room was merely that, a room in which to greet guests.

New guests were welcomed by the hostesses and left for a time to appreciate the atmosphere of the greeting room whilst enjoying the champagne, being shown to the couches to relax a little before being taken to the main entertainment room, or pit as it was lovingly known. A small passageway separated the pit from the greeting room, a solid door at either end preventing noise spilling from one area to the other. Guests were encouraged to use the facilities of the greeting room; perhaps to wait for a companion or maybe just to relax a little, as once a guest left this room, the calm and serenity was lost. Many preferred to savour it for a while. Many preferred to be seen as other guests entered. Many were eager to go to the pit.

The pit was a lively place, yet never boisterous. The stylish decadence prevailed, the peach décor so far removed from the usual reds which inherently dominated such clubs. Tables were spaced sufficiently that a limited degree of privacy was achievable, the centre–pieces ornate ashtrays of naked women in various poses.

For the pit was not about sophistication. It was about eroticism and sex, the calmness forgotten. The girls who entertained on the centrally–placed stage teased and goaded. High temperatures followed and the air became charged with anticipation and enthusiasm. This was the place to be — the most expensive and exclusive club in town.

Dayna had worked hard for the Jojoba Club. She had started, as most girls did, as a drinks girl in the pit, passing all evening between the tables and taking drink orders. She hadn't enjoyed the job; too close to the punters. Too close so that they could touch, which they frequently did, and she didn't like it. She felt uncomfortable as a drinks girl, felt vulnerable. Although the clientele were generally well-behaved, they were all the same once they'd had an evening of filling their faces with drink.

The stag groups were the worst, all out to impress

their mates at the girls' expense. The girls weren't allowed to retaliate. If they were seriously 'touched up' then they went to the bouncers who would have a quiet word in the offender's ear. This did more harm than good, since it only led to verbal goading when the girl next passed the table. The tips were okay, though, and the time passed quickly. Truth was, every man or woman in there knew that if they desired then they could get laid. Not so sophisticated or subtle after all, just dressed up that way.

She enjoyed watching the women who clung to the arms of these men; pretty women confident in their beauty, proud of being escorted by rich, maybe powerful, perhaps merely well-known men. Many were mistresses, some were wives. She often wondered why it was that these women thought themselves so different to the girls for, after all, they were providing the same service for the same reward, weren't they? She felt superior in her position as drinks girl and ignored the women with their smug looks, for at least she was earning her own living and not selling her body. She would smile back at them sweetly — fooled into the belief that she was a naive, simple girl — no clue that it was she who was laughing and looking down on them.

She had bided her time until one of the dancers had left and, thankfully, she had passed the audition and was now a dancer. 'Go-go dancers' they were called. She didn't have a clue as to why. She called herself simply a dancer. She danced, after all.

She was preparing for her next session on stage. They each did five sessions a night in two groups, making ten sessions in all, every half hour from 9.30pm. The sessions lasted for about fifteen minutes, depending on the routine, so by the end of the last stint every girl was exhausted. The routines were complicated, requiring stamina and concentration. One false move could mean the loss of the job.

The gaps between the routines were filled in, every

now and then, by two strippers. Dayna often stood and watched them, wondering at their confident and unashamed display of their bodies. She accepted that her body-wear didn't leave much to the imagination, but she felt that at least her most secret part was kept covered, even if only just! Somehow, that made showing the rest of her body okay, sort of justified it. It did to her, anyway, and that was all that mattered.

Dayna was concentrating on perfecting her elaborate make-up, carefully plastering and smoothing on as much as she could. It served as a mask, a barrier. She could freely dance without fear of anyone seeing who she really was. That was the aphrodisiac of doing this job, the thing that gave her the buzz — the fact that nobody knew who she was, nobody 'knew' her or anything about her. She simply danced for them and they applauded. She was a dancer, nothing more. She wasn't real to them. She only danced — danced where they couldn't touch her, couldn't harm her. The pay was brilliant and she only worked for four nights. She had all of her days free to do as she pleased; all of her weekends were free. She simply had to do as she was told — no more, no less.

She returned her concentration to her make-up. She loved her mirror, the mirror which she shared with Mandy on the other shift. She loved just sitting in front of it with its lights twinkling back at her, softly encircling her reflection. Most of the women watching, for all their position and wealth, couldn't hold a candle to her. She smiled confidently, evaluating the tassels hanging limply from her nipples, her nipples which stood firmly and proudly to attention on her perfect body. Of course, it had to be perfect or she'd never keep her job.

'Hiya, Day,' she heard from somewhere behind her. Mandy could never be bothered completing names. Not that it mattered since the name wasn't real.

'Hiya, Mands,' mimicked Dayna, 'you're a bit early, aren't

you?'

'Yeah, thought I'd drop by 'n' check out the action!' she said mischievously. Mandy was a dreadful flirt. 'Anyway, I thought I'd take a look at the opposition on the other shift 'n' see if you've improved to catch up with our grade!'

'You cheeky cow!' laughed Dayna. 'We're better than you any day. Probably cos we're not a set of old bags like you lot!'

'Watch out or I'll smudge your make-up!' threatened Mandy, leaving the room with a wave and a kiss.

The other girls were arriving now, preparing themselves for their performance. The room became heated with pre-performance nervous excitement. It never went away, no matter how many times the girls performed. It was always there, the knowledge that one slip could lose them their job.

They burst onto the stage as the music began and Dayna was hit, as always, by the sudden burst of adrenaline which threw her body almost unguided around the stage. She smiled, looking straight at the audience but never seeing them. She gyrated and wiggled, stretched and pulsated her body, confident in its motion, elated in the feeling that it gave her. She was exhilarated beyond anything that she had yet encountered; this feeling of power as the punters watched her, admired her, praised her. And they couldn't have her.

Her stint over, Dayna returned to her mirror briefly before Mandy came to evict her. She made her way to the rest room where the girls could lounge about, have a drink, take a coffee, take a fix, whatever, without fear of being disturbed by the punters. A bouncer stood guard on the door at all times. At the entrance to the door stood a small, glass table on which stood a silver tray. On the silver tray were several envelopes, each marked with a name. She browsed through them to see whether any of them bore her name. Sure enough, there were two for her. One was from a guy named Freddy who pledged his undying love if she would go and have a drink with him.

The other was from Barney and said that he'd see her after the show.

She smiled as she thought of him; sweet, gorgeous Barney. At least to her he was sweet, gorgeous Barney. Judging by some of the rumours which she heard he wasn't so sweet, but that didn't interest her. She didn't need to know about him, he didn't need to know about her. They just laid each other. Poor Freddy would have to be disappointed.

She didn't do much circulating between acts. Most of the girls did, but not Dayna. The girls could boost their income quite substantially simply by having a drink with a guy and making him feel nice. They always tipped well for the girls' company. She wasn't interested. She was only there to dance. She'd have a wander, though, and see whether she could find Barney. She just had time for a quick 'hello' before she'd be due on again. She pulled her short, peach tunic tightly around her and set off to find him. She had a good idea where he would be; in the table dancing–room.

Dayna hated table–dancing. She'd done it once or twice when one of the girls was off ill and she was 'told' to cover, but she hated it. It was the same as being a drinks girl; too close, too intimate.

The punters weren't allowed to touch, but that often didn't stop them and with the positions which she was forced to adopt during the dance, they often touched where a woman shouldn't be touched without permission! She liked the dancing part; it was just the erotic gyrations at eye–level which she hated. They were an essential part of the act, otherwise the punter felt cheated, felt that the act wasn't just for him/her. She was grateful for the bit of string which covered her dignity. She couldn't have done it naked, as some clubs expected.

The tips were very good, though, so when she had no choice but to perform she gave it her best shot and switched off her head, just going along with the pace of it all. She would usually take a joint before table–dancing, just to loosen her up a little, get her in the mood.

Barney enjoyed her table–dancing sessions. They always had a good time afterwards but she could never perform as well if she knew that he was around. Somehow, it made her self–conscious, as if something private was being put on display simply because he was there and knew every bit of her. Anyway, she didn't often have to do it so it wasn't a big deal.

She wandered through the room, aware that she didn't have much time before she was due back on stage. She loved to watch the other girls dancing, loved the way that they swirled their bodies, seemingly lost in their performance, concentrating solely on the person who had paid for their time, making him her world for that brief time. She wondered whether she looked as good when she danced.

There were ten tables in the room, each one occupied, but she knew exactly which table Barney would be watching. Sure enough, she found him at Eva's table, loitering in the background. He never paid for a table–dance, just prowled close, soaking up the leftovers.

'She good tonight, then?' asked Dayna, teasingly.

'Not as good as you, sugar.' He sneaked a gentle stroke of her elbow. No-one knew about them, what they shared. Barney didn't like problems and his wife would be one if she knew.

'I'll see you later then, shall I?' she both asked and confirmed.

'Yeah, I'll meet you as usual. Keep it hot, honey.' He winked and she left him to continue his biological analysis of Eva's finer points.

She slowly stripped her face of its mask and began to reapply her own makeup. She took off the bits of material which hung on her body and put on her own clothes, her tight, blue dress with the high neckline which she kept for coming to work. Plain but classy. She took the taxi which was provided by the club for each girl. She was only going about two minutes down the road, but she didn't want anyone to suspect where she was going. Besides, she didn't want to be mistaken for a hooker, unseen eyes looking her up and down, hookers as well as punters. The hookers were more of a threat than the punters if they thought that you were trying to steal their patch. No, she was safer in the taxi.

Barney was waiting for her as she turned her key in the lock of the flat door. He lay on the black, leather settee, devoid of clothes, his legs splayed with one hanging up against the back of the settee, the other one stretched out along it. His hand lay on the black, onyx table beside him holding a glass of what she knew would be whisky. A second glass stood beside it with the same contents, waiting for her.

Dayna casually threw her coat on the floor. She took the drink, swallowed hard and draped herself over him, gently teasing his firm phallus as she said hello to his eager lips.

'I see you're ready for me, baby,' she grinned.

'Aren't I always?'

Dayna loved her 'sessions' with Barney. That was all that they were. She had no illusions that there was a relationship here. They fulfilled a need within each other, a purely physical need. Barney got what he wanted without paying for it, and she got what she wanted without getting paid for it, which suited them both fine.

So without any preliminaries, they sought to sate their passion, no thoughts for anything except each other and their bodies.

Dayna woke at first light in the bed where she and Barney had finally run out of steam and fallen asleep. She looked down with affection at this man with his short, black, tousled, curly hair. His eyes, which were black, cavernous pools of hardness, were hidden from view as he slept.

Dragging herself upright, she pulled a stray, silk shirt around her and strolled towards the kitchen to make coffee. That was all that she needed right now. A good, strong cup of coffee.

She reached for the packet of cigarettes which had been tossed on the side and lit one. With great finesse and deliberation, she drew hard and let her hand drop as she exhaled. She caught sight of her reflection in the glass of the kitchen unit. Her tousled hair merely added to her simple, pure beauty. She gently ran her fingers through it, purring with contentment. She was happy with her lot. But it was daytime now, time for her not to be here, and she had better be making tracks.

'You awake, honey?' she asked, gently sweeping a kiss across his forehead.

'Yeah. Is that coffee?' he slurred.

'Uh-uh. You hungry?' She handed him his cup.

'No, I ate late at the club last night.'

'In the dining area?' she asked, cursing herself.

The other entertainment room in the club was a dining room, much the same as the other rooms, but with small booths around the edge whilst the main dining area filled the remaining floor space. Most guests ate in the main dining area. However, for privacy, for whatever reason — maybe simply for a romantic meal with a wife or mistress — a booth could be hired. Privacy was not the only thing which could be hired for use in the booths. Not advertised, rather common knowledge, but girls could be hired also. Some men hired the girls to act as companions to share their meal, have a laugh, make them feel wanted — like an added extra on top of dessert. Other men needed more entertaining, after dinner entertaining shall we say, and that was also for hire.

Dayna knew that the first floor of the building was more

of a hotel, yet the windows were disguised in such a way as to hide this. Sharif, the owner, was in this respect a glorified pimp, but no-one seemed to mind. The girls didn't mind. This was a much safer way of plying their trade without having to walk the streets and they were well taken care of by the hostesses. Even the police didn't mind. There was never any trouble. Many of their faces were familiar trade.

Dayna knew most of the girls. They were nice girls, pretty, good conversationalists, experienced at making a man feel important. She couldn't do their job, yet she had respect for them that they could. After all, she was selling what she was good at and they were selling what they were good at!

'Yes, I dined with Sharif. The chicken somethingorother was delicious,' replied Barney, breaking into her thoughts.

If he realised why she had asked, he pretended not to. Dayna had been dressing whilst they talked and now, her blue dress back in place, she was ready to leave.

'I'll have to be off now, babe. See you later.' A peck and she was gone.

'Hi, mum,' she shouted as she slammed the door of the house where she lived with her parents.

'Hi, love, good night at work?' called her mother.

'You know, same as usual.' A wry smile slipped across her face as she climbed to the slumber of the satisfied.

Chapter Five

Rose awoke to the sound of screaming and the pain told her that the screams were hers. Something had buried itself deep within her and was fighting to get out. Every muscle surrounding her slender bones tensed, pushing to evict this torture which overwhelmed her, kneading round and down. The sweat-soaked bedclothes struggled to cling to the mattress as they were yanked in an iron vice. She tried to open her eyes but the pain was too strong. What was happening? All that existed was the pain, nothing else.

She was oblivious to the presence of her mother beside her, holding and stroking her hand, gently 'shushing' as she tried in vain to comfort her deaf daughter. Rose was blind to the tortured face above her, which twisted itself and distorted the features, hiding the torment beneath though it burst through the grey, tired eyes — eyes desperate and crazed in anguish.

Rose winced through her teeth. The kicking again. Her left arm swung with a determination of its own, crashing the empty glass to cower by itself in the corner of the room. What was causing it? What was tearing her insides apart? Then relief as the mercy of unconsciousness fell.

A knocking downstairs. Bert was shaken from his futile hovering and ran towards the welcome sound. Rose lay unconscious when the doctor entered the room with his smell trailing behind him. Alice still stroked her daughter's hand gently, closing her eyes as she tried to take the pain for herself that her daughter might be released. As she became aware of the doctor's presence she stepped back, eager for him to hurry and remove the pain, her arms instinctively adopting their protective posture, folded across her chest. Her rigid stance a little back from the bed belied the fear which lay tethered inside the shaking body, hiding the love for her child.

She acknowledged the doctor with a curt nod. Bert had made the call to him not twenty minutes earlier, his mild manner struggling to stress the urgent need for the visit.

'What happened, Mrs Gallagher?' he questioned. He was now beside the bed and lifting Rose's eyelids gently.

'I don't know. Her crying woke us, and when we came to see what was the matter, we found her almost unconscious with pain. She finally passed out a short while ago. What's the matter with her, doctor?' she asked, knowing that this was a stupid question at this early stage and yet finding it necessary to voice it.

'Was she holding anywhere?' he asked curtly. He didn't appreciate being dragged out in the middle of the night.

'I think she was holding her stomach. She seemed to be trying to curl up, but I think it was her stomach.'

This piece of information did not surprise him at all. He had seen many pregnant girls in this state, many girls who were either miscarrying deliberately or by the grace of God. It was almost impossible to differentiate. The result was the same, so it didn't really matter. The first thing that he needed to do, the only real thing that he could do, was to alleviate the pain. He opened his time–weary, black case and took out a syringe, together with a vial.

His thoughts wandered as he routinely prepared the dosage for Rose. He was eager to get back home to his cosy hearth. He could still picture it; the fire softly burning, silently filling the air with its warmth and comfort. The generous measure of whisky poured and begging to be drunk. The thick, beige hearthrug with a pile to die in, nicely finished off with Mrs Johnson slithering in his favourite black lingerie upon it. This was the only night of the week that Mr Johnson stayed away on business, the only night when Doctor Pearce and Mrs Johnson could attend to 'business', staying up all through the night, grabbing bits of sleep amid their excitement, and now was not time to sleep. He involuntarily licked his pouting lips heavily. He could see her, lying as he had left her, her soft curves tempting amidst the delicate fabric, her warm thighs invitingly parted, her..... and then the telephone had rung. If he didn't speed things up, it would be morning already, and she'd be gone.

Doctor Pearce shrugged himself back to reality with a jolt. He despised these poky little houses with their poky little people, intruding on his evening. Urgently, he drew back the bedclothes, found Rose's arm and administered the painkiller. Pulling the well-worn stripes back further, he began his search for the tell-tale red patch. Nothing. So whatever she'd tried hadn't worked. Poor thing.

'I've given her a painkiller. I'll leave you these tablets, Mrs Gallagher. She'll need them every four hours for the next couple of days. She'll sleep for a while now, but she'll come round once the painkiller begins to wear off. Don't worry. It's nothing serious.'

'What do you mean, it's nothing serious?' spat Alice, her voice menacing. 'My daughter has been in agony, and has passed out in pain, and you expect me to simply accept your analysis of 'it's nothing serious'?' What is the matter with her? I demand to know.'

The fierce look on her face left the doctor in no doubt that she did, indeed, demand to know. Well, it didn't matter to him whether she knew or not. Rose should have told her.

'Since you must know, your daughter is pregnant.' He nodded his head in an 'I told you so' way as he uttered the words which dealt the devastating blow to this woman. 'She's either had a threatened miscarriage or she's tried to do something to get rid of the baby. Whatever the case may be, the fact is that she is still pregnant. Now, if you don't mind, Mrs Gallagher, I'll bid you goodnight.'

Alice was a statue, incapable of thought, movement or speech. Surely he was wrong, lying, drunk. She vaguely heard someone thanking the doctor, followed by footsteps down the stairs. The door banged. Footsteps up the stairs. An arm around her shoulders, leading her away — away from her pregnant daughter, away from her sleeping baby who would awaken once again in pain.

'Let's get some sleep, Alice, before she wakes up again and needs us.' The shock had drained her body and sleep swiftly released her from her agony.

She was asleep so quickly that the heart-rending, silent sobs of her husband beside her were forever lost.

The bright, winter sunlight shafted in to awaken Rose. The pain was there, now a dull ache fighting defiantly to take her body once again in its grasp. She tried to straighten her legs, which had become stiff from being bundled up tightly for so long, her instincts keeping them even in sleep where they might ward off the hurt inside. She heard the fiend within saying 'if you do that, you'll be sorry' as she felt the twinges, and decided that stiff legs were better than the dreadful grinding and returned them to their foetal position. She lay still, trying to remember what had happened during the night. What had she dreamt and what was real? She remembered her mother beside her. Where was she now? She didn't really care — she was too exhausted to care.

The sun teased the dancing, yellow flowers on the wall, making them jump as they played with her mirror. She could almost smell the beautiful day outside, crisp and fresh, November enjoying its glory before the harshness of December set in.

Then she remembered. The tablets. Slowly she slid her hand downwards towards the top of her legs. It was dry. She had the same night-clothes on. Nothing had happened. Only this pain for nothing. As if called by the thought, the serpent struck again. She lay back and wept, pain and despair overwhelming her in equal measure.

The door opened slowly. Bert smiled softly, his gentle, blue eyes creasing. Silently, he carried the tray to her bedside and set it down. On it was a cup of tea, a slice of buttered toast and two tablets.

''ello, love. You feelin' any better?'

'I'm still in lots o' pain, dad. I can't move much wi' out it 'urtin'. Why are you 'ere? Shouldn't you be at work?'

'It's Sunday, pet. Your mum's gone to church, but she'll be 'ome soon now.'

Rose nodded, hearing the unspoken warning.

'What's t' tablets for?' she shrugged towards the tray.

'They're painkillers. T' doc left 'em for you. 'e came to see you last night. We wer so worried 'n' you wer in so much pain, we 'ad to call 'im. Anyroad, I think it's time you took 'em now. Try to eat t' toast 'n' drink t' tea. It'll 'elp you feel better.'

Their eyes met. She needed no words to know that the doctor had given up her secret, had eagerly held her up as a harlot. The knife which now plunged deep inside hurt beyond healing, for she had hurt the man who did nothing but love her without demands, who had done nothing to deserve the disgrace of a pregnant daughter out of wedlock. The unasked questions lay written there for her to see, written along with the sorrow.

Bert reached for her, gently pulling her to him. His arms held her tightly, trying to surround her with protection, holding her head on his shoulder, trying to hold away her shame. He didn't want her to see the anguish within himself, not trusting his feelings to stay hidden if he looked at her. He held her for a long while, just sitting together, sharing their grief, trying to share each other's grief away.

'I'm sorry, dad. I'm so sorry,' she whispered as tears slid silently down her pale face.

'You will be, love, 'n' there's not much I can do to 'elp'.

He took her face in his hands and stared deep, wishing with all his strength to make her strong, to help his little girl.

'Now tek your tablets afore it starts to be bad again.' He cuffed her chin gently and left the room.

Bert leaned against the door which he had pulled closed behind him. He felt a void inside which he could not express. It swirled as empty as air leaving nothingness in its wake. He trudged down the stairs with leaden limbs and picked up the cup of tea which he had left. Why did people believe that a cup of tea would solve everything?

'My husband's left me.'

'Well, never mind, 'ave a cup o' tea and you'll feel better.'

'My wife's dead.'

'Well, never mind, 'ave a cup o' tea and you'll feel better.'

This cup of tea wasn't going to solve anything. He stared into its murky depths, trying to make some sense of things, trying to figure out what should be done next, what he should do next. His straightforward sort of a life had not prepared him for this. Life had just kind of happened to him over the years, allowing him to drift along the river of life with no stray driftwood to bar his way, nothing to force him to ponder which direction he might choose to go in. Then Alice had taken over and had ever since paddled his canoe down a straight, slow river and he had never had to worry.

He had adored Alice since the moment that she had strolled across his vision when they were both thirteen. She had lived in the same street as him, but she never knew he existed. She would say hello as they passed, and she would smile her smile, but she didn't notice him. He worshipped her as she grew and became a fine woman, never short of beaus to escort her for the evening. He would watch from the window of his room as she went out, her fine clothes clinging to her slender body, the body that he didn't even dare begin to think of. She was an angel on a pedestal, far out of his reach.

That was until the night when he had found her huddled

in the corner of a bus shelter. It had been dark and at first he hadn't recognised her with her head buried beneath a black, woollen scarf and her chin tucked into her coat. The head slowly raised and he saw her face, looked into the grey eyes so full of tears and sadness. His heart had leapt so hard, pounded so loudly in his body that he felt sure that she must hear. He had to say something.

'What you doin' out 'ere, Alice. It's a bit late to be out on your own.'

'I had to take a walk and I ended up here. I needed to get out to think, to be by myself for a while, but you're right, it is getting rather late.'

'Can I walk you 'ome, then, mek sure you get 'ome safe like?' he stammered.

'Thanks, Bert, that would be nice.'

An awkward silence hung for a while before Bert mustered up enough courage to try a conversation.

'Where's that American boyfriend of yours?' he enquired innocently.

He could feel the tension cover her like a blanket as her shoulders hunched and her step quickened.

'Didn't you hear? He's done the same as all the rest of the American boyfriends around here. His job here is over, he's nothing to stay for, so he's gone back to America.'

'But I thought you were engaged,' quizzed Bert, his tact lost amid his confusion and latent rising hope.

'So did I,' she said with finality.

'I'm sorry,' was inadequate, but it was the only thing that he could find to say.

It was a common story. The Americans had come, and then they had left, leaving behind them a trail of heart-broken girls, leaving the pieces for the long-forgotten men of the town to pick up and put back together. Alice was part of the flotsam.

When they reached her house, Bert shyly wished her goodnight. That was the beginning.

They had been courting for only a month when Alice had asked if they could meet in the park on Sunday. Bert had been confused; they usually went to the cinema or the dance hall. He expected the worst.

Sunday came at last. Bert arrived early, finding an empty bench beside the pond. He sat upon the names etched by hands of love now filled with grime and gum.

It was a glorious summer day and he gazed absently as a gentle breeze skipped through the daffodils surrounding the pond, weaving a yellow wave along its edge. Children played on the swings nearby, their squeals of delight breaking the languid, easy stillness, drowning the sound of the bees as they buzzed about their work. The sun warmed the earth, but couldn't warm his heart until he knew what she would say.

Then she appeared; an apparition, a vision in a lilac dress which hung around her body, stroking it yet never clinging to it. She sat beside him without saying a word, not even a greeting, her face sombre as she stared at him.

'Bert, I can't see you again.' There, the words which he had known must come but had dared to hope would not.

'Why, Alice. 'ave I done summat to offend you, summat wrong?' he beseeched.

'No, Bert. You've been so kind, so gentle. But I can't see you anymore. You see, I'm pregnant.'

The words crashed against him like a tidal wave, but he didn't waver. He didn't have to think about the words because there was only one thing that he could say, one thing that he had waited all of his life to say.

'Is the father the American?' She nodded.

'Does 'e know? Is 'e comin' back?' She shook her head resignedly.

'Does anyone else know? Does your mum know?' Again, the shake of the head as it hung despondently.

'Then marry me.' There he'd said it. He took her hand in his one hand and raised her head with his other hand gently under her chin, forcing her to look at him. 'Marry me, Alice.

Nobody need ever know that the baby isn't mine. All I've ever wanted is to marry you, so will you marry me? Please say you'll marry me.'

He was pleading, knowing that this was all that his life had been lived for, to be her husband. He could see the realisation sinking in to Alice's stern features. A mixture of amazement, relief, gratitude replaced the despair and anguish in her eyes. He held her protectively in his arms as she slowly leaned against him, firm in the knowledge that now he need never let her go.

And so he adored her.

The tea sat cold and untouched in the cup in his hand as the door banged, plunging him back to earth. Alice, hunched against the bite of the frost in her winter coat, managed a smile but her face was lifeless and ashen.

Church had helped — it always did. Somehow, as she perched upon the wooden hardness of the pew, tight against a pillar for comfort, the silent cocoon gave her control of herself, or handed it to someone else.

Being in the church had a soothing effect which restored the humble balance of the mind and body, reminded oneself of the control which one must have in order to survive, confirmed that life cannot be lived by falling prey to true emotions, feelings and desires. It just wasn't practical — too much effort on untethered emotions made the battle to carry on too arduous.

Alice knew that the rules which God laid down must be obeyed and then everything would be alright. She relaxed her tense body in supplication to her God and bowed her head, praying for His soothing which she received as she handed control of her life again to Him, the shock replaced by the calming effect of His mercy. She raised her head as Mary smiled down on her from a sun–streaked window.

Now she had strength to deal with the situation and help

her daughter to decide what was to be done. Forget the anger at the stupidity of her offspring, forget the sadness that her child's life would now be ruined. Forget it all. It was God's problem now.

'How is she?' asked Alice. 'Is she still in pain?'

'I took 'er some breakfast a while ago 'n' she still seemed to be strugglin', but I gave 'er t' painkillers. I wer just about to go up 'n' see whether they'd 'elped.'

'Don't worry, Bert. I'll go up and see how she is. You wouldn't mind making me a cup of tea, would you? I'm frozen stiff.' Calmly she climbed the stairs to visit her daughter.

Rose hadn't moved and still lay with her eyes transfixed on the glistening mirror. As her mother stepped into the room, thousands of butterflies in Rose's stomach took flight. She thought that she was going to be sick. She had dreaded this moment, dreaded it since she first knew that she was pregnant. She loved her mother, but was scared of how she might react, afraid of what she might do, scared that she would abandon her, evict her.

'How are you?' began her mother. 'Has the pain eased?'

''e told you, didn't 'e? 'e 'd no right to do that. 'e 'd no right to tell you at all. It's my business,' blurted out Rose savagely, choosing attack as a form of defence. Another pain rushed at her. She grimaced, trying to hide it.

Alice spoke gently.

'Yes, Rose, he did tell me. Perhaps you're right that he had no leave to tell me, but, then again, somebody had to. I know you're scared, I know you're upset, but I want you to know that you have nothing to fear from me. I know I don't always put my feelings on show, but you know how much I love you, and no matter what else I may feel, I do not sit in judgement, that isn't my job. I'll do everything that I can to help you through this. I'm your mother.'

Rose stared in stunned silence. She had expected anger,

lectures, shouting, abuse at her idiocy. She had expected to be thrown out — anything except this understanding. She knew that she was loved, but she also knew how much the shame and embarrassment of this would kill her mother — how she would feel every stare of the neighbours like a knife to her heart, her proud bearing brought under scrutiny because she had allowed her daughter to get into this state.

Her mother's understanding was harder to bear than her anger, delivered as it was in such a calm, resigned manner. Rose could not possibly know that this attitude had been learnt a long time ago — an attitude of resignation to one's lot, left only with compromise because she too had made the same mistake. Rose was simply relieved and grateful for her reaction.

'Does the father know about this?' asked Alice, breaking the silence.

'No, but I'll tell 'im soon,' replied Rose.

'Will he marry you?' continued Alice.

Rose thought for a moment as she considered how he would react.

'Yeah, I think 'e will,' she responded resolutely.

'Then the sooner he's told and we can start to make plans, the better.'

Chapter Six

Almost a week had passed and it was Saturday night. As she dressed to go out, Rose smiled at the pile of dog-eared books which slid from under the bed, reminding her that this was her weekly reward for the punishing studying schedule which she had meticulously followed and which would now become obsolete since she could no longer go to university.

She smoothed on her dark nylons and forced her feet into her white high heels. She loved these shoes, knew that they added height to her slender form and made the line of her lower leg like that of Marilyn Monroe.

A blue, tight-bodiced dress strained around her cleavage which stood prominently above her still-tiny waist. The dress spread wide below her waist, leaving the delights of her lower body and upper thighs to the imagination. The whole dress was covered delicately with a layer of lace, shrouding her tenderly. Her pale complexion had lost none of its lucidity. As she inspected the mirror she knew that she presented a portrait of beauty to the world.

Josie and Rose tottered arm in arm to the dance hall where they were to meet Alan and his friend, Jake. The evening was mild for November. A full moon penetrated the slate-black sky, accompanied by an army of shimmering stars which lit the cobbles and made their tread a little more gainly on the uneven pavements.

Rose laughed with Josie, hearing tales of all that she had missed during her week of imprisonment as she had been recovering. She lilted, as much as was possible in those high heels, her tiny handbag swinging carelessly back and forth. Her skirt swished as it swirled in the gentle evening whisper, briefly revealing the slender thighs beneath their disguise. A beam of self-satisfaction sat beneath her bobbing, black hair, accompanied by a lingering half-smile. Josie could contain her curiosity no longer.

'Are y' alright, then, Rose?'

'What d' you mean? Don't you think I look gorgeous? Don't I look as if I'm okay?'

'You know what I mean? Are y' alright, you know, alright?'

Rose smirked ironically and returned her friend's quizzical stare. The smile hid, the body stopped.

'If you mean am I still pregnant, then yes I am. If you mean did t' pills work, then no, they evidently didn't. I'll tell you summat, though. They med me bloomin' ill. I've never felt owt like it. If 'avin' a baby is 'owt like as bad then God 'elp me. If you mean 'ave I gone stark, starin' mad then yeah, I probably 'ave. You see, I decided that once I tell 'im — 'n' I'm tellin' 'im tonight — that I'm pregnant, then all t' laughs 'n' dances 'n' nights out 'll like as not disintegrate into a depressin' rush of arrangements for weddings, or arguments about 'ow to persuade 'im to marry me, or some such carry-on, so I've decided to 'ave a flippin' good time 'n' stuff this baby, at least for tonight. Does that sound like a mad person to you?' Josie laughed along with her friend.

'No, Rose, it sounds like t' best thing you could do for now. Just afore we start enjoyin' oursens, though, one more question. Does your mum know?' Rose stopped again and, taking both her friend's hands, she turned her to face her.

'You'll never believe it. She's been as nice as pie. She's been great. I can't believe she's t' same person. I knew she loved me, but I never thought she'd stand by me like she's doin'. I can't believe it. Anyroad, let's leave it now 'n' just 'ave one last good night afore t' beans are well 'n' truly spilt, shall we? By t' way, sorry for not comin' over to see you this week. I'm still strugglin' to get me 'ead round all this 'n' needed to sort mesen out for tonight. Forgive me?'

They hugged tightly, two young women dressed to the nines entwined in the middle of the street. They giggled, drawing a curious sneer from a trench-coated, umbrella-touting, small man.

'Don't be silly. We're best mates, pervert!'

When they arrived at the dance hall, Alan and Jake were waiting for them.

'Sorry we're late. We were propositioned by a 'Vogue' photographer who said we wer red 'ot 'n' would we like to be on t' cover, but we told 'im we wer busy wi' two red-'ot studs.'

Rose winked at Alan who responded with his crooked smile which somehow was attached to her stomach because it always leapt in response. It was a self-conscious smile but one which said more than words how much Alan liked her. His left hand dragged through his slicked-back hair, pushing it back into place, the kiss-curl gently falling onto his forehead. Alan returned her wink and Rose logged, not for the first time, that he was a good catch. She could do a lot worse, but then so could he. Jake hovered unassumingly behind Alan, taking Josie's hand as she stood tentatively close, his blonde curls already beyond control and a stark contrast to the mousey plaits beside him.

They pushed their way into the dance hall. Sweaty, eager bodies twisted and turned in every inch of space. The air hung heavy with cheap perfume and anticipation. They were steered through the rolling swell towards the bar, swimming through the waves of gyrations. The bar was infested with teasing girls as they were deprived of their inhibitions by drinks plied by expectant males, too eager to realise that their expectations would come to nothing once they had paid for enough drinks. The girls would make the boys feel wanted, tell them how wonderful they were, and then wave goodbye with a 'thanks for the drinks guys'. Only the stupid, immoral or sadistically desperate would risk getting pregnant. The guys would be left to go home and satisfy themselves alone, happy in the knowledge that for one evening they were masters of the universe.

The music was loud — the Beatles, the Stones — no-one really cared. It started a rhythm, a sensation somewhere deep inside which hypnotised the body into motion. The urgency of human flesh was drawn to human flesh to be entwined together to the ebb and flow of the sounds which filled them, lost in some carnal inner knowledge more eager than sex.

Rose and Alan moved metronomically, clinging to each other, savouring the intensity of shared emotion. Hundreds of bodies mingled around them, bottoms bumping, elbows jarring, swallowed up in the same sea of excitement. Rose attracted the usual amount of attention as the moths were drawn to the butterfly and she responded with sweeping waves of hands, accepting of her popularity which she had worked hard to achieve. Alan's eyes and attention never moved, focused on the girl who made him the envy of many.

'Let's go outside. I'm boiling,' shouted Rose, pulling Alan's shirt behind her. A side-door led to an alley behind the hall.

They both breathed gratefully and deeply as the cool air swirled mistily. Alan pulled her to him as they carefully picked their way down the narrow pathway, trying not to pry too closely on the fumbling dark shapes. But Rose saw a face that she could not ignore. Johnny. She had known that he would be there but was still not prepared for the sight of him nestled neatly amidst the extremely large bosom of a blonde.

Johnny was 'Jack the lad' — the cheeky chappy who all the girls adored, overflowing with charm and humour. There's always one. He was gorgeous and he knew it. He realised at an early age that he bore a strong resemblance to Elvis and he exploited this to his benefit in every way, even changing his voice and swagger to match. How could a girl resist? He flirted with any girl worth the time and effort, but had a long-term girlfriend, whose bosom he was now investigating.

One look from him and a girl would forget her modesty and morals as she became the focus, for that one moment, of his attention, seemingly bewitched — no matter which girl, and that included Rose.

The events of three months ago flashed vividly through her memory with alarming yet comforting clearness.

She had met Johnny in a cafe in town. She couldn't remember why she had been there, but she was there. And so was Johnny. She had wanted Johnny for as long as she could remember, but then hadn't every girl. Her astonishment was sincere when he came to her table and asked to sit with her.

They had talked — talked about anything and everything — losing their unfamiliarity within the first ten minutes and building into familiarity by the end of two hours. They had left together and made their way to his flat. She had known that she shouldn't go, but she couldn't bear to miss the chance to be with him alone. She had waited for so long. Besides, the familiar thrill of daring and excitement was already coursing through her veins and she was not in control.

Johnny had his own place and worked in the local factory. He talked about his work. He talked of his dreams and plans. She talked of her dreams and plans. And then the talk had stopped.

She hadn't realised what was happening until it was too late; so removed was this sensation from Alan's fumbled attempts at lovemaking. She was being swept along in a tide of pleasure which she had no desire to resist as tiny, tingling waves assailed her body. She had returned his searching kisses with like, their tongues delving deeper with the urgent need for discovery. She had explored his lean body with her hands, urging him with undulations to roam her slender curves.

Their clothes became a scattered pile on the floor, forgotten as they surrendered to the overwhelming need to satisfy their longing, his body probing deep within to complete the act begun three hours before, for they had known that this was where it would end.

Their passion sated, Rose uncomfortably gathered her clothes and dressed. The talk had dissipated along with the passion as the terrible realisation of her foolishness sank in. How could she have been so stupid as to believe that Johnny would want more than this from her? She had let herself be flattered by the attentions of this man just because every girl wanted him. She had been too confident of her own prowess as a siren, only now to realise, as she watched him dress nonchalantly, that she had been used.

'You okay?' she heard his voice through the ether of consciousness.

'Yeah, fine thanks.'

'Would you like me to walk you 'ome?' he asked, clearly in the hope that the answer would be negative.

'No, thanks. I'll be fine.'

'Okay, then. I'll see you around then, Rosie. 'n', well, thanks.'

She slowly pulled the door closed behind her as she left.

'Are y' alright, Rose?' Alan's voice broke into her trance. He had his arm around her, his face concerned.

Johnny's attention was captured by the figures standing for such a time so close to him. He lifted his head, seeing Rose. He smiled at her, his usual, charming smile which he gave to everyone. Then he returned to his groping.

The decision made she spoke.

'Alan, I've summat to tell you. You're gonna be a dad. I'm pregnant.'

Chapter Seven

Sharif gazed above him. He enjoyed watching, took pleasure from seeing the pale, white limbs entangled with his own brown body. He liked the movements from this angle; the gentle twists and turns as the two bodies slithered across the black, silk sheets and over him; teasing, pulling, sucking, biting, gracefully and silently performing their skilful witchcraft upon him. He mused at the contrast between the blonde hair strewn over his stomach and the tight, brown curls of the other head as it bobbed above him.

They worked well as a team, moving skilfully from one action to another but never fighting over the same piece of body. They seemed to revel in their power over him, at controlling the body of this powerful man. He was engrossed by the way that their buttocks would become rounded in a particular position and then tighten as they moved, reflected as they were in the mirror above him. After gazing for too long at the ceiling it would make him disorientated, but the alcohol had usually already had that effect on him a long time before. He was a fortunate man in that the alcohol never affected the performance of a certain vital area of his body. That apparently operated on auto-pilot!

He worked hard to keep his physique lean and muscular and knew that he was in good shape for a man of his years, even for a man perhaps five to ten years younger. He enjoyed sex, enjoyed the sensations of saliva and skin on him. Equally, he enjoyed his skill at giving pleasure to a woman — the sign of a real man in his country — feeling her squirm beneath his fingers as he expertly explored her body, gently stroking then firmly rubbing with supreme precision.

He needed two girls though; one was never enough. After all, there was only so much that you could do with one girl, only so much to explore. With two, the choices were doubled. He loved to experiment, aiming to change the intensity of physical sensation that he achieved for his own body, aiming to increase the enjoyment for his girls, taking pride in their fulfilment. They didn't seem to object to the two–some arrangement, being accustomed as most of the girls were to working the first floor at the Jojoba Club. He would argue that this was his method of 'quality control'.

His body shuddered with the relief of satisfaction.

'Go on, girls. Get yourselves a drink. Take a break,' he commanded, unsmiling and emotionless. Why did he never feel what he wanted to feel? Why did the intensity of feeling stop at the physical and never progress to the emotional?

He yearned for something that he couldn't quite grasp, something which eluded him. The girls were beautiful with perfect bodies. Their physical prowess, along with his own, could not be bettered. Then what was it? He had no answers, just feelings of something, some barren hole within him.

Then his thoughts drifted back to earlier that night, to the new girl. She had caught his eye, caught more than his eye. Why? She was as pretty as the rest and had large breasts — a necessity for his go–go dancers — but she was nothing extraordinary. Then why had he looked twice, looked hard, when she returned his stare with those eyes the colour of night? What did he see there that sought something within himself? Defiance? Reserve? Naivety? Vulnerability?

He couldn't tell. He could not judge this girl, this woman. She had captured his imagination and he felt the heat rising in his loins at the prospect of a challenge.

But for now he must concentrate on his girls. Their break was over and they were returning, eager to fall prey to his preferences and perversions.

Sharif was an enigma of a man. Little was known about him and that was the way that he liked it. He chose to be friendly yet guarded, never encouraging enquiries into anything personal. After a while, people had stopped asking and he was simply Mr Sharif, the owner of the Jojoba Club. It was suspected that he had a wife in his home country, wherever that might be. The colour of his skin gave little away, for the multitude of nationalities bearing the same was vast. It was presumed that his six–monthly visits — when he was away for three weeks — were to visit his prodigal wife and, perhaps, family. He never discussed himself, his life, his feelings, his thoughts. He simply was.

Men felt important in his company. His attire was that of a man of wealth and style. He favoured suits and ties rather than casual clothes, always wearing dark colours which satisfied his desire to blend into the background rather than attract any more attention than was necessary. He didn't need bright clothing to attract attention. He was a handsome man as well as physically appealing, having the dark, forbidding features which immediately produce images of Latin lovers or ethnic sheikhs, attracting women to him like a magnet, which obviously pleased his companions.

He was an avid gambler and dealt well with his losses as well as his wins. He frequently visited the premises of his friend, Marco, who owned a casino. Sharif didn't have a gambling room at the Jojoba Club as to do so would attract attention from the authorities who already turned many blind eyes for him. He was happy to go with his friends to Marco's and spend his time on the card tables. Anyway, it provided him with a welcome change of scenery, refreshed his outlook on his own establishment by comparing it to another.

Sharif was generous with his money and attentive to his companion's conversations, knowing that a man's weakness or problems can be unearthed by listening to liqueur–induced talk. He never drank too much whilst in company, drinking more than his share once he was in the sanctuary of his home where he had nobody to please or guard against except himself. Women didn't count as a threat. He treated women with contempt and, at the same time, with respect; contempt because they allowed themselves to be used by men, and respect because they did it without complaining and usually knew the rules. Women, oblivious to Sharif's opinion of them, looked forward to being chosen to share his company and his bed.

He placed women in two distinct categories; women with whom he would happily share a meal and conversation but did not take to bed, and women with whom he would share a meal minus conversation and drag away for a night of excitement. It would depend on his mood on a particular evening as to which type he would choose, for his sexual appetites were voracious but not daily. Should he choose a woman for company only, he often employed the services of his main hostess, Christine, to select a suitable candidate, not trusting his judgement when it came to non-physical attributes. She seldom chose unsuitably.

Even as his body devoured the two women, he couldn't stop thinking about the girl.

Chapter Eight

The day arrived. The bride and groom stood stiffly before the registrar. Relatives and friends fidgeted and whispered in the cramped rows, thankful for the crisp freshness of the February air which whistled through the half-open window. Impatience made the wide, awkward hats more of a nuisance than they might otherwise have been.

The bride was resplendent in cream lace which draped over her voluptuous body, an effort having been made to hide her swelling abdomen for the sake of decorum.

As she smiled radiantly at her guests, no-one could suspect the Oscar-winning performance which was taking place before their eyes, so in love and contented did she seem. No-one could know that behind the laughter was a little girl screaming to be anywhere but here.

The bride saw a handsome man beside her, a good man, who deserved to be loved tenderly. But he wasn't.

Alan stood before the registrar, unusually smart in his Sunday-best of grey with a bright red tie, laughing at Jake's nervous attempts at humour. Jake was the best man and was finding it hard to believe that Alan was actually marrying Rose.

'You what! She's pregnant! 'ow the 'ell did that 'appen?' asked Jake in amazement.

''ow d' you think, jackass. She didn't manage it by hersen, some divine miracle. We've bin goin' steady for ages now.'

'I know that. I mean, I thought we'd talked enough about 'avin' girls, fair enough, but bein' careful 'n' not getting' 'em up t' stick. What 'appened to 'bein' careful'?'

'I thought I wer. We only did it once. I must've bin worse for wear 'cos I could've sworn I wer careful. Accidents 'appen, you know. Anyroad, that's beside t' point now 'cos I'm gonna marry 'er.'

''ow can you be sure it's yours? I mean, she's well–known for bein' a flirt, Alan. Mebbe you're t' best bet.'

'Don't talk like that about 'er, Jake. I know we're mates, but don't push it. Course she wouldn't lie to me 'n' I want to marry 'er. I've alas liked Rose, more 'n that, you know I 'ave. You know what, I might even've married 'er even if she 'adn't bin pregnant, though with all 'er fancy university talk she probably wouldn't 'ave 'ad me, so p'rhaps this kid's doin' me a favour, okay?'

Alan had loved Rose forever, or so it seemed. He found it hard to believe his luck when she had noticed him and they had started to go steady.

He had finally managed to persuade her to 'go all the way' with him on a freezing cold night in the back of Jake's beat–up old Morris. A Morris was not exactly his idea of a 'passion–wagon' but it was the best that he could do.

They had driven to a secluded spot known as 'Lovers Lane' which was actually just an old dirt road that led to a quarry. Alan had been nervous. He knew that it wasn't cool to be nervous, but he hadn't done this with anyone before and, to be honest, he wasn't exactly sure what he was supposed to do, not in detail.

He did, however, know that 'he' was the one who had to do the 'doing'. He began by kissing her. He kissed her gently at first but, as their bodies begged for each other, their kisses became eager. This seemed to go quite well.

He'd then carried on to Phase Two. At least, this was how Jake described it when they had their 'man to man' talks. He held his breath and ventured to move his hand down — down towards the breasts which he had touched a thousand times in his dreams. His dreams did not prepare him for the reality, for the firmness and enormity of these mounds. He breathed a sigh as his body responded to the warmth beneath his hand, to the feel of the small, erect tissue which he could feel pressing hard to escape from the restraints of Rose's clothes.

Fumbling, he unbuttoned the blouse, struggling with the strange device which held his objects of desire. He did not dare to rush anything; she might scamper like a scared rabbit suddenly caught in headlights as she realised what was happening. Up to now, he was doing well.

A small moan escaped her lips and he knew that things were proceeding as they should. He relaxed as he stroked the soft flesh of her breast; so soft it was like touching nothing, like running a hand across silk. He was finding it increasingly difficult to control his urges, finding himself motivated by a need to have her now, this minute.

With one hand he continued to caress her, afraid that if he removed it she would wake from the spell which she seemed to be under. With the other he tugged at clothing as the pending eruption grew within him like a pressure-cooker. Kissing her almost frantically, he delved beneath her skirt — noting somewhere gratitude that she wasn't wearing her usual slacks — and wriggled her out of her underwear.

No further thought could penetrate his frenzied torment as he entered her, no longer aware of anything except the sensation which crawled through his body. Emotions, strange tingling which he'd never felt, overcame him; intense, surging, urgent.

Instinctively, his senses returned as he realised what was about to happen. Pulling away, his body exploded with the intensity of a champagne cork released after being restrained from its vice.

Afterwards, he had felt such a love swell within him for Rose, a love which had always been there and had now been fulfilled. He had known then that he never wanted to lose her.

But he thought that he had been careful.

'Alan, are you there?' came Jake's jibe from beside him. 'Is there anybody in there. Time to get married.'

'Yeah, Jake, I'm 'ere. Ready, willin' 'n' able.'

The ceremony passed uneventfully. The registrar said the appropriate words, Rose and Alan said their 'I do's' and it was done. They were husband and wife. Till death do us part.

A banner had been hung across the entrance to the local club where Rose and Alan spent their Saturday nights out. It was home from home and the only fitting place for the reception. Fred, the steward, had tried his best to make the place look festive which was no easy task in a place so often used and rarely decorated.

The walls of the room were a colour which could best be described as 'smokey', being the distinct yellow which paints any room where smoking is the prime activity, which also accounted for the many tiny holes in the brown, fake-velvet chairs which were scattered around the room, circling the brown Formica tables like attacking Indian tribes.

A few bunches of drooping daffodils had been thrown unceremoniously into jam jars and placed on the two window ledges. Jake had dragged one of his friends along to be a disc-jockey for the afternoon and evening so they would get the compulsory 'knees-up'.

Fred had tried his best with the food, having battled heroically with sandwiches, sausage rolls and various things on cocktail sticks, all of which now sat hidden under red tissue paper on a wooden trellis table in the corner near the bar.

Weddings helped the years go by, grabbing together people joined by blood or friendship to celebrate. For one day, all was forgiven as they became part of something positive, the day-to-day drudge forgotten.

As evening fell, the club filled with Rose and Alan's friends, all eager to wish them well, which meant that they saw little of each other throughout the whole afternoon and evening, busy playing host and hostess, making sure that everyone enjoyed themselves. They managed to grab a quick peck every now and again as their paths crossed. Plenty of time to be alone together later.

Alan's parents Tom and Emma found themselves a table tucked into a corner with Bert and Alice — hardly quiet, but away from the drunken staggering which was spreading like a disease and away from the descending cloud of smoke. Polite exchanges exhausted, an awkward silence threatened to engulf them.

'Lovely do, don't you think,' smiled Emma

'Could have been worse,' replied Alice.

'Sorry 'bout all this Bert,' Tom smiled apologetically, hands lifting the burden of air.

'Don't be daft, Tom. It teks two to tango. 'e's a good lad your Alan, gentle-like, a good grafter.'

'Aye, your Rose is a belter an all. 'e couldn't 'ave got better 'n' she'll keep 'im on t' straight 'n' narrow, I'll bet.'

'Thanks for sorting t' 'ouse out for 'em Tom. It meant a lot wi' t' baby an' all.'

'A mate owed me a favour so t' rent's cheap 'n' our Alan's job's safe wi' me in t' shop. Alas need butchers they do.'

'Aye, I think they'll do alright. Bit of a bad start but they'll like mek best of it. Let's 'ave a toast to our Rose 'n' your Alan.'

Glasses and hopes were raised for their children as they began their bumpy journey together.

Towards the end of the evening, Rose found Josie who had dutifully helped to entertain and attend to Rose's guests and was exhausted.

'I hope you'll be 'appy, Rose,' she whispered as she hugged her friend tightly.

'I think I will be, Josie. I'm comin' to terms wi' it all

a bit now. Well, there's not really much I can do about it, is there? At least Alan's a good man. I 'aven't seen 'im all night, y' know. Keepin' out o' my way already!' They laughed.

'I know what you mean. Jake 'n' me 've bin so busy doin' t' rounds we 'aven't seen each other either. 'e's walkin' me 'ome, though. Anyroad, it'll be time for you 'n' Alan to go soon. You can't be t' last to leave on your weddin' night. You must 'ave better things to do!' Josie nudged her friend and winked.

'Aye, I think I'd best find 'im 'n' we'll start mekkin tracks. Did I tell you we booked an 'otel for t' night since we can't afford to go away, with t' baby an' all?'

'Well, enjoy yoursens n' don't get up too early in t' mornin'. If you're payin' for an 'otel room, mek most of it!'

Rose and Josie set about rounding up their men just as the 'smoochy' records started which made it difficult to evade the haphazard meanderings of the couples as they clung together in the hope that they could manage to hold each other upright. Uncle Ernest and Mr Turner's blonde, busty, new wife had been unsuccessful, and lay in a heap together on the side of the dance floor. Still, they looked as though they had enjoyed themselves.

Josie eventually found Jake, together with Alan and half a dozen of their friends, laughing together at a corner table, no doubt giving Alan some last minute, though belated, advice on his expected performance for his wedding night. Rose caught up with them at the same time, and the girls exchanged an 'I guessed as much' smile before dragging their men reluctantly away.

'See you tomorrow, Rose, 'n' good luck,' shouted Josie over her shoulder as they both struggled to keep their men vertical as they went their separate ways — Rose to her wedding night and Josie to her home.

The night was silent, shattered occasionally by snippets

of raucous singing which became muffled as they walked. Jake wasn't quite as drunk as it had first seemed — Josie suspected that he had probably faked his drunken state to maintain his macho reputation as a drinker.

As they walked, Jake put his arm firmly across Josie's shoulders.

'You must be freezin', lass. Let me warm y' up a bit,' he said lovingly.

'Thanks, Jake. I should've put a thicker coat on.'

'Listen Josie. Mum 'n' dad 're still at t' do. They won't be 'ome for ages yet. D'you fancy comin' back to mine for a cuppa? We've 'ardly seen each other all night.'

'Okay Jake. That'd be nice,' she smiled, recognising a warm, fuzzy anticipation at the thought of their restrained clinches.

They soon reached Jake's house. The fire was almost to its embers but had kept the room warm and welcoming. With tea in hands, they curled up together on the small, red rug. A small lamp at the back of the room gave a rosy light. They were contented. At least, Josie thought that they were.

Jake took Josie's tea from her meaningfully, placing it next to his on the hearth. He gently put his hand to her face, caressing attentively the features before him. She leant into the hand like a cat being stroked, trying to force its body deeper against the warmth. Her eyes were closed as she savoured his touch, thinking not for the first time how surprised she was at his tenderness. He kissed her fleetingly across her lips, kissing then stroking, kissing then stroking, until he judged that the time had come to kiss her deeper, eager to continue, still in the grip of liqueur, forgetting propriety.

He let his hand wander downwards which was gently, but firmly, pushed away. It descended again and this time received a more forceful shove. Undeterred, he tried again, certain that Josie wanted the same thing that he did; she just hadn't realised it yet. This time Josie pulled away from his grasp and moved to the settee.

'I think it's time you took me 'ome now, Jake. It's gettin' late.'

'Come on, Josie. Let's 'ave a bit o' fun. You know you want to. We've bin goin' steady for months now. Don't ya think it's about time you stopped t' virgin till death act? What's matter wi' you?'

Josie was used to fending off Jake's advances, but he'd never protested so adamantly before. She felt nervous, uncertain of this man whom minutes before she had trusted completely.

'You know 'ow I feel, Jake. I'm sorry it upsets you, but I don't agree wi' knowin' a person afore bein' married.' She could never bring herself to say the actual words. 'I'd never forgive mysen if I gave in to this. You know 'ow I feel about you, you know it's not you, it's just t' way I feel.'

She was close to tears now, unsure of what to say or do, only knowing that she must remain steadfast.

'Well that's just tough, isn't it, 'cos I'm tired o' waitin'. You want to save your precious virginity, well save it for someone else 'cos I've 'ad enough o' bein' prick–teased. That's it, Josie. Forget it, we're through.'

Josie couldn't believe what she was hearing from this stranger before her. They'd only been together for a few months. That wasn't enough time to consider if this was the right man to whom she should give her honour. He had no right to expect that of her. She was stunned yet, after a struggle, won the fight to retain her composure.

'If that's t' way you feel, then you'd best get me coat. I suppose it's too much to ask for you to walk me 'ome?' she asked, hoping that he could at least do that for her.

'Course I'll walk you 'ome. Just 'cos we're finished doesn't mean I don't care what 'appens to you. What kind of a bloke d' ya think I am?'

She couldn't answer that one.

Rose opened the hotel room door and was transported to a world of beauty and luxury. A solid-oak double bed filled the large space, with a cabinet on either side. On the top of the cabinets sat delicate, white, lace mats protecting them from the bases of two huge, pink lamps. The pink lamp-shades had tassels all around the bottom, their glow bathing the room in dusk. Rose thought that they were the most elegant things that she had ever seen.

The bedspread was a silky material, delicate and pink, again with tassels dripping from the edges and draping onto the floor. A sink sat in the corner with two fluffy white towels neatly beside it; one for him, one for her. One for him, one for her. For them. Two champagne flutes and a bottle of champagne on ice glinted on a small, collapsible table.

Her father and Alan's father appeared in the doorway with her husband slumped between them. Alan lamely lifted his head, threw a wan smile her way, and dropped his head again. They carried him into the room and dumped him unceremoniously onto the bed.

'D' ya want us to get 'im undressed, lass,' they asked rather sheepishly.

'No, it's alright. I'll sort 'im. Thanks very much, both o' you.'

'Sorry 'bout this,' said Alan's father as if it was in some way his fault, ''e 'll be fine in t' mornin', 'n' sorry as 'ell. You wait 'n' see.' She got the feeling that he was talking from experience.

'Y'alright, love?' asked Bert, concern and love brimming.

'Yeah, dad. I'm fine,' she lied as they left them alone.

She struggled to open the champagne — she had never opened champagne before — and filled the glass to the brim. She took several long, hard gulps of the cold, bubbling liquid as she perched on the edge of the bed. What was all the fuss about? It wasn't that fantastic; champagne.

She poured herself another glass, not quite so careful

this time, and the frothy liquid spilled over the sides. The glass wasn't full for long as she poured again. Why shouldn't she get drunk? After all, he was. She plonked back down onto the bed.

'Look at ya. The man I've married,' — she raised her glass in toast — ''n' look at ya. Pissed as a fart. Unconscious. I'm 'ere on me weddin' night all alone. I've got a thing inside me I don't want. I've got an 'usband I don't need. I've got a life which is over. I might as well get drunk 'n' forget about it. Forget about it all.'

Uncontrollable sobs wracked her body unbidden; sobs of hatred for the unborn child, sobs of anger at her lot, sobs of frustration and self-pity.

Staggering to the champagne bottle she found it empty. She clumsily staggered back to the bed and collapsed upon it. They were a sorry sight; both drunk, still clothed in their wedding outfits which were now crumpled and creased.

She allowed herself to sob until there were no more tears to cry. She vowed that this was the last time she would give in to crying over spilt milk. She had made her bed and would have to lie on it, get on with it as thousands before her had done.

But she refused to let the old Rose die. She could be a good wife and still be herself sometimes. She couldn't live otherwise — she would simply die.

As she drifted into the sleep of the drunk and weary, she decided that marriage would not stop her having a life. She would not lie down and play married. She would lead their lives down a path which followed her rules. She would find a way to have a life *and* be a dutiful wife because she knew that she was better than the life which had been handed to her.

Chapter Nine

Sharif strode into his Club, sub-consciously noting that the greeting room was full. Christine quickly explained that it was a stag party and they were waiting for the whole group to arrive before they went in. Everything was under control, as he would have expected, since his staff had great respect for him despite his exacting rules. They respected him because he treated them fairly and paid them on time. Or perhaps they respected him because everyone had heard the tale of the drug-dealer who tried to deal in his Club. Sharif found out about it and confronted the dealer in the Club, in front of everyone. The dealer had mouthed-off, eager to show how big he was and how small-time Sharif was. Sharif had leaned over to him and whispered in his ear. The dealer turned pale, got up and left. Nobody knew what had been said, but the dealer turned up dead the next day in the canal. Apparently, he had fallen in a drunken stupor and drowned. At least that was what the coroner decided.

As Sharif moved on into the pit, he watched Clarissa as she did her stint of stripping on the stage. He stood for a moment, assessing her performance. Yes, he thought, just as good as ever. He chose his strippers with care. Go-go dancers can hide behind each other's performances, but the stripper is out there on her own under the direct scrutiny of every male eye in the room, and also under the scrutiny of every female eye as they wait for a slip, a mistake, eager to hurl criticism at the object of so much attention.

He found himself watching for longer than he intended and realised that he wasn't watching. He was waiting. Waiting for what? For who?

Before he could finish the thought she was there on the stage. Who was she? What was her name? He stood transfixed as she danced along with the others, oblivious to anyone except her. Her body gyrated, her gold tassels twirled. God, but her breasts were gorgeous, so full yet firm. He had to have her. Something inside, not just his body, was straining with the urge to possess her. Why? He didn't know, he only felt; felt himself becoming rigid with the exciting anticipation of owning the woman, not just the body. As the show ended, he made his way to the rest-room. Dayna sat in the corner with her arms around the torment of his thoughts. She waved at Sharif as he came in.

'Hi, Mr Sharif. How's tricks?' she asked.

'Fine, thanks. And you?' he returned politely.

'Great.'

An uncomfortable silence.

'Well, aren't you going to introduce me to your friend?' he asked, almost coyly.

'Sure, this is Bonita. She's new, so I was just giving her a pat on the back. I thought she did very well, didn't you?' Dayna grinned mischievously.

'I wasn't really watching, but I'm sure that she did fine.' He challenged her stare as he spoke and she returned his intense attention; looking, searching, for what? 'Since you're new, I was wondering if you would care to dine with me when you have finished, if you have no plans?' he asked courteously.

'I'm real sorry, but I've got summat planned already. Mebbe another time, if that's okay?' She smiled at him. Was that a smile of triumph or a smile of regret? Who did she have plans with? Why was he bothered that she had plans?

'Sure, another time.' He turned and left the room.

'Another time' came the following week. She held his arm dispassionately as they strolled together into the dining room. She wore her own clothes now, her sessions having finished. The cut of her attire was demure, the neckline high and the hem low, yet there was no hiding the figure beneath or the enticing eyes above.

They were seated at Sharif's usual table in the corner; he didn't like to be overheard. He found himself filled with anticipation at the prospect of holding a conversation with her, finding out about her. With the ease of someone accustomed to such behaviour, he pulled the chair from the table and allowed her to sit, expertly pushing the chair to follow and cushion beneath her. Once seated himself, he opened the menu.

'What would you like to eat?' he asked politely.

'You choose,' she replied without expression. She simply stared at him. He ordered for them both; chicken in white wine sauce by some fancy name. Champagne arrived as if by magic which he poured as he spoke.

'How do you like working here?'

'Very much, thank you. It's nice 'ere, not a bit rough like t' other strip– joints.'

'So that is how you consider this place, a strip–joint?'

'At t' end o' t' day, no matter 'ow fancy you mek 'em, that's what they are. Not that there's 'owt wrong wi' 'em, y' understand. I wouldn't be 'ere otherwise, now would I?' She grinned at him questioningly, or perhaps teasingly.

'Have you done this type of work before?'

She considered a moment before replying, as if repeating a long–practiced speech.

'Yes, but a while ago. I 'aven't worked for a few years. Bad back, but it's fine now.'

'That's lucky for us, then.'

'Yeah, I guess it is.' Yes, she was definitely toying with him — flirting or toying.

''ow long 've you owned this club, if you don't mind me askin'?'

'Many years now. It was only small when I began. I have built it up with much hard work and the hard work of my staff. There isn't a club as respectable as this in the whole town, wouldn't you agree?'

'It certainly does 'ave an up–market feel, Mr Sharif,' she replied, adopting the 'Mr' with which all staff were obliged to address him.

'Please, no 'Mr'. It's not necessary tonight. Sharif will suffice. And You? Shall I call you Bonita?'

'Yeah, that's me name.'

'Such a pretty name. Where did it come from?'

'One o' those old romantic movies wi' a Spanish lover in it, but t' lover wer female in this film for a change. Bonita Venecheta.'

'And you, Bonita, do you live up to your romantic name with a romantic nature?'

'It is my belief that there aren't many women born who don't 'ave a slight romantic nature at least. That's part o' what meks 'em female, wouldn't ya say?'

'Possibly so,' he agreed, nodding and smiling.

The meal was interspersed with verbal fencing, parrying away unwanted questions with ease, both experts it would seem. As the meal drew to its conclusion, Sharif could not decide whether to ask her back to his house and risk her turning him down or, worse still, being offended, or should he simply wish her goodnight and put his fantasies on ice until another time. To perform the second would be to act totally out of character. He wasn't used to playing waiting games, guessing games, but this time was somehow inexplicably different.

'Thank you for your most enjoyable company, Bonita. I do hope that you will honour me with your company on a future occasion,' he found himself saying before he had consciously made a final decision. He watched for a reaction. What did he see? Was it relief or rejection? Did she want him to ask her or not? Her ice–maiden was a match for his ice–man. She gave nothing away by action or word. He found this highly exciting and, as his member rose in agreement, he couldn't believe that he was actually letting her go home.

'Thanks for a lovely meal, Sharif. Could you get my taxi for me now please? Thanks again.'

'Goodnight then, Bonita. Sweet dreams.'

Chapter Ten

Rose awoke to the smell of alcohol, her husband's face looking down on her. For a moment she struggled to recall where she was and why Alan was there. She dragged her forearm across her face in an effort to open her eyes properly as they seemed to be resisting. Then she remembered.

'Sorry, love. 'ope I didn't wake you. I wer just watchin' you sleep. I've never seen you asleep afore.' He grinned coyly. 'I'm real sorry about last night. I know there's no excuse for it. It must've bin wi' drinkin' all day. Forgive me?' He gently stroked her face and grinned that irresistible grin.

She smiled up at him, the smile of the half-asleep and hungover. He looked so vulnerable, hanging there waiting for her forgiveness.

'Course I forgive you. I was tired mysen, so don't worry about it. It's not as if it would've been t' first time we'd done owt, is it?' They laughed.

'What's that smell, anyroad?'

'That's brekky. Either me dad or your dad must've ordered it last night. They brought it a bit back. D'you fancy some?'

'No ta. Just tea 'n' toast, please.'

They shared in silence. Rose wondered why he didn't seem as hungover as she was.

'He must be used to being drunk,' she thought, then shook the thought away. He was trying hard to be nice.

''ow d'ya feel this mornin', Mrs Knowles?' Alan asked with a posh butler's accent.

'Very well, thank you, Mr Knowles.'

'Care for a bit of 'anky panky, Mrs Knowles?'

'Don't mind if I do, Mr Knowles,' she giggled back at him. Their breakfast abandoned, they rather belatedly turned their attention to consummating their marriage.

They shared precious time together, locked away from

the world, enjoying the feel of holding each other. They hadn't had much chance to be alone over the past three months, what with the baby and planning the wedding. It surprised Rose that she really did like Alan, maybe love him even. She had blamed him so much for her predicament that she had been unable to see past it and hadn't given herself the chance to contemplate that she might actually enjoy being married to him. She could have chosen a lot worse.

They had little in common so shared a mutual, companionable silence whilst they gently got to know each others' body, sharing the need to be close physically. Alan relished the chance to be near his baby, laying his head on Rose's huge mound and stroking it, overwhelmed by the enormity of his emotions for the unborn child.

The time came to leave the hotel. They took a taxi home, their last extravagance allowed for their wedding. After all, they couldn't very well catch a bus dressed in their wedding outfits. When the taxi reached 21 Leicester Street, they stood together hand-in-hand for a moment just staring and imagining.

Neither of them had been inside before. The previous tenants had only moved out a week earlier, and the landlord had busied himself cleaning and decorating the little house to make it pleasant for his friend's son and his new wife.

If they were honest, they were as scared as they were excited, for they both still felt too young to have such independence thrust upon them. But this was an adventure, their new life together. Alan unlocked the door and turned the handle. With a wide smile he swept Rose into his arms and carried his new wife over the threshold.

The house was in the same style as that of Rose's parents; in fact, it was only two streets away from them. The small room into which they had stepped was spotlessly clean, the smell of polish still lingering. There was a red settee in front of the fire. A small dining table was folded up and pushed against the back wall, just like home. A small television set perched on a buffet in the corner.

'Hey we've got a telly!' whooped Alan. 'Good job 'cos we won't be able to go out much.'

'Party pooper! Shall we open t' prezzies yet?'

'Not yet. Come on, let's see upstairs.'

A large painting looked down from above the fireplace. Children played in a narrow street, the sun shining down and lighting tiny candles in the puddles around them, the street bursting into life after a downpour, the children eager to be at their play after being restrained. It felt like home already, and the adventure no longer seemed quite so daunting.

The upstairs differed to Rose's in that her parent's house had two small bedrooms, whereas this had one big bedroom. There was room to move about, room for her dressing table and still space for wardrobes. The bedspread was candlewick like hers but fresh and new, pale-blue with the tassels still intact and each of the lines unbroken. Pale-blue curtains to match hung at the windows.

Rose twitched the curtains on the front window, the street empty apart from the few people hurrying past who were late for church. The back window held no surprises; still the dismal back yard with its prison walls.

Rose sighed contentedly. So this was their house, at least for now; for Rose had plans.

They went for a stroll down by the canal. Nothing disturbed them, the only sound being the chug of houseboats as they coasted along, weather-beaten by years of exploring. The walkway along the canal was lined on one side by tall, thick, mature trees which either provided shade from the sun or shelter from the rain, depending upon the weather. They couldn't protect the couple against the cold though as it bit at their entwined fingers.

They called at the 'chippy' on the way back home,

ravenously eating fish and chips smothered in salt and vinegar out of the paper bag as they walked. The day ended with a cosy evening snuggled together on the settee, warmed and comforted by the sizzling fire, their arms around each other. They went to bed early, tired from their walk, and eager to once again be close.

And so their life together began its predictable pattern, the way life does. Rose got up every morning to make Alan's breakfast. The initial attempts weren't very appetising and consisted of black sausages, crispy bacon and brown eggs, but she soon got better with practice. Rose packed up his favourite corned beef sandwiches for lunch and then kissed him goodbye as he traipsed the few minutes to the next street to his father's butcher's shop.

Rose was then left alone for the day. She was playing the part of the perfect housewife and so she cleaned, becoming obsessed with keeping her house spotless. Every week without fail, come rain or shine, she would clean her windows and her front doorstep, the sign of a good housewife. She experimented with cooking, attempting varying dishes for Alan's evening meal which were always ready and waiting for him when he returned home from work. Alan wasn't too sure about some of the meals which Rose cooked — they were a bit too fancy for his liking — but he never said anything because he was grateful for her efforts; chopping and peeling the various ingredients, weighing and measuring on the tiny scales which someone had bought as a wedding present.

The tiredness which everyone had warned would soon befall her never came and, when she had spent the allocated time each day on her house cleaning, she would go into town on the bus to shop for the baby. She had to make sure that she was prepared for its arrival. She could not be seen to be anything less than the perfect mother, carefully choosing the tiny clothes, the cot, the bedding and the pram. Especially the pram. Anything less than a Silver Cross carriage pram made it obvious that you couldn't afford it. So Rose bought a Silver Cross carriage pram.

The shop delivered it for her because it was too big for her to take on a bus. As she looked down into the empty space, she had an overwhelming desire to vomit. Her head bubbled like a volcano, the pressure forcing the top to explode through her mouth. Incapable for a moment of moving, she remained glued to the handles, her eyes dark with dread, never leaving the small space before her. Unable to control the eruption any longer, she waddled to the sink and threw up.

Each day, Alan would return from work to find that another item for his child had mysteriously appeared in his house. He didn't complain, because he was so pleased that Rose had taken to being his wife so well.

He hadn't expected this at all. The house was always spotless, his meal was always on the table waiting for him, she kept up to herself despite growing bigger every day and her appetite for him hadn't dwindled in the slightest. What more could a man ask for? The least that he could do was to allow her to spend his money on their baby and not complain.

Although Alan enjoyed working alongside his father, the work was very demanding and it didn't stop from eight till seven. Alan was contented in his work, chopping and cutting, making his sausages, which were becoming renowned for their thickness. Alan had never quite got the knack of making thin sausages and customers would even ask Alan, quietly, if he had made the sausages before they decided whether to buy them or not.

Alan enjoyed dealing with the customers and was always cheery and chatty, aware that for some of them, especially the old folk, shop people might be the only people who they spoke to all day. He would joke with them and chat up the young wives who came in. His father kept in the background, adding his 'hellos' to the regular customers but leaving most of the serving to his son.

All in all Alan was pleased with his lot. Yes, he was a very contented young man and happy with his life.

Once a week, Alan and Rose allowed themselves a night out even though money was tight. They were both still young and needed to escape being grown-ups for a while. Sometimes they would go to the cinema, sometimes on a 'pub crawl', or they would spend the evening in the club. They usually ended up at the club by the end of the evening anyway, as that was where all of their friends usually ended up too. It gave them a chance to be with their own friends, the boys and the girls, as it wasn't really seemly for a married woman to go out without her husband and this was the only way that Rose had a chance to be 'one of the girls' for a little while.

Rose was relieved that Josie had started to come out with them again.

Rose hadn't seen Josie at all and realised that she missed her, having spent most of her time in her company until she married Alan.

So one evening she decided to tread carefully over the cobbles to reach Josie's house. Josie's mother answered the door, a smile of relief spreading across her face. She beckoned Rose inside.

'Oh, Rose, am I glad to see you,' she began.

'Why?' asked Rose with concern. 'What's t' matter? Is summat wrong wi' Josie? I would've bin over earlier, but ya know 'ow it is. Time just flies. I've bin so busy.'

Josie's mother glanced upstairs and, taking Rose gently by the arm, led her without a word into the front parlour. She closed the door quietly but firmly behind them.

'It's Josie. I don't know what's t' matter wi' 'er. She goes out to work on a mornin' as normal, but when she comes 'ome she just goes to 'er room 'n' stays there. She teks 'er meals up there on her own. We never see 'er. I've tried to talk to 'er, but she just doesn't want to know. Please talk to 'er, Rose. I'm real worried about 'er. In fact, if you 'adn't come over soon I wer gonna come 'n' tell you about this. I don't know what to do to 'elp 'er.'

'Don't worry, Mrs Green. I'll go up 'n' see 'er now, if that's okay.' She rubbed Mrs Green's shoulder reassuringly.

Rose gently tapped on the door of Josie's room.

'Josie, are y' in there? It's me, Rose. Can I come in?' She waited silently, but there was no response.

'Well, that's just tough 'cos I'm comin' in anyroad.'

Josie was standing by the window, staring out into the dark. She was still dressed in her work–clothes. She didn't turn as Rose walked over to the window and stood beside her. She carried on staring at nothing. Josie's face was drawn, tired, grey; a mask of sadness.

'God, Josie. What the 'ell's matter wi' ya? Ya look awful. Come on, what's up?'

Rose cautiously put her arm across her friend's shoulders and gently pulled her closer. Josie began to shake. Nothing more. She just shook. There was no sound, no tears, just shaking. Rose continued to hold her friend, not knowing what else to do.

The sound which eventually escaped Josie's lips froze Rose to the bone. It was the cry of an animal; a frightened, tormented, crazed animal, the yell of indescribable anguish, stifled to a harrowing moan by the desire not to be voiced yet breaking out of Josie's body which was being crippled by the need to keep it inside. Rose felt the distress physically through the sound, felt it seeping through every pore of the body which hung in her arms. The moan kept coming, the sound that said the pain could never heal, that the soul inside had been mortally wounded beyond repair.

Rose thought it would never stop. And then all at once it did, to be replaced by heaving sobs as Josie clung desperately to Rose, sobbing so hard that she found breathing difficult, taking great gasps of air as she struggled to control something which was killing her. Josie buried her head into Rose, trying to hide from the pain, hide away safe and protected in the arms of her friend.

They clung together for what seemed like an age, and then, little by little, the sobs began to subside and left only the struggle for air. With each breath a new wave would hit Josie and she would be forced to submit to a new bout of sobs.

Gradually, the sobs became weaker and weaker. Rose steered her friend to sit on the bed beside her and stroked her head, comforting her like a child, Josie not moving. Josie wanted to stay where she was forever, to stay buried away where nobody could hurt her again. Rose did not dare to speak, afraid that anything that she might say would cause her friend to once again feel the pain which was eating away inside her. She was prepared to stay sat as she was, stroking her friend, for as long as she had to.

'Sorry, Rose. I'm sorry to lay this on you,' spluttered Josie quietly. 'I didn't want to come 'n' bother ya, wi' sortin' your 'ouse out 'n' all, so I couldn't tell anyone.'

'Don't be silly. You should've come. You know ya come first, Josie. You know I'm always there for you. You don't 'ave to tell me, anyroad. I know what's t' matter. When I told Alan I wer comin' over 'ere, 'e finally decided to share wi' me t' fact that Jake told 'im a week ago that you'd broken up. I'm sorry, Josie. I'd no idea. 'e should've told me, but that's men, isn't it? They never think, do they?'

'Alan didn't know why, did 'e? Why did Jake say we'd finished?' Josie asked, her voice anxious.

'I don't know, Alan didn't say, so Jake can't 'ave med a big deal of it. Why? D'ya want to tell me why ya finished or not?'

'Oh, Rose. It's t' same old story. They all want one thing, 'n' I'm not ready to give it. I wer stupid enough to think p'rhaps Jake was different. I really cared a lot for 'im. I thought we might've stayed together. I wer such a fool.'

'He didn't....'

'No, it didn't get that far, but I wer frightened. Anyroad, it's all over now. I just couldn't face anybody though in–case I wer t' laughing stock, little Miss Goody Twoshoes. D'ya think I'm stupid, Rose, lettin' 'im go like that when I cared about 'im so much?'

'You don't even need to ask me that question, you idiot? You know I've total respect for ya. You stand by what ya believe to be right. Believe me, it's far easier to give in, 'n' look what a mess it can get you into!' Rose rubbed her protruding stomach and laughed. Now feeling better after being unburdened, her friend smiled.

So Josie had returned to the fold on Saturday nights and they joined together with their other girlfriends to have a laugh and a drink at the club whilst the boys stalked the local talent at the other side of the club, stupidly thinking that the girls didn't notice, and thinking, even more stupidly, that they would be bothered.

It will always be the case that whenever a few women get together, the talk will eventually always turn to men and sex. Men would be shocked to find some of the conversations which take place between women. Whilst men are busy talking about 'cor, she's a bit of alright', with immaturity, women are getting down to the 'nitty gritty' of how many times, where, when and how!

'So, Rose, 'ow's married life treatin' you?' enquired the group, with a wink and a smile.

'Very well, thanks very much,' winked Rose.

'Is 'e alright, then, your Alan.'

'Not bad at all, thanks. Why, d'ya want to borrow 'im?' They all laughed.

'Doesn't it put you off, bein' pregnant?'

'Not so as you'd notice,' she laughed.

'But 'ow d'you do it wi' your belly in t' way?'

'Sorry, love, you'll 'ave to use your imagination on that one!'

And so the banter carried on, becoming smuttier the more they had to drink. For a while, they talked little about boyfriends for fear of upsetting Josie, but once they realised that she could cope with Jake in the same room quite easily, they felt on safe ground again.

Josie had found it difficult at first to go into the club with the girls, knowing that Jake would be there, but after the first time that they bumped into each other she had coped well.

She had been dreading seeing him, but knew that it must come. Making a beeline for her, he had asked politely how she was.

'I'm fine, thanks, Jake. 'ow are you?'

'I'm fine, too. Listen, Josie, I'm real sorry about t' way I acted wi' ya. I 'ope you'll forgive me. I acted like an idiot. Anyroad, still friends?' He put out his hand to her and she shook it. She realised that she would never be just friends with Jake for she really did love him, but this would have to do and was better than nothing.

Maddy was part of their group sometimes, when she had nothing better to do. It was unusual for her not to have a date on a Saturday night, but once in a while her date was one of the boys who came to the club, so whilst he went to the boys corner, she came to laugh with the girls.

Maddy never suited the club; she looked out of place because of the way that she dressed. She always made an effort to attract attention, wearing her skirts as short as she could without revealing her underwear, her tops as low as she could without her breasts falling out and her heels as high as she could without falling over.

Her confidence sparked from her, almost tangible, which bred inferiority in most women around her and made her unpopular in certain circles. However, girls who took the time to get to know her knew that she was a gentle, good-hearted person who liked to flirt and have a good time at nobody else's expense. Most of the girls in Rose's particular group accepted her willingly. There was always the odd one who didn't, but you can't please everyone.

Rose remained grateful for the help which Maddy had given her.

'Hiya, Rose. I see they didn't work, then,' Maddy said quietly, nodding at Rose's bump.

'No, they didn't, but thanks for tryin' anyroad, Maddy,' smiled back Rose.

'I heard you got married.'

'Yeah. Alan Knowles. 'e's over there.' She pointed him out in the group of males in the far corner.

'How's it going? Are you finding plenty to do?'

'Yeah, fine. There never seems to be enough time to do everythin'.'

'What, like cleaning and such,' smiled Maddy, eyebrows raised. Rose got the distinct impression that she was being mocked.

'Amongst other things. Bein' 'ousewife's a very busy life, ya know,' she responded defensively.

'Well when you get bored and you want to do summat a bit different, let me know, won't you?'

Maddy knew girls like Rose. She wouldn't be happy just pottering for long. She'd soon get fed-up and want some fun. Just wait and see.

Rose didn't understand what Maddy meant, but laughed and tried to dismiss the remark which left an uncomfortable trail in her thoughts.

Towards the end of Rose's pregnancy, Alan started to get nervous about going out on Saturday nights, petrified that Rose would start having the baby whilst they were out and he wouldn't be able to help her if he'd had a drink.

'C'mon, Rose. Let's stay in tonight.'

'Don't be funny. It's Sat'day night. We alas go out on Sat'day night.'

'But what if ya start wi' t' baby.'

'Don't worry. I won't.'

'To be 'onest, Rose, we might 'ave to start stayin' in a bit more. We might 'ave to make it every other Sat'day instead of every Sat'day night.'

'What on earth are you talkin' about, Alan?'

'Well, I don't earn tons, 'n' wi' t' money you've spent on t' baby, everythin' I 'ad saved 'as gone now. We've only got t' money as I bring in every week. That won't go as far as it does now once we've got t' baby.'

'Are ya tryin' to tell me I'm extravagant? Is that what you're sayin'?'

'No, love, don't be daft, but we don't want to end up wi' money troubles, do we?'

'So you mean this baby isn't even 'ere yet an' already it's spoilin' me one night a week when I can actually go out 'n' enjoy mysen 'n' be summat more than a domestic drudge 'n' moron 'n' dress mysen up 'n' see me friends 'n' 'ave a laugh 'n'.....'

She gasped sharply, a knowing, frightened stare replacing her snarl.

'What's up?' Alan asked anxiously. Her hands clung to her stomach as she bent forward.

'I think it's startin'. I'm not sure, but I think so. I think you'd best call t' midwife. Go next door 'n' borrow t' phone. Quick.'

She couldn't remember what the lady at the hospital had told her to do. She was having the baby at home, so she thought that she had been told to ring the midwife as soon as she felt anything. Anyway, she wanted her here because she was scared. Her mind had gone blank and she couldn't remember what to do, what was going to happen. Were you supposed to know?

Another contraction. It was the same pain as when she took the pills but worse. She hoped that this was about as bad as it was going to get, because this was bad enough.

The midwife arrived, sending Rose upstairs to lie on the bed. Alan was summarily despatched to make them all a cup of tea. She didn't really want one, but it helped to keep the husband occupied and out of the way with these home deliveries. The midwife examined Rose, the contractions coming about every ten minutes.

'There's no reason to get excited just yet, then. I'll just take a look and see what's happening.'

Rose was about to feel embarrassed and humiliated when another contraction came, and she couldn't have cared less about anything. Why was the midwife taking so long? She eventually reappeared from between Rose's legs, a concerned look on her face.

'When did you last go to the hospital for a check–up?' she asked accusingly.

'About three weeks ago. I kept forgettin' to go.' She hadn't forgotten at all. She'd got tired with being prodded and poked about. The baby would come when it was ready whether they prodded and poked or not. 'Why, is owt wrong?'

'It's breach. You're too small to deliver this baby here. If there are any complications then I won't be able to help you. The baby could die. It's lucky your husband telephoned me as early as he did. There's still time to get you to the hospital.'

'But I don't want to go to 'ospital. I want to 'ave me baby 'ere.'

'Listen here, young lady. Your baby could die. More to the point, you could risk dying yourself, 'cos, believe me, as small as you are that's always a possibility, and I don't want that responsibility.' She was glaring at Rose now, trying to make her see the urgency of what she was saying. 'Now, where's the nearest telephone.'

'Next door. Me 'usband 'll show you.' A knock on the door......

'Tea's ready,' Alan beamed innocently.

'Never mind the tea now, son. Show me to the telephone. You, Mrs,' she said, turning to Rose, 'had better pack a bag and be quick about it.'

Everything was going too fast. The pains were not coming any faster, but Rose dreaded every one. When she reached the hospital, there were nurses everywhere it seemed. She was prepared and examined as though she was a spectator, being tugged, prodded and poked this way and that.

The pains became stronger and pure terror gripped her. She sucked hard on the gas and air in the hope that she might go to sleep and miss all the excitement, but they made sure that she stayed awake. Spoilsports. She struggled to hear what they were saying and realised that this was the intention. Something was not right, and panic set in. What were they going to do to her now?

'What's matter? What's wrong?' she cried, voicing her fears. One of the nurses came to stand beside her and took her hand.

'Baby is getting too tired. If we don't get it out soon, then there could be problems,' she explained.

'You mean it could die?' she asked with a mixture of feelings that she did not wish to assess. The nurse hesitated. Should she tell her how serious the situation was, that her life could be threatened too? Of course not. She simply nodded.

'We're going to give you a little injection which will speed things up for you. There's nothing to be worried about, dear.'

Within seconds the injection was administered. Rose was too busy dealing with another contraction to be too bothered about what they were doing.

Then it hit her. She was in hell. Somebody was tearing her apart from the inside, scraping and tearing. Then someone was tearing from the outside. She could feel nothing other than agony as her body struggled to eject its occupant.

She heard a voice screaming, begging for it to stop. And then it did. The demand to push stopped as quickly as it had started. There was still pain, but the intense pushing, shoving pain had stopped. Was that it? Had she survived? Wasn't there supposed to be a cry? Why was there no cry?

As she struggled to see over her straddled legs, she froze in horror at what she saw. Surely she had not given birth to that thing? That couldn't be a baby; that tiny, blue creature with flesh wrapped around its neck, dangling like a piece of Alan's meat?

The nurses were frantically unwrapping the cord which was strangling the child, preparing the life–giving oxygen to pump into its tiny lungs.

There was no cry. They placed the child in a glass box and wheeled it away to a place where they could continue the struggle to save its cherished life.

'Where's t' baby? What's 'appenin'?' asked Rose when she recovered from the shock of what she had seen, the picture that would stay firmly entrenched in her memory forever.

'Don't worry, Mrs Knowles. The doctors are doing all that they can for your baby. Now, let's have a look at you, 'cos you're in quite a mess yourself and you must be exhausted. We're just going to put you to sleep for a little while now whilst we finish sorting everything out down there. You're far too tired to help now. Just have a nice sleep, dear.'

Alan was still waiting in the room for 'pregnant fathers'. He had heard the screams emanating from the delivery room and cursed his bodily desires that they had forced such pain upon the woman he loved. He had seen the team of doctors and nurses rush from the delivery room with the glass box and head for some place down the hall.

He did not hear the cry of his child. It never came.

After some time, a length of time which seemed to tick

by so slowly and during which he became more and more agitated as his fear for his family mounted, a bed appeared from the room and was pushed off down the hall, closely followed by a nurse who came to seek him out.

'Mr Knowles, there were some problems with the birth. Your child is being taken care of in a special unit. Everything that can be done is being done. Your wife has also suffered badly. She has lost a lot of blood and has been sedated. She will be asleep for a while, but if you come this way I'll take you to where you can wait for her to wake up. I'll let you know the minute that we know more about the baby's condition. Don't worry, Mr Knowles. We're doing everything we can for your wife and child.'

'Please, nurse, could you tell me what we 'ad? I mean, is it a boy or a girl?' he asked almost reluctantly, as if knowing would make it all so much worse if there was no baby.

'Oh, I'm so sorry. Did I not say? It's a girl, Mr Knowles. You've got a beautiful baby daughter.'

Chapter Eleven

Alice busied herself preparing the sandwiches. Her hands were becoming an enemy to her already. She hadn't expected that things would progress this quickly, or rather she had hoped that they wouldn't. She could no longer fool herself that this thing would go away. It was attacking her body more vigorously with each passing month now and she was feeling the effects.

She had managed to hide her illness from Rose, but the time was drawing near when she would have to tell her the truth. Worry furrowed her brow as she contemplated Rose caring for Lydia full-time as she and Bert had practically raised her over the past twelve months.

The pattern had just sort of developed with Rose leaving Lydia for some reason every single day of the week, maybe for an hour, maybe for five. She always had some excuse;—

'Mum, I need to go to town 'n' I don't want to drag Lydia wi' me. Just 'ave 'er for a few 'ours.'

'Mum, I need to clean summat 'n' I can't do it wi' t' baby around. Please 'ave 'er for me.'

'Mum, we're goin' out tonight. D'you mind 'avin' 'er to sleep over. Thanks.'

Always an excuse, a reason. But Alice knew the reason. She had known from the very first time that she had seen Rose with Lydia.

Anyway, Lydia was where she should be right now, with her mother and father. Alice was on 'butty' duty for the christening which Rose had reluctantly agreed to after much persuasion.

'Why should I 'ave t' baby christened?' Rose had argued. 'I obviously didn't care enough anymore about God to get wed in 'is church, so why the hell should I want 'im to bless me child? I'm not an 'ypocrite.'

'This isn't about you for once, Rose. This is about the soul of your child, and just because you don't believe in heaven and hell any more, maybe, just maybe, I do and maybe, just maybe, I need you to do this, if not for your child then, for once, for me. It's not much to ask. I haven't exactly asked you for much over the years, have I?'

Rose had eventually acquiesced and the christening had been booked. Everybody was coming back to Alice's house afterwards since there wasn't enough room in Rose's house because of all the baby's clutter. There wasn't really room at Alice's either, but they'd manage.

'D'ya need 'and, love?' called Bert as he came down the stairs.

'No, I'm alright for now, thanks,' Alice replied, smiling at him as he came into the tiny kitchen.

'How're your 'ands?' he asked carefully, knowing that she didn't like to admit to the illness.

'I hate to admit it but they're getting worse now. I'm going to have to tell Rose. I don't know how much longer I'll be able to take care of Lydia properly. I'm getting afraid I'll drop her.' She looked at Bert, looking with hope that he would disagree with her and tell her that she was mistaken, that she was imagining things and she would be fine, but she knew that he couldn't. 'Anyway, let's forget it for today and concentrate on the little mite. She'll look beautiful in the shawl that I bought. I know I should really have made it, but what the heck! If I can't, I can't, can I?'

Bert was lost in his own thoughts and didn't reply, trying to decide whether to raise something with Alice which had been bothering him, but he couldn't bring himself to add to her burden.

He had thought for some time, just like Alice, that things were not quite right with Rose. More to the point, not right with Rose and the baby. He had realised, as had Alice, that they seemed to be caring for Lydia almost as much as her parents. It didn't seem right. It was as if Rose didn't want to be with Lydia.

Then he'd noticed them when he was bathing her for bed. The bruises. Only a few at first, but there always seemed to be bruises. He hadn't really bothered at first — babies were always falling and bruising themselves — but then the bruises had become larger, always somewhere on her tiny body.

He couldn't bring himself to think what he was thinking, the notion too horrific even to contemplate. He must be wrong. What did he know about babies? He refused to believe that his beautiful, gentle daughter would hurt her child deliberately. He'd wondered why Alice and Alan hadn't noticed anything, but it dawned on him that they didn't bath her; Alice because she couldn't and Alan because he was always at work.

He decided to put aside his fears and hoped that the christening would make Rose realise how special her baby was. He wondered whether she loved her child, then remonstrated with himself. Of course she must love her. How could anyone not love their child?

'You alright, Bert?' asked Alice, concern on her face.

'Sorry, love, I wer miles away. Aye, I'm fine, ta. Just 'ope today goes okay for 'em. 'Ere, I'll give you 'and.' He smiled, closed his mind and joined his wife on 'butty' duty.

'Shut up, you stupid little sod. Shut up!'

The child was thrown face down into the cot. She continued to scream; loud, pleading screams. She managed to roll herself over, her thin body shaking with the exertion of her cries.

Her mother paced frantically backwards and forwards across the room, drowning in anger, clenching her fists in a vain effort to control the mounting rage which threatened to overwhelm her. She was forcing herself to stay away from the cot, but the screams were drawing her like a magnet, teasing her with the knowledge that the tormentor lay there. That's where the cries were and she had to stop them, had to stop them because she couldn't take it. Her head was going to explode, her guts were going to erupt with this rage unless she let it out, let it out where the screams were.

She strode towards the cot and fiercely grabbed the tiny bundle from within. She held it roughly in front of her in the air and shook it.

'For God's sake, bloody shut up. Just stop it, stop it, stop it, stop it!'

The door opened. Alan stared in horror.

Rose remembered the first moment that she had set eyes upon her daughter. The nurse had brought her in and placed her gently in Rose's arms. She was sleeping, so delicate, so vulnerable.

Her small face was yellowish, but apart from that everything was where it should be. She had two eyes in the right place, which she'd been told were blue but that this meant nothing, they could change colour; a small, pink slit where her mouth should be and a tiny mushroom for a nose.

Rose stared down at her daughter. She knew that she should feel something, but she didn't. She felt absolutely nothing. She remembered the mixture of feelings when she had thought that the baby might die, and realised at this moment that the hope had been that she would. She had hoped that she might at least feel like a mother to make up for having this child, had hoped that all of a sudden this awe–inspiring 'bond' which everyone talked about would materialise. But no, she didn't even have that.

It began to stir from sleep and Rose stiffened in response.

'It's wakin' up. What do I do now?'

Panic began its slow swirling in her head, gathering pace as she waited to see what would happen next. The movements increased, the body twisting feebly, and the baby finally awoke. It looked up at no-one in particular, although Rose thought it was at her, and let out an almighty scream.

Revulsion is not strong enough to describe the feeling which filled Rose as the sound hit her ears. The sound was annoying, distressing, putting her jangled nerves on edge. She wanted this thing out of her arms and fast. She didn't know what to do.

'What's matter wi' 'er? What do I do to stop 'er cryin'?'

'Feed her, silly. Babies only cry when they're wet or tired or hungry. I know for a fact that she's not wet because I've just changed 'er, and she's not tired 'cos she's just woken up; so she must be hungry. There's a bottle made up for her in the nursery. I'll go and get it for you whilst you two become acquainted.'

Rose was relieved that she had been unable to breastfeed. That would have been more than she could take, the little mouth pulling at her, tugging at her body and drinking. The idea was horrifying. Luckily, she and the baby were both initially too ill to instigate breastfeeding and so bottles had been introduced immediately. Maybe there was a God after all.

As she waited for the nurse to reappear, she tried hard to stop the panic from rising within her, but it was being fuelled by the crying which wouldn't stop. Rose rocked the bundle up and down — she knew that much at least — but it didn't work. Of course it wasn't going to work until the hunger had been fed, but Rose needed it to stop now.

After what seemed like hours, the nurse trotted back, bottle in hand, and gave it to Rose. She gave instructions for performing the task of feeding, and Rose tried her best to follow them. She must have done it properly because the baby started to guzzle and the crying stopped.

Although the baby was feeding, it was obvious that she was not content as she continued to struggle. However, after a while, the tiny body reacted to the liquid which was filling it and it gave in to sleep before the bottle was finished.

Rose heaved a sigh of relief. She could put it down now, put it down and leave it for a while. How long did they sleep for? Hours? Minutes?

She placed the baby in the glass cot and lay back on her bed, her eyes closed, her hands covering her face.

'Come on, Rose,' she said to herself, 'you've dealt with marriage and coped well. You're a good wife. Now it's time to learn to be a good mother. So you don't love it. Big deal. You've still got to look after it because no-one else will, will they? Now pull yourself together and start trying.'

And so she lay, planning her act, putting together the requirements for the role of a good mother, once again adding another layer of persona.

Yet she knew that it would not be easy.

She realised that she had a problem with the child — Lydia they called her — when she was three months old. Up until then she'd been coping well. She would listened to every scrap of advice from the nurses, the health visitor, her mother.

She had learnt to control her desperation, rage and anger at the screaming which governed her life. She steeled herself against reacting to the screams, forcing her brain to ignore them. She carried out all of the tasks which were expected of her, hoping that by caring for her baby she would come to love it.

After three months she was told that it was time to introduce solid foods, so after carefully preparing the mixed mush she sat Lydia in a corner of the settee, bib on, ready and eager.

Rose dipped the spoon into the dish and placed a pea-sized blob on the spoon. She pointed the spoon towards Lydia's mouth and her mouth dutifully opened then closed around the spoon. The attempt at swallowing came, followed swiftly by a cough with ballistic force which ejected green goo straight onto Rose's face.

For the first time, Rose's anger became uncontrollable, breaking free from its tight reign. She picked the child up and then .... she couldn't remember.

As if awaking from a dream, she slowly turned her head towards the noise which was calling her. She stared blankly at the screaming baby which squirmed on the settee, vacantly questioning the two large welts which were painfully rising on its legs, welts the shape of fingers. Deaf to the distress calls, Rose walked away towards the kitchen and cleaned her face.

Over time Rose learnt how to cover her actions so that nobody knew; learnt when to make sure that nobody saw her or the baby for a few days; learnt when to have it in trousers even on a sunny day; learnt never to hit its face.

Once released from its cage, the anger had refused to be tamed any longer, although Rose continued to fool everyone with the perfect mother portrayal undiscovered.

When the 'incidents' occurred, which she considered was not too often, she pretended that they hadn't happened. She told herself that the baby had fallen, the baby had trapped itself on something, the baby was accident-prone.

It wasn't long before she believed her stories. She believed the excuses because she wasn't the sort of person to lose control. She wasn't the type of person who would hit a baby. She was too clever, too well brought-up and gentle to resort to such behaviour. Such behaviour was for the poor people who didn't know any better. She would never do it, never.

She relieved herself of the burden of the baby as often as possible, grateful to her doting parents for taking care of Lydia as often as they did. She needed time for her new pastime which relieved the jumbled messages which swarmed inside her head and scared her; shopping.

After her curvaceous figure returned, she developed

a burning desire to buy clothes, not just for herself but for her husband and the baby. She would spend hours searching for just the right dress for Lydia, just the right dress which told the world that her mother must love her. Everybody must have wondered how Alan and Rose had so much money to spend on their wardrobe, but nobody wondered as much as Alan.

'Come on, Rose. Did I really need another jumper? 'n' look at that dress for Lydia. She's got one almost exactly t' same upstairs,' Alan would reason.

'D'you want us to go around like urchins, eh? D'you want me to sit at 'ome all day 'n' then when we do go out, go out lookin' like a bored, borin' 'ousewife?'

'You know I don't, love, but money doesn't grow on trees, you know. Me wage can't keep pace wi' your spendin'. I love you, Rose, 'n' I want to give you all t' things you want, but I can't work any harder, can I?'

'Then change your job.'

The statement hung in the air as they reached the old, familiar battleground, and Alan knew what was coming next.

'Go 'n' work wi' dad. T' money's ten times better on t' lorries. You're never 'ere anyroad, so what does it matter if you're away a few nights a week. We'll never get out o' this pokey 'ole as long as you work for your dad. T' money's crap. You could be well-off on t' lorries.'

'I've told you a thousand times I'll not leave me dad. 'e's bin good to me 'n' 'e couldn't cope wi' out me 'n' anyroad, I like bein' a butcher. I can't think of 'owt more borin' than drivin' round t' country fightin' me way through traffic all day. End o' story. Forget it. You'll just 'ave to stop spendin' so bloody much.'

Rose didn't stop it. She discovered catalogues which meant that she could search the shops for the latest styles and then come home and order from the catalogue. Easy payment, you see. Everybody was doing it nowadays. Besides, she couldn't stop shopping as it was yet another cruel disease which was now beyond her control. She kept the house nice, she had the meal ready on the table for when Alan came home, she was still the perfect mother, so she had a right to go shopping. She deserved it, after all, didn't she?

Alan couldn't believe what he was seeing.

'What the bloody 'ell fire d' ya think you're doin'?' he roared. He dashed across the room and grabbed the baby from Rose. He held Lydia tightly to him and gently kissed her head. She was still screaming and he gently rocked her as he spoke.

'God, Rose, what's got into you?'

'Nowt, silly,' replied Rose, guiltily. 'I'm sorry. It's just wi' t' christenin' 'n' all. I don't know what got into me. It's never 'appened afore. I just sort o' lost me temper a bit, love. I'm real sorry. I didn't upset 'er, did I? I'll never do it again, I promise. I'd never 'urt 'er. I'm just uptight, that's all. Don't look at me like that, Alan, like I'm some mass–murderer. I said I'm sorry. Please forgive me?'

She began to cry, all the time watching his reaction, waiting to see what he would say. He walked slowly over to her and put his arm around her.

'I'm sorry, love. You just gave me a shock, that's all. I understand. It's all a bit much, int it? It'll soon be over. Come on, now. I'll get Lydia ready. You go 'n' sort yoursen out. Why not 'ave a nip o' that brandy in t' cupboard downstairs? It might do you good.'

'I might do that,' she responded with relief. 'Thanks, Alan, I really am sorry.'

Alan and Rose arrived at the church, Lydia laughing in their arms; beaming, 'Vogue' creations, they were the perfect, happy family.

Maddy had shown her face at the christening. She'd sat

at the back where she had hoped that no-one would notice her; wouldn't do her image any good being seen in church, yet she'd wanted to be there.

She and Rose had become quite close over the past months. They both shared the same passion for clothes and often went shopping together; Rose's choice of clothes now mirrored the short, tight skirts and low tops which Maddy wore.

'How d' ya manage to afford to buy so much?' Rose quizzed. 'I've an 'usband to pay for mine.'

'I work, course,' Maddy laughed.

'But when? 'You're always out shoppin' wi' me in t' day 'n' you're always out on a weekend, so when d'ya work?'

'I work evenings and night shifts, silly. It's good money 'cos it's shift work and it's a doddle of a job. So I never feel as though I'm working, just taking a paid night out.'

'I could do wi' some o' that mysen,' sighed Rose. 'I can't get a job durin' t' day 'cos o' Lydia 'n' Alan's always 'ome of an evenin'. We could really do wi' t' extra money, too. 'e won't give up 'is stupid job 'n' it doesn't pay very well.'

'Well, when you decide to take the plunge, let me know. I'm sure I could get you something and you know you're bored to death.'

'Thanks Maddy. I might just do that. You comin' back to me mum's?'

'You know she hates me. Think I'll give it a miss.' They shared a laugh knowing that the words were true, so Rose hugged her goodbye and went to find Josie.

Josie had spent a long time trying to get over Jake and decided that perhaps she never would. The longer that she was separated from him, the more she realised that he was all that she wanted. She would see him around town with his 'bits of stuff', the easy girls who would definitely not be in the 'no' category.

He even brought them into the club. She pretended not

to notice, pretended not to care, but the hurt still punched her inside. It wasn't pain any more, just hurt. It made losing him a little easier for Josie to bear seeing this obvious craving for an easy lay, and made her relieved that she had stood her ground. If that was all that he wanted, then he was welcome to it. She'd had a lucky escape.

All that changed with one conversation.

'Josie you've a visitor, love,' her mum whispered with a puzzled frown.

'It's Jake. Says 'e wants to speak to you. D'you want to see 'im? Is everythin' alright wi' you two now?'

'Yes, mum, everythin's fine. I'll go to t' door.' Maybe there was something wrong with Rose or Alan?

''ello, Jake. Everythin' alright?' She didn't know what to say.

'Aye, Josie. Everythin's fine. I just wondered if you'd like to tek a quick walk wi' me, just for a while. I wanted to talk to you about summat, if that's alright wi' you like?'

Josie felt her heart quicken and caught it in a tight rein. There was no reason to get her hopes up; they had been finished for ages now. He probably wanted to talk about one of his floozies.

Josie snuggled into her coat for moral support even though it was a mild, May dusk. She didn't want to start the conversation, didn't want him to know her thoughts. He wasn't entitled any more. Anyway, he was the one who wanted to talk so let him talk.

'I've bin such a fool, Josie,' he burst out. ''ow could I 'ave bin so stupid as to let you go. I 'aven't stopped thinkin' about you. I know I've bin out wi' almost owt that moves, but I wer tryin' to get you out o' my 'ead. Can you forgive me, Josie? I only want you. I love you, I want you 'n' only you. Josie, will you marry me?'

Josie couldn't believe what she was hearing, couldn't

believe that the words which she had dreamt about every night had been uttered by the man that she loved.

'Jake, what d'you mean? Are you sure?'

'Course I'm sure. I've never bin more certain of 'owt in me life. Alan told me when 'e married Rose as 'e would've married 'er even if she 'adn't bin pregnant, 'n' I thought 'e wer mental. Now I know what 'e meant, what 'e felt like. 'Cos I feel like that too, Josie. Please say you'll marry me. No, don't answer now if you need time to think. I understand. But will you promise me you'll think on it.'

Josie took his face in her hands. She could see in his eyes the reflection of love which shone and she knew that this was meant to be.

'Jake, you idiot. I don't need to think. It's all I've wanted since I met you. I love you too you nut-case. Yes, I'll marry you.'

They threw their arms around each other and clung together, a hug that would hopefully last a lifetime.

Rose found Josie hand-in-hand with Jake.

'Hi, Rose. 'ow's baby? Did she enjoy 'er 'ead-wettin'?' Her long plaits had been replaced with a stylish cut just below her shoulders and she had make-up on. Rose had never seen Josie with make-up.

'She's fine. Quiet for a change. 'Ow are you, Josie? It seems ages since I've seen you? 'n' what's all this?' she asked, pointing at the hands entwined around each other. Josie and Jake shared a secret smile.

'We're gettin' married, Rose. Can you believe it? We're actually gettin' married.'

Rose thought that Josie's mouth would split in two so wide was her smile. She was radiant, her innocence so pure and endearing, and obviously very much in love. Rose felt a pang of unbidden jealousy rise. Was it jealousy for her friend's joy, or jealousy at losing her best friend? Was it regret that she couldn't wait to search for the excitement of sex instead of waiting for .... for what because she didn't know what it was that she wanted. She only knew that the empty hole inside her was being filled with anger and frustration in the place of love.

'Oh, Josie. I'm so, so pleased for you,' she gushed. She hugged her friend and grabbed Jake into the hug too, hoping that they felt her joy for them, nothing more.

'It's about time you got your act together,' Rose nudged Jake. 'You're gettin' a good woman 'ere, you know. The best.'

'Don't worry. I know,' he grinned as he gently yet protectively encircled Josie's shoulders with his arm.

Alice found Rose upstairs checking that Lydia was still asleep. There was something strange in her daughter's stance, something not quite right.

Then she realised. Rose didn't bend over the cot to stroke the baby's head, or perhaps kiss her, or even just bend as parents did with the in-built, unheeded need to be close to their child. She just stood there, staring down into the cot.

'Everything alright?' whispered Alice.

'Yeah, she's fast asleep, thank goodness.'

Alice braced herself to tell Rose what she knew she must tell her.

'Rose, I've something I need to tell you.'

'Funny enough, mum, so do I.'

'What you grinning at lass? You'd best go first I think.'

'I'm pregnant,' laughed Rose, 'only this time it wer sort o' planned. You're gonna be a grandma again.'

Alice hugged her daughter and felt desperation rise deep within. How could she tell her daughter that she would not be able to help her this time, would not be able to share the burden?

'Sorry mum. What wer you gonna say?'

'Oh, it doesn't matter, Rose. It'll wait. It'll wait.'

Chapter Twelve

Three months passed before Sharif found the courage to ask her to visit his house. After their first meal together and their cool game–playing, it had become increasingly difficult to change the basis of their relationship. They had undoubtedly become closer. Closer? What did that mean? He didn't know, but he knew that it was so.

They had discussed everything that it is possible for a man and a woman to discuss, everything except their real lives, their lives outside the Club. The latent tension between them grew with each rendezvous, begging to be satisfied as their desire for each other grew. They would kiss goodnight; small, intimate pecks which held so much in chains.

'Bonita, I would like to ask you something and I don't want you to be offended by what I ask?' Why the hell was he so nervous?

'I can't promise that, but carry on.'

'Bonita, will you do me the honour of coming back to my house with me this evening.'

'Yes.' There it was. No hesitation, no pondering. Yes.

And so it had begun. One night every week, Bonita would accompany him to his house. Just Bonita. No other girls, no threesomes. Just the two of them. Sharif was satisfied with only her, with what they shared as they explored each other.

He revelled in the joy of what he had found with this woman. He couldn't call it love, for he wasn't sure what that meant. It was a feeling, a deep feeling which surpassed the physical, made their bodily contact more intense and pleasurable simply because it existed.

They experimented in every way, hungrily stroking, plunging, fuelled by the illicitness of their affair. They would caress untiringly, eager to convey their feelings for each other yet unable to express them verbally for there were no words, no adequate words. They were simply content to be entwined, cocooned, for a short while each week. Of course, Sharif still entertained his girls, but his desire for them had waned and the lure of the physical explorations with them had lost its temptation.

Nobody knew about them. People saw them in the dining room together. People saw them talk to each other. But people did not see that they shared their minds and bodies.

Sharif maintained a major presence and vigilance over his club and over his girls. He would never allow himself to be distracted nor his good sense overpowered when it came to his business.

As he took his usual spot so that he could watch the stage from a distance, he noticed that Dayna was missing. Why hadn't Christine told him that she hadn't come in? She always kept him informed about staff changes. Having sought out Christine he asked his question.

'Where's Dayna? Is she ill?' he asked.

'No, Mr Sharif, she's here, but she's having a little trouble with her make-up this evening. She'll be on for the next session.' Christine looked uncomfortable.

'Trouble with her make-up? Come on, Christine, what's going on?' Christine hesitated and glanced around furtively.

'You'd better ask your friend Barney what's been going on because I'm damned if I know.'

The penny dropped. So he was getting rough with her, was he? Well, that was all well and good but not when it affected his club. Dayna was a good dancer and worked hard. He didn't want her being knocked about.

Detouring around the tables, stopping to greet several of his regular customers who were oblivious to his frustrations, he eventually reached the dressing-room. Silently, he stood and observed as Dayna concentrated on mending her broken face. She had made a start on disguising the blackness around her eye, but had not quite managed it yet. She had done a good job on her lips, making them fuller to hide the swelling which still lingered.

'Hi, Dayna.'

Dayna jumped and turned all in one movement, startled by his voice breaking into her crashing thoughts.

'Oh, hi, Mr Sharif. Listen, I'm really sorry that I aren't out there. I'll be ready by the next performance, honestly. I was a bit late getting here, but it won't happen again, I promise,' she explained, nervously.

'Barney?' he both asked and stated.

She registered the fact that he was not supposed to know about her and Barney and was alert enough to react accordingly.

'Oh, no, Mr Sharif. Just some girlie fight that got out of hand. You know how it is?'

Yes, he did indeed know how it was and he had the confirmation that he needed.

Barney was where he was always to be found at this time of night, in the table–dancing room. Sharif spotted him immediately at Eva's table. Eva looked uncomfortable and the reason why soon became clear.

She was trying to remain professional whilst being provoked by Barney. He insisted on touching her, which was strictly forbidden. Eva was no novice at dealing with such situations, but she was unsure of how to react to Barney in his drunken state as she knew that he was a friend of Sharif's.

Her relief was obvious when she saw Sharif approaching.

'Come on, Barney. Let's go and have a little chat, shall we?' Sharif took his arm and dragged him firmly, leaving Barney in no doubt that he was going.

'Oy, what d' you think you're doing? I wer watchin' that tart. Come on, Sharif baby. Leave me alone.'

Sharif said nothing; he simply continued to take Barney out of the room. He firmly led him through the pit and into his office. Once inside, he sat him down on the black, leather settee which filled the whole of one wall.

Sharif's stance was solid as he stared long and hard at his drunken friend without saying a word. Barney was only half-conscious and lolled groggily, waiting for a voice to speak to him from somewhere in the room, but he couldn't quite decide from where.

'What's going on?' fumed Sharif. 'You come into my club drunk and insult my girls. Then I find that one of my dancers has been beaten up. I don't suppose it had anything to do with you, did it?'

'She deserved it!' spat Barney.

'And why did she deserve it?' asked Sharif, struggling to keep his composure with this pathetic creature.

'She's pregnant, up the stick, fucked-up, whatever you want to call it. Not only is she pregnant, but she's only gone 'n' told me wife, the silly fuckin' cow. 'ow could she do that? She knew it wer only sex, nothin' more. 'ow could she drop me in it? Don't you think she deserved it?'

Sharif was torn. These girls knew what they were doing. If they got pregnant, it was their lookout — but to tell a man's wife? That simply wasn't part of the rules at all. It wasn't on to beat up on a woman, but it wasn't on for her to tell his wife. So who was worst? Barney was his friend, after all.

'What's she going to do? Am I to lose one of my best dancers?'

''ow the fuck should I know? I told 'er I don't want anythin' more to do wi' 'er. I'll 'ave to stay 'ome 'n' stay clean for a while. You know 'ow it is. I love me kids. You know 'ow it is.'

That night, a sad, young woman lay down on her bed. In her hand she held a glass of whisky, full to the brim. In the other she held something white. She took the something white and placed it in her mouth. She gulped down a mouthful of whisky and choked — choked quietly so that no-one would hear her. She took another handful of the white something and swallowed again, gulping down more whisky. She didn't remember which came first; the loss of consciousness or the finishing of the handful of the white something.

Dayna had a week off work. Flu, she said, a bad bout of flu. Then she came back. She danced as well as she ever had. She was as slender and agile as she ever was. Barney only came in once a week now and never went into the pit. His enjoyment in there was over, the episode concluded.

Sharif and Bonita stood back and watched their friends. They stood back and secretly wondered what they would do, what would happen if they were in the same situation. They refused to wonder for too long. After all, it was all over now, wasn't it?

Chapter Thirteen

Darkness had fallen lazily onto the day. Bert and Alice had just settled down peacefully together in front of the open fire, the bronze flames dancing before them. They were contented in their silence and hadn't even bothered to put the television on. The air outside was cold and damp, a typical March evening, not yet willing to let in Spring and determined to remind everyone that winter was not yet over.

Alice had her nose thrust into a book — a romantic novel telling of loves lost, loves found, loves discovered by accident — painting illusions of perfect happiness between two people; fantasy.

She read her books, as lots of women do, to escape into a world of peace and love, where washing-up, cleaning and ironing didn't exist, where husbands or lovers brought flowers every day and kissed their loves tenderly every night before making passionate love to them.

The readers would, of course, eventually be forced to lay down their books in order to perform the afore-mentioned chores which had not disappeared, only to climb finally to bed with their snoring husbands, who may sometimes raise the effort for a quick fumble about before falling quickly to sleep and dragging all the bedclothes away.

Alice was presently preoccupied with the plight of Juliet who was waving goodbye to her soldier boyfriend as he left to fight in the war, bundled with his soldier friends onto a train destined for who-knew-where, leaving Juliet to contemplate whether she would ever see her love again. Bert was preoccupied with trying to decide whether Liverpool would win, lose or draw next week as he contemplated his pools coupon.

They jumped at the frantic pounding on the door. A pleading yell accompanied the banging, but they couldn't distinguish the words. They exchanged a look which asked 'who, why, what?' as they opened the door together.

It was Josie, tears running down her face. She grabbed Bert's hand. He felt the trembling which had taken over her body. Bert opened his mouth, about to ask what was wrong, but Josie beat him to it as she spat out her words in haste.

'Come quickly. Please, come on. It's Lydia. She's fallen.'

Alice was already pulling on her coat and threw Bert's coat towards him as they left the house, not even stopping to lock the door. Bert ran as Alice followed as fast as she was able.

They found Rose in a heap on the floor at the bottom of the stairs. A baby's demand for attention seized their ears, coming from somewhere within the house, and was ignored. Their concern was with the child which lay amongst the heap, a silent child with blood covering her face. Her tiny body was crumpled into a mangled pile, arms and legs all crossed together.

Neither Bert nor Alice could move. All that they could do was to register fear and horror at what lay before them. They couldn't think or move or speak, immobilised for what seemed like minutes but was, in fact, only seconds.

Then the bubble burst.

'Did you call an ambulance, Josie?' asked Bert, trying to remain calm.

'Yes, I rang from 'ome. It's on its way. Is she alright?' she asked, needing someone to say 'yes'. She didn't get a response. Alice placed a comforting arm around Rose's cold shoulders.

'Are y'alright, Rose? 'ave you fallen?' Rose lifted her head. A glazed expression hid Rose somewhere far away, somewhere safe and warm.

'No, mum, I'm fine. It's Lydia. She fell. I wer carryin' t' baby 'n' Lydia just fell. I 'ope she's alright. Is she alright?' Her words were stilted, monosyllabic as she again lowered her head. Tears rolled unnoticed down her face.

The silent girl looked broken, like a doll long used to being thrown about by its owner. Bert gently lifted Lydia from Rose's lap, carefully moving the tiny frame, eager to hold her yet fearful of causing any more damage. At least she wasn't dead. It looked as though she was sleeping, oblivious to everyone's fear.

'I think it looks worse than it is, Rose,' said Bert in an effort to give some comfort. 'It looks like most o' t' blood is comin' from 'er nose. I can't see any other cuts or 'owt. It's just a matter o' whether any bones are broken, but she's only little so she like as not won't 'ave done much damage.' He hesitated, but knew that he needed to continue. ''ow did she fall? Weren't you 'oldin' 'er too?'

'I wer 'oldin' t' baby. Lydia's bin goin' up 'n' down t' stairs by hersen for ages now. I didn't need to 'old 'er. I 'ad to carry t' baby. She just fell. I don't know 'ow. She must've tripped. It wer an accident.'

Rose would not have understood the expression which crossed her father's face, the questions which lay there which he didn't want answering, questions which he wouldn't hear right now. He had to deal with Lydia.

'Rose is in shock, I think. I wish that ambulance 'd 'urry up.'

Josie reappeared with the baby in her arms, holding a bottle to its hungry mouth. Alice raised her head, absently thinking that she hadn't heard the baby stop crying.

'Josie, could you mind t' baby for us. D'ya mind? It's just we'll need to cope with these two at t' 'ospital 'n' t' baby needs lookin' after,' asked Bert. Then, a thought struck him. 'Where's Alan? 'e should be 'ome by now, shouldn't 'e?'

Nobody knew where Alan was.

The ambulance arrived and took Bert and Lydia, Alice and Rose to the hospital. Josie set about packing a few of the baby's things to take over to her own house where her mother could help her to deal with Annie.

Before she left the house, Josie quickly scribbled a note for Alan to tell him briefly what had happened and where to find everyone. Alan never read it.

Bert and Alice sat alone in the waiting-room. Their daughter and grand-daughter had been whisked away by efficient-looking nurses and they were left alone to wait. They sat beside each other in silence, each gaining comfort from the presence of the other.

The room was sparse but clean and smelt of the hospital. Alice thought of the people who had sat on these seats before them, waiting to be told the plight of their loved ones, the people who had slowly, inadvertently counted the black and pink coloured squares which lay scattered on the floor — just as she was now doing — their minds drifting to anything except the thoughts of what might happen next.

They had no way of knowing that a man and his mother sat in a waiting-room just like this one, in the same hospital, waiting for news. They too sat side-by-side in silence, the son holding his mother's hand to comfort her.

After about an hour had passed, Rose stepped gingerly through the door, like someone elderly afraid of falling. The blank expression which Alice had seen earlier remained. Rose was supported by a doctor who held her elbow. A plain-clothed woman accompanied them. The doctor spoke first.

'Mrs Knowles has had a shock, but she is fine. She has been given a mild sedative just to calm her down a little so she may seem a bit groggy. Will you be staying with her?'

'Yes, at least until we can find her husband. We don't know where he is but we're sure that he'll be here soon. We've left word with a neighbour,' Alice answered.

'That's fine. With regard to the child, we're still taking a look at her. She's badly bruised and we suspect that she may have a slight fracture or break in her arm, but the main concern is that she is still unconscious. It's nothing to worry about yet. This quite often happens when children have a trauma. It takes a little time for their bodies to recover and wake up, so we're keeping a close eye on her. Most of the bleeding was from her nose which she gave quite a bang, but no major damage there. Anyway, that's the position for now. We'll let you know the minute that she comes round. In the meantime, this is Mrs Turner. She's a social worker. Apologies for having to put you through this right now but it's standard procedure in these cases for her to interview the parents — a matter of paperwork, you know, so she may have some questions to ask. Well then, I'll leave you to it for now.'

Rose was reeling. How did she have a broken arm? Unconscious? Where was Alan? Who was this woman? What questions?

'If you 'd all like to take a seat,' began the woman called Mrs Turner, whose beige, tweed suit spoke of middle–class interference, 'then we'll begin. I just need to ask a few questions, just for our records, and then I'll leave you alone.' She gave a reassuring smile which did nothing to reassure. They all sat obediently.

'Now, Mrs Knowles. Suppose you tell me exactly what happened.'

'I wer comin' down t' stairs. I wer carryin' t' baby 'n' Lydia wer walkin' down by 'ersen. She can do that quite easily, y'know. She's bin doin' it for a while. She fell. I don't know 'ow. I wasn't rightly lookin'. I wer 'oldin' t' baby, 'n' then Lydia wer fallin'. My friend 'appened to be comin' over to see me 'n' called t' ambulance when she found us.'

'What did you do with the baby?'

'I put 'er down on 'er blanket in 'er room.'

'You went to put your baby down before seeing to Lydia? Why was that?'

'I 'ad to put t' baby down first. I couldn't sort Lydia wi' t' baby in me arms, could I? I couldn't just throw t' baby down. I 'ad to lay 'er somewhere safe, didn't I?'

'Lydia has quite a few old bruises on her. Does she fall a lot?'

'She's alas fallin' over or bangin' into summat'. Typical two year-old, isn't she?' Rose smiled at the social worker, sharing a secret knowledge of two year-olds.

'Well, she's almost two anyroad,' continued Rose.

'She's right,' interrupted Alice, 'she is always bumping herself. We've noticed it as well, but as Rose says, that's quite normal for a toddler finding its feet, wouldn't you say?'

The social worker sat writing in her notebook for a minute and then stood.

'Well, that seems to be about everything. Sorry to disturb you when I'm sure that you must be worried about Lydia. I'm sure she'll be fine. Next time though, Mrs Knowles, you might try taking the baby down the stairs first and coming back to stand with Lydia whilst she comes down. After all, it's better to be safe than sorry, isn't it?'

Mrs Turner smiled, turned and left. Rose sighed wearily.

Bert and Alice went off together to find a cup of tea and to telephone Josie's house to see whether they had seen Alan yet, leaving Rose by herself, guessing that she'd need a little time alone.

She remembered coming down the stairs. She had been in a rush. She hadn't done Alan's tea yet. She'd been shopping and taken the two children with her and it had taken much longer than she had anticipated. Lydia had moaned and whinged all afternoon. Rose had been forced to carry her most of the time and push the baby in the pram. Sometimes Lydia would sit on top of the pram and that was a bit easier, but she soon got restless and wriggled about too much making it impossible for Rose.

She should have left Lydia with her mother, but had decided to try with them both for a change. She should have known better. Now she was rushing to get the tea on the table in time. Lydia was going down the stairs in front of Rose.

Lydia had decided halfway down the stairs that she didn't want to walk down — she wanted to be carried. She stood rigidly, refusing to move, and even though Rose shouted she would not budge.

She had deliberately goaded Rose, had tried to get her angry. She had forced Rose to lose her temper. She should have moved. The child should have moved. It was her fault. She knew what happened when Rose got angry.

Lydia didn't have the aforethought or time to catch the handrail as her mother's foot struck her back.

The man and his mother rose as the doctor came into the waiting-room. They willed the doctor to tell them that everything was alright.

'I'm so sorry, Mrs Knowles. I'm afraid that your husband never recovered. He had a massive heart-attack. We did everything that we could for him, but I'm afraid that he passed away. You can see him if you wish.'

The woman began to sob, silent sobs as she leant against her son. He wanted to scream, wanted to cry, wanted his mother to hold him, but he was the man now. He had to take care of her. His father, whom he loved so much, was gone.

He held her gently as she wept against him, patiently waiting for the initial reaction to subside, waiting for her to move. After some time she raised her swollen eyes to meet his.

'Let's go and see your dad,' she said. He nodded and they followed the nurse who had waited discreetly just outside the door.

Bert and Alice returned to the waiting-room to find the doctor with Rose.

'Mum, dad, Lydia's awake. She's gonna be fine,' smiled Rose. 'Shall we go 'n' see 'er?'

'What about 'er arm?' asked Bert.

'I'm afraid that it's fractured, but it's only slight. We've placed the arm in a pot until it's healed, so she'll be fine. No lasting damage.'

They followed the doctor to Lydia. She was in a hospital cot which resembled a cage. When she saw them, she stood up and beamed as bright as a star.

She called for her mother and stretched her arms out to her through the bars, apparently oblivious to the thick, white appendage. Her mother put her arms around her, genuinely pleased that she was alright, filled with the guilt which always followed an 'incident'.

Lydia looked dreadful, her bruised face bearing witness to the fall along with the pot on her arm. Still, Lydia didn't seem any worse for wear. She snuggled close to her mother with the adoration which only a child can give to its parent; the unquestioning, loyal love which asks for nothing in return and bears no grudge.

Bert could barely contain his anguish as he watched. Maybe he was wrong. Surely Lydia wouldn't love her mother if she hit her and Lydia's love for her mother was evident, even in her battered state. Yes, he must have been wrong. How could he think such a thing? Anyway, they'd offer to give Rose a break for a while and look after Lydia for a couple of days because Rose must need a rest after this, mustn't she? That was the only reason for offering, wasn't it?

'Rose, we'll 'ave Lydia for a couple o' days 'n' give you a break. It must've been an awful shock for you an' all. Anyroad, Lydia'll just think she's 'avin' 'oliday. What d'ya think?'

'That'd be great, dad. Thanks a lot.' She couldn't look at him. She was afraid that he would see, etched on her face, the fear of being near her child. She didn't hate her. She didn't mean to hurt her. It would be good for her to have a few days away, though, out of harm's way.

'They're keepin' 'er in overnight, just to keep an eye on 'er, but you could get 'er tomorrow. Thanks a lot.'

As they talked, Lydia lay down and fell asleep. The day had obviously taken its toll on her and she had thankfully been delivered into the peaceful arms of slumber.

Rose knew that Alan hadn't yet come home as the note lay unread on the settee. It was by now almost midnight. Annie was sleeping soundly across the road and so she was alone.

The house seemed strangely empty and cold. Where was Alan? It was not like him to stay out so late. He never went out during the week. She picked up the note which Josie had left and threw it away. What would he say? He would be furious that she had let Lydia fall.

He was always accusing her of being careless with her, as though Lydia falling was all her fault. The child was clumsy.

No, she wasn't always clumsy. She couldn't help but admit what sometimes happened. Why did she do it? Why did all of her anger, which continually stirred within her, choose to vent itself upon a defenceless child? She didn't need to ask the question for she already knew the answer.

She blamed Lydia for being born. Rose believed that everything that happened to her was as a consequence of Lydia existing. Her life could have been so different. She could have....well, it could have been different.

So try as she might, Rose could never get past this resentment enough to allow herself to love her child. She did try, she knew she tried, but she couldn't.

Rose made a pot of tea to warm her hands, her coat still on against the cold as it was too late now to light the fire. She stared into her mug, angry at Alan for not being there to comfort her.

She dozed fitfully as time drifted by until five o'clock in the morning when she shivered awake.

A hundred scenarios flooded in huge waves across her head as to where Alan might be. Had he been in an accident?

Had he heard about Lydia and gone to the hospital? Was he with another woman? No, she doubted the last very much.

She was just thinking about worrying when his key turned in the lock and he appeared in the doorway.

Something was wrong, she could tell. He looked terribly weary. He still wore his work–clothes, which were by now rumpled like rags. His tousled hair fell unchecked onto his forehead and deep, purple colouring splattered his eyes. The grief which ran unchecked across his face suffocated her anger as she strode over to him.

'Alan, what's t' matter, love? What's wrong?'

He took her in his arms and pulled her to him. He held her tightly, clinging as though his life depended upon it as he buried his head in her hair. She returned his hold. As he shook gently she realised that he was crying. She had never seen Alan cry. She couldn't cope with this, not from a man.

She remained silent, simply holding him, giving what comfort she could give, wishing that he'd stop because she couldn't bear it. At length, he did stop. He swished his head against her head in an effort to remove the tears, pretend that he hadn't been crying, trying to save his dignity and pride before his wife.

'What's wrong, Alan? What's 'appened?'

'It's dad. 'e's dead.'

The rain had started early and already a thin film lay across the road as they left the house to make their slow, sad journey to the church. It wasn't cold. There was only the rain, dropping and jumping back up to catch the legs of the mourners, wetting them from the bottom up as well as from the top down. It didn't matter though. Nobody seemed to notice. It was irrelevant.

The hearse came, carrying Tom asleep in the back. As it pulled up in front of the house, a line of neighbours flowed silently onto their doorsteps to say their last 'goodbye' to a man whom they respected, a man who had served them dutifully for the last thirty years. As they stood waiting for Emma to appear their umbrellas stood to attention, lined up to send off a good man on his final journey.

The door to Tom's house slowly opened and Emma stepped out into the street. She was grateful to the residents who had come out into the rain. She acknowledged that they were there with a turn of her head and a nod in their direction. She then gracefully stepped into the car which was behind the hearse, followed by her young daughter, Joanne, who was being held protectively by Alan, followed by Rose.

Rose felt like an outsider. She loved Tom and was sorry that he was dead, but she could not possibly feel the pain that the family felt, could not share in their united bond.

Nobody spoke but the silence was not morbid; Tom wouldn't have liked that. He was a kind and gentle man who had served his family and friends without complaint; never questioning his role in life, just content to have no worries. He would not wish for them to be morbid — sad maybe — sad for a while that they wouldn't see him again, that they couldn't share their lives with him, sad that he had gone before them. The silence was one of remembrance of shared times together which could never be stolen, not even by death.

Emma was vaguely aware of the figures as they passed. There seemed to be people all the way to the church; so many acquaintances. She couldn't really call them 'friends' for Tom shared his life with her and her alone. What would she do now? She had lost her husband and her best friend. Who would comfort her when the wind howled at night and she was scared? Who would help Alan and Joanne with their lives, for she had loved them, fed them, clothed them, tidied after them, but it was Tom who had guided them. Would she be able to do that in his place?

At least she still had Joanne at home; someone to look

after and distract her worrying away from herself; somebody to wait for at the end of the day.

She sighed. This day wasn't about her worries, her fears for the future. That would come later. This day was here for her to say goodbye to the man who had been her faithful companion for so many years; who had been her lover, her confidant; who had chosen her to share his life with, and now that life was gone. It was a day to be filled with the love which they had shared, a day to remember joyously the life that they had shared. As she turned to their two children she smiled thankfully, for she could not be sad since Tom had left her the most precious gift that anyone can bestow upon another human being; he had left part of himself in his children.

The service was performed by the Reverend Vindage. His rounded body belonged at the front of a church, hidden under his black and white garments. His lack of hair and blessing of wisdom made him old for his years.

Reverend Vindage did actually know Tom, which was comforting; no sympathetic, hypocritical, meaningless words from a stranger.

Tom didn't go to church but the Reverend did go into the butcher's shop, and many was the time that they had shared a conversation when the shop was quiet. It wasn't that Tom didn't believe in God. It was just that he only had one day to share with his family, and he chose to share it by doing something with them other than going to sit in a church and sing. Reverend Vindage understood this, and set about recounting conversations which he had shared with Tom as they attempted to put the world to rights from their different viewpoints.

Alan stood. The Reverend had asked him if he would say a few words. He walked nervously to the front. He wasn't used to speaking out loud in front of people and he was unsure of himself, but he wanted to do this for his mother and father.

'Dad was, as I'm sure you all know, a good man. 'e wer also a good father. Course, there were times when 'e 'd tell us off, even give us a quick, sharp clout. We'd sit for ten minutes watchin' 'n' waitin' for 'is massive 'and mark to disappear from our leg. But 'e wer never unfair. 'e never punished us wi' out tellin' us why. Then 'e'd ask if we agreed, sort o' like askin' for 'im to smack us 'cos we deserved it! As we grew older, 'e didn't need to smack us. 'e earned our respect. 'e 'ardly ever lost 'is temper, except for odd times, like when our Joanne thought it'd be a good experiment to put dad's favourite pipe in t' fire to see if 'owt 'appened to it, 'cos, well, it didn't burn when dad lit it. Or the time when I wer ten 'n' I decided it might be a good idea to 'ave a smokin' party in t' privy so's when dad next went in 'e got gassed!

Best thing about dad wer 'e loved everyone. 'e weren't a mushy man 'n' wouldn't say 'e loved us, but we knew. We knew 'e loved mum, too, 'n' that meant a lot. We didn't 'ave to put up wi' blazin' rows or nowt. Anyroad we'll miss 'im but we won't be sad 'cos we know 'is love is within us 'n' 'e 'll carry on guidin' us from somewhere else. 'Till death do us part' is a daft thing to say. Death doesn't part owt, 'cos what 'e gave to us all, 'is friends included, is still livin' inside us.'

Rose put Annie to bed, Alan made the fire and a pot of tea, and they settled down in the comforting glow to recover from the day.

Rose was grateful that Lydia's accident had been skimmed over, almost gone unnoticed in the aftermath of the past week's events. With Lydia staying at her parents, Rose and Alan had not been forced to discuss the accident as it didn't put itself in front of them. Like they say, out of sight, out of mind.

'What you gonna do now then wi' yer dad gone. I mean, you won't 'ave a job now, will you?'

'What d'ya mean, won't 'ave a job? I've got a job for as

long as I want one. Dad left t' shop to me to run for as long as I want to. 'e alas told me 'e put it in 'is will that I can run t' shop 'n' then when it's sold, t' money would be split. I've to provide for mum out of t' takin's, but then t' rest 'll be ours.'

'What rest? Why d' ya think 'e paid you such a pittance? 'Cos 'e wanted to? I've 'eard your mum talk afore sayin' 'ow things 'aven't bin as good over t' last few years, sayin' 'ow 'ard they find it to manage. 'ow d'ya think you're gonna manage to support a wife 'n' two kids 'n' your mum on what t' shop meks?'

'It's what dad wanted!'

'I'm sorry, Alan, I know 'ow upset you must be, but don't ya think it 'd be best to sell t' shop? Your mum 'd 'ave enough to live on, 'n' you 'd each get your share. I'm sick o' livin' in this 'ole, all cramped up. Don't ya think I deserve better than this? What about yer children? They need their own space. I can't stand this for much longer, Alan, 'n' it'd be years afore we could afford to move wi' you runnin' t' shop. I'm sick 'n' tired o' mekkin do when all you 'ave to do is sell t' blinkin' shop 'n' go to work on t' lorries 'n' we'll be fine. We could get a bigger 'ouse then, too. Look outside, just look out t' back. D' ya like 'avin' to go to t' toilet outside, 'cos I don't. Don't throw this chance away jus' for t' sake o' nostalgia. You can't do that to me. I won't let you!'

'Won't let me? It's my choice, my decision. Mebbe I want to try to mek me own livin' instead o' bein' told where to go, when to come, 'avin' a boss. Mebbe, just mebbe, I don't want that.'

'Well mebbe, just mebbe, it's either that or me, 'cos I'm fedup o' livin' like this, 'avin' you gettin' at me for spendin' money on t' kids 'n' on clothes, bein' stuck 'ere all day 'cos I can't afford to go nowhere, to do owt. Mebbe, just mebbe, I might get a job if you can't bring enough in.'

'I don't want you workin'.'

'Oh, I see, I can't tell you what to do, but not t' other way round. Well think again, 'cos if you don't sell t' shop so we can move, then I'm out of 'ere. Get it!'

Rose stormed upstairs, leaving Alan alone in his grief; grief at the loss of his father, grief at the loss of a mentor. He didn't feel old enough to be making decisions — decisions which would affect his whole family.

Yet he accepted without much argument that the decision had already been made for him after all.

Chapter Fourteen

Another blob of bright-green, sticky jelly, encrusted with slimy, cream blancmange hit the floor. Rose pounced, cloth at the ready, diving on it before a stray foot inadvertently stamped on it, plastering its definition forever into her pale-pink carpet. Diving was difficult in her present condition, as her protruding stomach tended to get in the way. She straightened stiffly, placing a hand into her lower back in an effort to revert her spine into a linear column.

'Come on, Rose,' she said to herself, 'nearly there now. Only another half hour to go.' She ran the dishcloth under the tap to dislodge the offending food and wrung it, now ready for its next rescue attempt.

She surged back into the fray, wondering what 'little incident' would land on her next. What could be worse than the four year-old girl, Jessica, who, in her eagerness to win musical chairs, had forgotten to go to the toilet. Her only reward was wet knickers and socks coupled with chapped thighs. Rose had thrown the offending items unceremoniously into a carrier bag in readiness for Jessica's mother to deal with them. The sweet smell of disinfectant still lingered.

Then there was the child who had been thumped by Jonathan Smith for some reason best known to Jonathan Smith. The child, now sporting an ever-reddening right eye, refused to cease wailing at high pitch. His eviction to the back garden imminent, he had been saved by sleeping logs. What a wonderful idea. God bless the inventor of sleeping logs! Silence was indeed for a short time golden. Rose's shoulders momentarily lost their knot, but all too soon the magic spell wore off. Once a few of the older boys were out, they decided to begin yet another rampage.

Tea-time had been the solution, at least for ten minutes. Curiosity stilled their bodies if not their tongues as they did a survey of the neatly spread sandwiches and things not on sticks. Little had she realised that they were assessing each mouth–sized morsel as a prospective projectile and soon the children from hell had begun their attack. Rose found herself on 'missile patrol', dodging and catching the small pieces of food which landed anywhere except in the childrens' mouths. Helplessly she watched as Jonathan Smith attacked her settee with a head–dive, all six stones of him, his jam sandwich exploding between his podgy fists and plastering the fluffy, pastel cushions. What on earth had possessed her to have a party for Lydia's fifth birthday?

Of course, she knew perfectly well the reason for the party. Rose had spent the last three years renovating her beautiful new home. The party was the first time that she had had the chance to show it to the world at large; well at least to the world at large down her road.

Alan had given in to her desire — no, her need — for a bigger house and they had moved to Wykon, a moderately exclusive area of town; suburbia. Most of the money which the sale of Tom's shop had given to them had been buried within the house, but Rose didn't care for she had the house which she had always wanted.

It was much larger than the rabbit hutch where they had started their married life together. It had an indoor toilet; no more nocturnal outings to the privy. It also had three bedrooms. The rear garden swept away in a narrow sloping strip, but it was their narrow strip. Rose extended the perfect, neat order of her household down to the bottom of the garden, the military rows of strong, tall daffodils standing to attention against the fence, leaning over fragile pansies, superior in their colour as they sheltered meekly in the shadow of their handsome cousins.

Inside the house she had carefully sought out each piece of furniture, every ornament, the colour scheme of each room in unison with the next. The subtle hues of delicate pastels flowed as each door was opened. Yes, she had been impressed with her creation.

She was, however, at that particular moment, musing that perhaps pastel pinks were not a good idea as long as children roamed the earth. In fact, at that moment in time, with ten children attacking the room, it seemed a particularly bad choice. Or maybe it was just the party that was the bad choice?

No, she had needed to have the party. She had needed to show the world, her world, what a good wife and mother she was. Why else would she put herself through this torture?

She basked in the praise of her peers at her domestic achievements, at her wonderful children who were always immaculately dressed, always dressed the same. If it was good enough for the Royals, then it was good enough for Rose and her children. They boasted little red knicker–bocker outfits with frilly, white blouses, pristine sailor dresses with knee-high white boots, their hair bunched in tidy pig–tails. They walked hand–in–hand, respectful, well–behaved, untouched dolls.

Rose was so attentive to her children. Everyone knew. How else would Lydia already be able to read and write? Of course, it was purely due to the time and effort which Rose had invested in her daughter that this achievement came to pass, made difficult by the fact that Lydia wasn't the brightest of children. Still, she had persevered and had a literate five year–old. Wasn't she clever? And here she was giving a party for her loving daughter.

Rose was losing the battle to control her rising anger at the unruly and disrespectful beasts before her. Didn't these children have any idea of how to behave? How could they possibly daub chocolate–stained fingers on her wall? Lucky that the paper was washable. Her children would never do such a thing.

Snatching her arm to her face to see her watch, she

realised with relief that she only had to hold on for a short time longer. It was almost time for them to go. Time to cut the cake.

Eagerly, anxious now to finish the ritual, she escaped into the kitchen and grabbed the cake, whisking it unceremoniously into the dining room. Calm now, counting the minutes, she placed it carefully on the table. It was a solitary square of peach perfection amidst a swell of debris which threatened to engulf it. A tiny angel danced daintily on the top and the disorder faded into insignificance. Rose concentrated on the tiny angel. Not long now.

She lit the candles. After yelling herself hoarse to be heard, the children finally gathered round. They dutifully groaned 'happy birthday to you' and then Lydia blew out her candles. She smiled at her friends, her rare smile curved and gentle, excitement popping from her piercing, blue eyes at being the centre of so much attention.

Josie had been nominated, under protest, to provide sane adult assistance at the party. Her attempts to remain unobtrusive by guarding the washing-up bowl had so far succeeded.

She would have volunteered anyway to help out Rose. They were still best friends, if that's what grown-ups called it, and they lived on the same road. Not in the same type of house, though. Josie and Jake had managed to afford only a small, terraced house, but they were happy there with their year-old son, Charlie. It had taken all of their savings to pay for their wedding and then they had struggled together to save for the deposit on their home. They didn't mind. It had brought them closer together, struggling and sharing the good times and bad.

Everything had fallen into place at the right time. They had just managed to save enough for the house and get moved in when Josie had discovered that she was pregnant. The timing couldn't have been better.

Josie and Jake were so happy; best friends as well as husband and wife. Josie wished that Alan and Rose were happy, but she knew that they weren't. She didn't know why, but she just knew, and so she helped Rose whenever she could, as she always had. And so there she was, yet again, providing support to her friend.

She 'd helped Rose a lot over the last few years, especially with babysitting. That was really the only time that Josie and Jake argued, when they argued about Josie looking after the children for Rose whilst she worked.

'I don't see why you need to look after t' kids for 'er durin' t' day when she works at night,' he would argue.

'It's only for a few 'ours whilst she gets a bit o' sleep. It's 'ard work at that factory 'n' t' graveyard shift is t' worst. That's why t' money's so good. She gives me a bit o' summat for 'avin' 'em, too, so it's not like I do it for nowt. Anyroad, she's me friend 'n' if I can 'elp 'er out then I will. Please don't mek a fuss, Jake. You're at work so it doesn't bother you, does it? Please don't be cross eh?'

'That's not t' point. It's not right 'er bein' out at night when Alan isn't 'ome. She might be your friend, but I wouldn't trust 'er as far as I could throw 'er. Got fancy ideas, that one.'

'There's no law against 'avin' fancy ideas, Jake. Anyroad, what can she possibly get up to in a grotty, stinkin' factory. You must 'ave a good imagination 'cos I can't think of owt. Well, she'll have to stop now she's pregnant.'

Josie was tugged sharply back to her red bowl of cold, soapy water as she ducked to avoid being hit by a low–flying bun which just missed her head. She decided that it might be wise to check on Charlie to make sure that the children hadn't devised a new game of 'eat the baby!'

At last the party was over. The children had disappeared, transported away by some wonderful magic spell, and the noise had ceased. Rose and Josie stood in the middle of the room wondering where they should start. They looked at each other and burst out laughing with relief that at least it was all over and they had survived.

'Whose stupid idea wer this, then?' laughed Rose.

'Whose stupid idea to volunteer me to 'elp? Next time, I'll leave you to get buried under t' bun attacks by yoursen. Remind me never to 'ave a party for Charlie.'

'By the way, where is 'e, Josie?'

'Sound asleep in bed wi' Annie. They did really well to sleep through that lot, don't ya think?'

'Yes, little darlin's.'

'By the way, where's your mum? I thought she wer comin' to 'elp.'

'So did I. She 'asn't been very well lately, though. She's like as not chickened out. I'll give 'er a ring later.'

They set about the unenviable task of returning the room to its former glory.

They didn't give a thought to Lydia. The party over, she was now forgotten, her usefulness finished.

Lydia was so tired after her party. She wearily took off her party dress and hung it on a hanger in the wardrobe. She loved her dress. She thought it made her look pretty. It was made from peach taffeta, her mum had said. Lydia gently ran her fingers down the front of it, feeling the smooth coldness of the material against her skin, stroking the dress lovingly. It wasn't dirty. She never got dirty. Mum didn't like it. More washing, she would say.

She smiled the smile of the sleepy as she thought of all of her friends who had sung her happy birthday. She hadn't known she had so many friends. How nice that they all came. They must all like her or they wouldn't have come would they? And her mum must love her so much or else she wouldn't have made her a party would she?

Silently she crept to the bathroom and washed herself, making sure to wash her neck and behind her ears because mum would check. Then she brushed her teeth, making sure to do all the way to the back or else they would surely all fall out and leave her toothless. That's what she'd been told.

She squatted down on the landing when she'd finished, curled tightly, unseen in her favourite place, clinging to the banister. She often sat here listening when she was supposed to be in bed. She could never hear the words, unless mum and dad argued, but she liked to hear the voices downstairs. She didn't know why — it just made her feel less lonely. She listened to her mum and Aunt Josie downstairs, laughing as they tidied up. She liked to listen to her mum. She missed her because she never really saw her very much. Nanna and Grandad looked after her mostly, or Josie, and mum was always busy; busy cleaning, busy tidying, busy seeing to Annie. Lydia knew that her mum had lots to do. She tried to keep out of her way so that she wouldn't call her a nuisance and get angry. She didn't like it when mum got angry because she hurt her. She didn't mean to hurt her, but she did.

She never told anyone. It was their secret, hers and mums. Mum had said so. Mum really loved her, she said so, and so she couldn't let anyone know their secret. Lydia knew that mum only hit her when she annoyed her, when she got in the way, so it was Lydia's own fault after all. She just had to learn to behave better, to be a good girl and not bad. Mum said that she was bad, but she did try hard not to be. She tried hard with her reading and writing although sometimes it made her head hurt so much. She didn't care, though, because mum said that she was good if she got it all right. She nearly always got it all right. Then mum liked her. Then they smiled together and sometimes mum would even hug her.

She hadn't done very well last week, though. Lydia winced as she remembered the iron. It was very heavy and she knew that it was boiling hot. She was scared of it really, but she didn't let mum know. Mum had lowered the ironing-board and told Lydia that it was time that she learnt how to iron. Mum had told her how to lay the clothes out and then run the heavy iron *over them to make the lines and bumps disappear. The clothes had changed before her eyes. That was until she had stopped concentrating and burnt her finger. She had screamed out in pain. Mum had called her an idiot and thumped her on her arm, on her shoulder bit. She'd managed to carry on with the ironing with a throbbing finger and a throbbing shoulder. It made her concentrate very hard so that she wouldn't do it again. She had managed, but dad's trousers were bigger than her so it was hard work trying to get them lined out on the board. It had taken nearly five minutes just to get them straight. Still, she did it and mum was pleased. Mum had smiled at her. It had been worth the sore thumb.*

The room door opened. Lydia scuttled back to her bedroom. She knew that mum was cross with all of her friends for throwing food so she decided to stay out of the way. But her mum had, after all, given the party for her, hadn't she? She knew that her mum loved her. She must because if she didn't love her then she wouldn't have given her a party, would she?

Lydia snuggled down in her bed with a smile on her face, the sheets held tightly against her chin; happy from her party, happy that her mum had thought of her.

The party over and the mess finally gone, Rose went to check on Annie. As she bent over her, she felt compelled to stroke the wispy, soft, blonde curls. She looked so peaceful, so beautiful. Rose felt the familiar jump in her stomach just being near her.

The miraculous 'bond' which had seemed a figment of some poor, frustrated spinster's imagination at Lydia's birth had pounced tenfold upon her when Annie thrust her tiny head into the world. She had loved her since the moment that she first saw her; a wriggling, slimy bundle of life. Rose craved cuddling her, snuggling close to her, loving her. Annie had been part of Rose's plans, a wanted and timed baby. She smiled, stroked her head once more and crept from the room.

She realised that she hadn't seen Lydia since the end of the party. Hopefully she was in bed. She 'd better check though, just in-case. You never knew what that child might get up to. Rose snaked her head round the door. Sure enough, Lydia was tucked up in bed.

'Ungrateful child,' thought Rose, 'she never even came to say thank you for t' party or to say goodnight. Why do I bother?'

Rose stole another secret, indulgent look at Annie. As she leant over the bed and listened to the hushed, rhythmic breathing of her daughter, deep in sleep, she was torn from her absorption by the sound of the front door banging closed.

'Hiya, love. It's only me,' came the familiar voice.

Rose sighed. She wasn't going to get her peace and quiet after all.

Alan was tired after his day. He had wanted to be back in time for Lydia's party, or at least to see her before she went to bed, but the silence of the house told him that she must already be asleep. Lydia always came running to kiss him when he came home, always made him feel welcome and wanted. Now he was met with only stillness. Damn the warehouseman in Liverpool. If he had got off his fat backside sooner to unload instead of making Alan wait until he finished his lunch-break, and hadn't unloaded an earlier delivery first, he would have been back. Still, nothing he could do about it now. He would just have to ask her about her party in the morning. Fatigue began to settle on him as he sat to take the weight off his legs.

'Don't even think about sittin' down on that settee til you've changed yer clothes 'n' 'ad a wash,' came the command from around the door. He sighed wearily and turned to greet his wife.

'Alright love,' he said. He didn't want to upset her. He was too tired. 'ow did t' party go?'

'Dreadful. They wer little monsters. I've got a stinkin'

'eadache too.'

'Did Lydia enjoy it?'

'I suppose so. She went straight to bed so it must've tired 'er out.'

'Okay, then. I'll go get washed. Any chance o' some supper? I'm starved.'

'You'll 'ave to get summat from t' fridge. I'm too tired to do anything. I'm off to bed.'

Alan washed and changed and made himself a sandwich. He fell gratefully into the warm comfort of the settee, carefully avoiding the wet patches where the jam stains had been cleaned, and turned on the television.

He couldn't understand Rose. He had tried so hard to do everything that he could to please her. He had sold his father's business as she asked although it had ripped away small pieces inside of him. It had been a major part of his life, his life with his father, the embodiment of the man he had loved so dearly. It had provided for so long for all the family, been a retreat from the rigours of his personal life, a safe haven in a sea of self-compromise.

Telling his mother that they would have to sell had been one of the most difficult jobs of his life. He had lied, telling her that he felt too young to take the responsibility of a business, but they both knew that she wasn't fooled as to the reason; Rose. He needed to keep her at all costs. He loved her and, well, he was quite happy with his little family. Contentment for Alan never went further than having a roof over his head, his wife at home waiting for him with tea on the table and his children taken care of. Most of this was achieved most of the time.

He'd even gone to work on the lorries to earn more money to keep pace with her spending. It wasn't hard work, just long hours, but he'd got used to it. The hardest part was spending nights away during the week. It usually averaged out at about two a week, some weeks three, some weeks one, which were long and lonely nights, bundled and cramped into the tiny sleeping cot in the cabin, freezing and uncomfortable.

He had plenty of offers to help to heat up his cabin for him, but he wasn't interested. Some of the drivers did take advantage of the offers, steaming up their cabs and performing like contortionists, but most were simply family men just the same as him, simply earning a living in the best way that they could. It wasn't that bad though. In a way, he still felt like he was his own boss. Once on his journey, it was just him, his lorry and his radio. He quite enjoyed his own company, singing along to the music.

He had come to fit in well with the other men at the depot. They were good blokes and had made him feel welcome, maybe because he was Bert's son-in-law, maybe because he was the baby of the bunch. Most of the men were a similar age to Bert; long-time shackled, solid workers. They made Alan the butt of their jokes, but they watched out for him too.

''Ey young Alan, 'ow come that young missis o' yours is pregnant again? When did ya find time for that then? Thought you'd be too tired — y'always say you're tired! Not too tired then eh?'

Alan had wondered the same thing. Well, he must have made the effort in the right place at least once, mustn't he, or else she wouldn't be pregnant!

Being pregnant had meant that she had been forced to give up her job which he was pleased about as he didn't like his wife working. He felt that he worked hard enough for all of them and couldn't understand why they could need any more money. He never asked — and never knew — where all of his money went.

Anyway, she would hopefully not have time to work after this baby was born. He would be able to show her that they could manage. He wanted her at home, and thankfully he now had her at home.

He smiled, contented that he was warm and cosy, that his family slept soundly upstairs. Yes, he had a lot to be pleased with in his life.

Rose wasn't asleep. Her breath came short as her chest heaved under the force of the eruption inside. How could he just walk through the door and expect her to leap up and look after him? Didn't he know that she had been taking care of his children and Lydia's friends all day? Didn't he realise how demanding children could be? And she was having another.

She was fed-up of being pregnant. She hadn't wanted to be pregnant, not again, not ever. She couldn't believe her stupidity. She thought that they had been careful.

She had been left with no choice but to give up her job too, give up the cork which held the rest of her life firmly squeezed into sanity.

She knew that Alan hated her working, but she didn't care. It wasn't many hours and the extra money paid for the clothes which Alan thought extravagant. For just a few hours it took her away from the house, away from the kids, away from the cleaning, from the boredom, from being a wife, from being a mother. For just a few hours, she was allowed to be Rose.

She felt stifled now that she had lost this outlet, the vent for her frustration. Why did her life keep taking these turns, throwing these insurmountable obstacles in her path? Did some joker somewhere relish watching to see how she would get out of each hole which was dug for her, or did she dig them herself? She would be back to the beginning again. Always back to the beginning.

The baby kicked savagely, tormenting her ribs. She wished that it would hurry up and be born. She was sick of carrying it around inside her.

She heard Alan turning off the lights downstairs and

automatically turned over to feign sleep.

Why couldn't she love him? He was a good man and she had tried so hard, but the intimate spark which unites two people simply wasn't there. Had it ever been there? She could no longer remember. It all seemed so long ago. She knew that she needed him, and yet when he was around he annoyed her by existing. Still, there were marriages worse than theirs. At least they didn't argue all the time. They'd managed for five years, so she felt justified that she was trying

Alan went to lock the front door. His hand hung in midair as a knock fell upon it and it slowly opened. It was Bert, his face strained and ashen.

"'ello, Bert. Come in. It's a bit late for ya to be visitin', int it?'

'Sorry lad, but I thought Rose might be wonderin' where 'er mum wer.'

'Well, she might've bin. I don't know. She's in bed. Why? What's t' matter?'

'Ya best get Rose down afore I tell ya, if that's okay lad?'

They didn't need to get Rose down. She had heard the door close and was now downstairs, her fleecy, pink dressing gown pulled tightly around her.

'What's up, dad? Where's mum? Is there owt wrong?'

'You'd best sit down, love. There's summat we shoulda told you ages ago.'

Bert began hesitantly, searching for the right words.

'Your mum's real ill, Rose. We've known about it for a few years now, but it never seemed like t' right time to tell ya.'

'I knew she wer ill, but I didn't think it wer owt serious. She never said owt.'

'Well it is serious. I don't know 'ow to tell you this so I'll just say it straight out. Your mum's got multiple sclerosis. It's bin gettin' worse over t' years, but this mornin' she tried to get out o' bed 'n' couldn't. 'er legs've given in t' fight now.

'er 'ands've bin bad for years. She's managed to struggle on 'n' 'ide it, but now she can't walk.'

He took a deep breath, struggling to continue, the emotions which lurked so close to the surface threatening to burst through his tear–filled eyes.

'She's at t' 'ospital now. There's not much they can do except check 'er, give 'er a wheelchair.'

The word 'wheelchair' filled Rose with horror. The thought of her mother — her strong, independent mother — being pushed about in a wheelchair for the rest of her life was too much to take in. Why hadn't she noticed? Why hadn't she seen the pain which her mother was in? She knew that she had been too wrapped up in her own life to bother about her own mother.

The silent tears turned into sobs which turned to a wail, the wail of a child for its mother when no-one else can heal. Alan put his arms gently around her shoulders, but she didn't want Alan. She wanted her mother. The pain was physical, a pain deep in the pit of her stomach, growing more urgent, threatening to overpower her. Then she realised.

'Oh God. It's t' baby. It's comin'.'

'Don't panic. Don't panic,' soothed Alan. 'Your bag's all packed 'n' ready. Don't worry. We've just got to get you there. Bert, can I borro' yer car?'

'Course, lad. Don't worry about t' girls. I'll look after 'em. You just look after Rose.'

Bert sat alone, staring at nothing, staring at the future which could no longer exist as they had planned. He was lost in some faraway place where he and Alice were young and in love with their lives before them, trouble–free and exciting. A place where Alice could walk beside him.

The birth was swift. The baby broke free of its prison and filled its lungs with air to scream its first scream of life.

'Congratulations, Mr Knowles,' lilted the nurse as she handed the baby to Alan. 'You have a fine baby boy.'

Alan held the baby with tender, practiced ease and marvelled for the third time at the miracle of life. As he looked down upon his son, a voice in his subconscious wondered who in his family tree had such dark skin.

Chapter Fifteen

The day began just as any other. Who could have known that after that day their lives would be forever changed.

Lydia sat motionless on the edge of her bed, staring without blinking across the muddy playing fields. Her eyes followed a golden dog running backwards and forwards behind a boy. They ran into the distance and out of sight. She didn't notice and stared after the ghosts which were left behind.

She heard the shouting and tried to use her trick to turn the loud voices into silence in her head. They were arguing again.

A tug on her leg dragged her head around to her baby brother. Jack offered a gurgling smile which let loose a snake of dribble from his mouth onto his teddy-bear pyjama top. Lydia would have smiled back but she was scared that she might make him excited and she didn't want them to hear him, didn't want her mum to hear him. Lydia had grabbed him from his cot and put him beside her feet on the rug with some toys when he awoke, so he wouldn't cry. She didn't want her mum to come up. Because they were arguing again.

Lydia dared to peek over at Annie in her bed, scared that her stare might awaken her, but thankfully she was still sleeping.

Lydia was numb from sitting so still for so long. She couldn't move her body because she had stepped outside of it, not too far in-case Jack or Annie needed her, just far enough so that she could move inside her head, to a secret place where she felt protected, locked away where nothing could harm her.

As she stared across the field, her body a deserted shell, she shouted to the ghosts and ran with them, chasing the dog. She no longer heard the shouts. She no longer feared the anger. She was locked away in her safe world where nobody could get in and hurt her. Her 'safe world' had been sent from God a long time ago so that she could go there when her mum hurt her, because her body just sat there and she could watch from Godland without being scared.

Godland was what she called this special place, a place where only she could go. When she was hurt, she would close her eyes and walk in her mind to this place where she felt loved and safe, open the door and feel nothing. It was an empty place, just a space, but a warm, cosy, safe space. It felt like being wrapped in cotton wool.

Because Godland lived in her head, no-one knew about it so no-one could take it away. She knew it was real because she felt it all around her. At first she had needed to sort of go on a trip to get there, say goodbye to her body and jump outside and then knock on the door and go in. Now she simply faded away into it whenever she needed to hide.

She could keep Annie and Jack safe too because if she let her mum get angry with her then she left them alone. Lydia would smile because she knew how silly her mum was that she couldn't see how she was being tricked. She loved her Godland. Because she could go there she didn't need to be scared of her mum and so she could love her.

Another tug at her leg dragged her back down the big, long, yellow chute which meant that she had to go back. She smiled quietly, shushing Jack, and found a new toy to put in his hand. Thankfully he just smiled back and stuffed the toy in his mouth then shook it and did it all over again. She sighed with relief. Hopefully the shouting would stop soon. It couldn't last for much longer now, could it?

And then the silence fell. She feared the silence almost as much as the shouting before it. She always feared that they had hurt each other, feared what would happen to herself and her brother and sister. She would wait, holding her breath, until she heard both voices. Then she would know that this one was over.

The mumbling of two voices wriggled up the stairs. She breathed. It was over.

She hurriedly picked up her brother and placed him gently back in his cot with his toys, satisfied that now he could be heard and it would be okay.

A glance at the bedroom clock told her that she would be late for school again. She kissed her baby brother firmly on his bald head, picked up her school-bag and crept quietly down the stairs. Unnoticed, she left the house. She had learnt long ago not to bother her mum with 'goodbyes'.

And so she began her lonely journey to school, on her own, as usual.

'What d'ya mean, you've swapped your shift 'n' you'll be workin' on Sat'day? What d'ya want to work on Sat'day for? Don't you work long enough 'ours, leavin' me 'ere wi' these kids all on me own? What sort of an 'usband are ya?'

'Obviously no preliminaries today — straight in with the real thing', thought Alan.

'I'm off on a stag night tonight, so I've swapped one o't' lads for a local run today 'n' I said I'd do 'is Sat'day run for 'im. And, I'm tekkin tomorrow as a day's 'oliday, just in-case I need to recover. Okay?'

He glared a glare of false bravado, defiant yet wary. He judged that Rose was about to explode like a small incendiary device and splatter all over the kitchen. He realised that he should have thought this out better as he saw that the breakfast things were still on the table in front of them, including the bread-knife which she may well use at any moment, probably on him!

'Where's t' money comin' from for a stag night out, then? I thought ya wer still complainin' we wer broke.' She paused for breath and time to think out her next line of attack.

'You're never 'ere, Alan. A woman needs a man to be around, y'know, otherwise she gets lonely. We never sleep together any more. Ya never give me a love or a kiss or tell me ya love me. Ya know what 'appens when a woman gets neglected. She'll go 'n' find someone who won't neglect 'er.'

'Come on, Rose, It's you who wanted me to work on t' lorries in t' first place. Your dad got me t' job. It's a bit late to complain now. We need t' money 'cos you spend it as fast as I earn it.'

'Work days, you idiot. Work days 'n' then you aren't away. I've bin tellin' you for ages. Why are you so thick? Can't you see what's 'appenin'?'

'You're right, Rose. I am thick for puttin' up wi' your demands all t' time. Puttin' up wi' you changin' yer mind every time summat doesn't quite suit ya. I like me job 'n' I'm not changin' it.'

'Well, you'd better change it or you'll come back one day 'n' find I've gone. You'll be sorry then.'

'Like 'ell I will,' he lied. 'What d'ya suppose we'll do for money if I change jobs? Where will all yer fancy clothes come from then, madam?'

'We'll manage. We always do. I don't want to bring these kids up on me own. I'm stuck 'ere all week wi' 'em by mysen. You wanted 'em as well, you know. Why should I 'ave to look after 'em all t' time whilst you're off workin'. It's not fair. I've 'ad enough. Change your job, Alan. I need you 'ere wi' me, not away all t' time.'

There was no more that he could say. He was tired of arguing. They had been having this argument ever since the baby was born. He should feel flattered that she wanted him around. Instead, all he felt was manipulated.

He was relieved to hear the baby crying. That would divert Rose's attention, at least until he left for work and escaped.

Alice sat in her chair by the front room window, eagerly awaiting the return of her husband, desperately awaiting the return of her husband. The clock must surely have stopped, travelling so slowly on its circular journey.

She strained to see further down the road, clumsily pushing herself up a little higher on her wheelchair arms.

She knew the owner of every car in the street now. There was the little, blue, battered Volkswagen beetle which was driven rather erratically by a tall young man, often in the company of a leggy young lady who insisted on displaying her lingerie as she stepped into it.

Then there was the silver Audi which rolled up to number seventeen every other lunchtime. It would rest unquestioningly outside the house for the allotted hour, and would then be driven away quickly, anxious to disappear unobserved and without arousing any curiosity. A silver Ford something came to rest at the end of the day in the place kept warm by the Audi.

Then there was Mr Howard's Reliant Robin. Mr Howard was not the sort of man who would have the confidence or ability to take his driving test. He had therefore committed himself to a life as a Reliant Robin driver, tentatively steering his course from home to work every day and back again but never venturing further.

Alice laughed at the uncanny way in which the cars reflected their drivers; the carefree, student young man, the professional assured strut of the Audi driver, the timid demeanour of Mr Howard daring to dip his toe into the adventure of driving.

The same could be said of animals, even wives. All are outward demonstrations to the world at large of how the man wishes himself to be perceived. Alice had always thought men to be nothing more than large children, eager for recognition and attention, and since she had been forced to spend much of her day in contemplation, this opinion had been fortified, aided by her observations from her window.

She often wondered what people passing by thought of her. Did they feel sorry for her, stuck all day in her wheelchair alone, or did they think that she was a nosy old cow spying on them? How did she feel about herself?

That question had been asked and faced every day

for the last fourteen months since the day that she had been condemned to this contraption. At first, she had been angry, at who she couldn't decide. Her feeble body would shake gently as her sobs were hushed so that Bert wouldn't hear. She didn't want him to hear. She knew that he felt useless, as if somehow he could have done something to save her from her disablement.

She wanted somebody to blame, someone at whom she could aim her anger and frustration, but there was only God and she refused to place blame at His door. But surely that was where the blame should lie? Surely all things were brought forth as wishes of God.

She had considered this thought regularly for a long time until she finally accepted that yes, this was indeed deemed fit for her by God and who was she to question His judgement. Somehow she found peace in her acceptance and began to come to terms with her situation. It wasn't easy, though. She had known for years that she would eventually be unable to walk, but it had still come as a shock when the reality of it struck her.

She had always been so busy; cleaning, washing, ironing, painting and, of course, she had been kept busy looking after her grandchildren. Her wonderful grandchildren. Lydia — so clever, wise beyond her years, helpful to everyone but prematurely a mother before her time. Annie — sweet, cute, cheeky Annie with her blonde curls and angelic face. Such a joy. Then there was little Jack — a beautiful, dark enigma and such a good baby, sleeping when he was supposed to, feeding when he should, gurgling in all the right places.

Alice chuckled to herself as she remembered the shocked looks on the faces of everyone when they first saw him. Alice had simply smiled and gone immediately home to rummage in her photograph albums. She had scanned the relevant years until she found the photograph that she needed. Cyril. Her cousin. She hadn't seen him for years, but she remembered him distinctly. She remembered him because they often played together as children. She remembered him because he was always being called names at school because of his dark skin and the sight of Jack had reminded her. Once the family had seen the photograph, their questioning looks disappeared in shame that they had been there in the first place.

The day had been never-ending, the minutes struggling to become hours. Alice was due to baby-sit and was eager to have tea and then have Bert take her down to Rose's house.

Rose left for work at about seven-thirty and left her mother in charge of the children. Alice felt confident being alone with them as long as they were put to bed before Rose left, and she was grateful to Rose for letting her still be useful.

At first, they hadn't left their beds, but then Annie had begun creeping downstairs, peering around the door, trying to be invisible but eventually sleep had forced her to seek refuge curled up on the floor by Alice's feet. Once Lydia had realised that their disobedience was not reported to her mother, she had gained confidence and she, too, would tiptoe to sit with Alice. In whispers they would talk for what seemed like hours.

Alice delighted in her conversations with her grand-daughter, glad to give her some much-needed attention. They discussed school and the work which Lydia did there. Alice loved to see her so animated as she recollected her lessons. She was usually so quiet, not sullen just quiet, yet she came alive when she talked about her school-work. Her hands became pencils in the air accompanied by vibrant contortions of her face as she artfully painted visions of her days. Their conversations would draw gradually to a close as Lydia fought sleep. Alice would send her to bed with a kiss, asking that she took her sister with her.

Alice slept on the settee as she could easily pull herself

onto and off it when she needed to. Jack lay in a small collapsible crib beside the settee where Alice could reach if she needed to comfort him during the night.

Alice felt a tingle of independence when she baby-sat. There was nobody to turn to, nobody to jump to help her before she really needed it. She loved the sound of the children in the morning when they awoke and began scuttling around upstairs; fresh, untouched innocence as they clambered downstairs with the sleep still clinging to their eyes and bodies.

With a little help from Lydia she would make breakfast and Rose was always back before Lydia needed to leave for school as Alice couldn't deal with a wriggly, squirming baby alone, that she would admit!

Alice relished these two nights a week, although she knew that Alan wasn't keen on Rose working. Alice couldn't help her rare display of selfishness in this situation and always took her daughter's side when the disagreement arose, but somehow she knew that Alan understood why.

Alice saw Bert long before he opened the door. She never lost her excitement at seeing him step out of his Vauxhall Viva and stride solidly towards their home, towards her, bringing an end to her day of loneliness. As he closed the door behind him, Alice shouted her greeting to him. Even after all these years, Bert still loved to hear her call to him and he smiled to himself.

'Hiya, love,' he replied. 'You okay?'

'Yes, fine thanks, but I thought that you were never coming home tonight. What kept you?'

''eavy traffic on t' motorway. Must've been an accident or summat earlier 'n' everythin's jammed up. Sorry, love. Owt nice for tea?'

He knew that Alice spent a great deal of time preparing his meals for him, struggling to keep control over her ever-errant hands, so he always made sure to compliment and appear eager for his food.

'I made a salad since it was such a nice day. Is that alright for you?'

'Course love.' He bent to kiss her cheek. She always felt so cold these days, even though the weather was warm. Still, she seemed perky enough.

'Lookin' forad to tonight?' he enquired needlessly, for he knew how much she would be eager to have tea and leave for her daughter's house.

'Silly question, isn't it? Come on, let's get sorted and have tea.'

Alice was distressed to find that Alan was at home. He was nearly always away midweek — that was why she slept over. Alan laughed as he saw her face drop to her knees, thinking that she would be redundant for the evening.

'Don't worry, Alice. I'm not stayin' in. I'm goin' on a stag night tonight 'n' stayin' wi' a mate, so yer baby–sittin' services are still needed, if that's okay wi' you?'

'You great lummox!' she laughed, amused by her own disappointment. 'You gave me a turn, you did that! Go on, get yourself ready and be off with you. Where's Rose?'

'She decided to go in a bit early tonight wi' me bein' 'ere. T' girls are all tucked up in bed, 'n' Jack's over there in 'is usual 'ideaway. Right, I'll go 'n' mek mesen look gorgeous for all these women as I'm gonna 'ave to fight off tonight!'

'You dare, my lad, just you dare!' laughed Alice.

The cool freshness of the evening air engulfed Alan as he closed the front door behind him. He felt like a young man again as he lilted down the path; a butterfly about to escape the prison of its cocoon and fly away if only for a while. He looked handsome in his trendy, light–blue suit with a fashionable, thin tie and his hair slicked back. On his feet shone a pair of black shoes which Rose had only purchased for him a few days earlier from the catalogue.

He breathed deeply, relieved to be on his way out with his friends, especially after this morning. Why was it always one demand after another? Was this the price that he would forever have to pay for having a wife? Having said that, Rose had never faltered in her upkeep of the house or taking care of him and their children, although the other wifely duties had been rather thin on the ground just lately. To be fair, though, he had to admit that he was equally at fault. They were both always so tired.

Still, he was free from it all for tonight. Jake was going too. It seemed a lifetime ago since they had been out together, chasing the girls and getting away with as much as they could. They had made a good team.

'Hi, Alan. We thought you'd blow us out, bein' an old married man!' laughed Chris, Alan's friend from work.

'You cheeky sod! What about 'im? 'e's an old married man too,' he laughed, pointing his finger towards Jake, who was already settled with a pint in his hand. 'Anyroad, stop blabberin' like a woman 'n' get me a pint, quick. Best mek it two so 's I can catch you lot up!'

There were ten of them altogether; all local lads who had know each other for years. Johnny was the man getting married. Usual story. Girlfriend pregnant. Alan didn't know him as well as some of the others there, but Jake did and had asked Alan to come.

Their third pints were slipping down smoothly whilst Alan struggled with his second. He knew that if he tried to keep pace with them he would end up legless, but who cared. It would give her something different to complain about, give her a change of record for once.

'What's on t' agenda for tonight, then?' asked Alan.

'Didn't I tell ya? Johnny's a member at this classy strip joint so we're goin' there. It's open early 'ours so I 'ope you're not under curfew.'

'Well I wer sort of 'opin' I could doss on your settee.

Alice is on ours wi' t' baby 'n' I don't want to wek 'em up drunk like. Will it be okay wi' Josie d'ya think?'

'You know Josie. There's not much she'd complain about. Course it'll be alright. Just don't throw up anywhere or she'll kill you.'

'I'll do me best. Thanks mate.'

A few pints later and worse for wear, Alan found himself talking to Johnny.

'Congratulations, mate. 'ope you'll be very 'appy,' laughed Alan. 'They all say that, don't they, but once she's got a weddin' ring on she'll start naggin".'

'No, she's alright is Donna. You'll 'ave seen 'er around. You can't miss 'er. Tits t' size o' buckets. Know who I mean?'

'Blonde 'air? Alas wears an 'eadband?'

'Yeah, that's the one. Gorgeous, int she?' Alan nodded in agreement.

'Who's your missus, then?'

'You prob'ly won't remember 'er 'cos she dunt get out much these days but she used to. She's t' same as your Donna, a big girl. Rose, 'er name is. She wer Rose Gallagher.'

'Don't remember 'er? You must be jokin'. 'ow could I forget li'l Rosie? I dint know it wer you that married 'er.'

''ow come you remember 'er so well? I don't think she's ever mentioned you.'

'No, she wouldn't 'ave. You see......'

'Come on, you two. 'urry up wi' those pints. It's time we were off to this club o' yours, Johnny.'

The moment was gone, the question forgotten.

It was already well after eleven when they reached the club. Johnny had warned them that if they seemed drunk they wouldn't be allowed in. The size of the bouncers on the door soon sobered them temporarily, as did the pain in their wallets as they paid their door fees.

'Oy Johnny. We 'ope this is worth t' brass.'

'You must be jokin'. This is no backstreet sleaze joint. These birds are real classy. Wait till you see t' table–dancers, then there's t' stripper 'n' t' go-go dancers. Don't sit too near t' front when they're on, though. They'll 'ave your eyes out wi' their knockers!'

They were shown to a table in the main room, the pit they were told it was called. A lapse in conversation hung for a while as each man got his bearings. Heads jerked sharply left and right as they struggled to embrace everything at one glance, fearful that the beautiful girls serving the drinks might disappear in a puff of smoke.

Johnny had been right. They were goddesses.

They didn't notice one of the girls making a hasty dash for the small office beside the bar.

'I need to take a break for a minute, Christine,' blurted the girl hurriedly. 'I won't be long.'

'Okay, love. You're alright for a few minutes, but don't be too long, eh?'

Christine didn't mind. They weren't over–busy and the girl was, after all, only helping her out for an hour since one of the waitresses hadn't turned in.

The girl hurried as quickly as she dared, not wanting to lose her decorum and her job, searching for her friend. She reached the dressing–room, her eyes seeking the girl but not finding her.

'Where's Bonita? Quick, I need to find her.'

'Don't know,' sulked one girl. 'Prob'ly wi' Sharif, don't ya think?' She pulled a derisive smirk, betraying her jealousy.

Dayna reached the rest room. Again no luck. Then it was too late. The music had started for the go–go dancers and wherever Bonita was it was too late to warn her. She would be on the stage. Sure enough, Dayna glimpsed her dancing into the spotlight from the other side, a smile on her face, presumably put there by Sharif.

The music started. The group of men smelled sex like a pack of wolves on heat as their attention became focused on the stage. Whistles swooped and sighed as the girls danced out.

Yes, Johnny had definitely been right. Their bodies were undeniable female perfection. They all looked the same with their heavy make-up and blonde, bobbed wigs as they swayed seductively, teasing the audience.

Alan's table was near the back and, coupled with the alcohol, he was finding it difficult to focus. He liked the way that they moved, bending and bouncing, yet so graceful.

Something about one of the girls was familiar. He didn't know what, but there was something. He followed her movements, the other girls blurred by his concentration on this single body, struggling through the ether of alcohol, struggling to see straight and think.

Then he knew, as a flash struck his memory and begged him to forget. She reminded him of Rose. No, she didn't just remind him of Rose; it could only be Rose. He was certain it was her. But how? Why? Was he hallucinating? Had he drunk far more than he remembered? He strained his eyes, his brow furrowed, refusing to evade the torment which danced before him, greedily consuming every movement, every gyration, every inch of the body which he knew so well.

Jake sat still, not daring to move until he cleared his head. He was the only other man who knew Rose well enough to recognise her under the make-up and wig. The others hadn't seen her for years.

Jake didn't know what he should do, other than keep quiet and wait for Alan to make the first move or comment, and then react accordingly. Could it be that he was too drunk to notice? No, Jake saw the puzzled, hurt expression which betrayed his blatant torment. There was no question that he had seen her.

The audience stood. Thunderous applause and stamping was the reward as the girls left the stage. Alan slowly pulled himself up.

'Where ya goin', Alan?' asked Jake, grabbing his arm protectively.

'I 'ave to know for sure. I 'ave to find that girl.' He ignored the jibes of the others around the table jeering for him to 'go and get some'. Jake knew that it would be useless to confront or try to stop Alan, and anyway, he agreed with him. He needed to know for certain.

Jake covered their actions by saying they'd seen someone they knew and that they would be back, and then he followed his friend.

They reached the stage door. The bouncer put his arm out to bar the way, his black jacket far too tight for the chest which filled it.

'An' where d' ya think you're goin' boys? If you fancy owt go pay for it like everyone else,' he laughed, obviously pleased with his hilarious comment.

Alan's face reddened with the pressure of the frustration which was about to break free. Jake quickly stepped between the bouncer and his friend. He whispered conspiratorially, eager to diffuse the situation.

'Look, mate, 'is old lady's in there. She doesn't know we're 'ere. It's kind of a surprise, ya know, 'cos 'e's bin workin' away for months. You know 'ow it is — can't wait to show 'is missis 'ow pleased 'e is to be back, know what I mean!' confided Jake, winking.

'Straight up?'

'Course, pal. Listen, we'll come straight out once she's seen we're 'ere. Give us two minutes, that's all.' Jake slapped his shoulder as if they'd been friends for years. The bouncer thought it over for a moment with his limited capacity for thought and decided that they couldn't do much damage in a couple of minutes.

'Okay, but if you're not out in two minutes I'll be in 'n' throw you out. Capisch?'

Jake nodded and dragged Alan behind him.

Neither of them knew what they would do if they found the girl and it was indeed Rose. They both hoped they were wrong. Trying to avoid attention, they checked around the backstage area. The scantily-clad women floated by unnoticed as they searched for just one woman. Their two minutes was looming when a door opened behind them. Together they turned.

A dark-skinned man and a woman with short, black hair stood just inside the doorway, tightly wrapped in an embrace. The woman wore a light-blue, silk dressing coat.

She turned to leave the room, smiling, and came face to face with her husband. She stopped dead, holding her chest, and stared uncomprehendingly.

Alan returned her stare without seeing.

All of the answers to all of the questions fell on the ground like confetti between them. The evening job which she wouldn't surrender. The darkness of his son. Could this be the reason why? Was Jack this man's child? Did she love this man? Was that why she couldn't love him?

The discovery that she was a go-go dancer paled into insignificance. Tears slid slowly down his face as he turned and walked away. Jake followed.

'Alan, please wait. Please don't go. Just let me explain,' begged Rose.

Alan carried on walking and never looked back.

Chapter Sixteen

A lone dancer moved before him on the stage. She was beautiful with short, black hair and deep, brown eyes which peered into his soul and stripped him bare as she danced for him alone.

He was mesmerised by the gentle swaying of her silver tassels, hypnotised by the frantic gyrations of her body. The twists and turns gracefully rolled into one another, like a gentle wave flowing before his eyes. Her eyes never left his face, watching, knowing, leaving him naked before her.

A man came onto the stage behind her, a dark man. He purposefully strode up to her and pulled her to him. She continued to gyrate in his arms, bending and weaving, leaning into his body, lost in passion. The body reached heights of latent fervour, desperate to escape and reach its peak. The man took the woman's face in his hands firmly and bent to kiss her. No, he couldn't. He mustn't. It was his wife. She was his. He couldn't have her. He wanted her. Let her go.

'Alan. Alan. Wek up, love. Wek up,' whispered Josie as loud as she dare, 'wek up, you'll wek Charlie.'

'No, no. Leave 'er alone,' he yelled as he sat up.

He opened his eyes and searched the familiar room, struggling to understand why Rose had disappeared and trying to remember why he was there. His head was spinning along with the room and it took a minute before he had Josie in his sights. She was leaning over him, a concerned expression clouding her face.

'Are y'alright, Alan. You wer cryin' out. Sorry to wek ya, but I didn't want Charlie to wek up 'n' 'ear ya. D'ya want a cup o' tea?'

Alan tried hard to understand the words which were coming from Josie's mouth, but found the conflict too much for his befuddled head.

'Sorry, Josie love. What did ya say?'

'D' ya want a cup o' tea?'

'Yes, please. Ta love.' He paused for a moment. 'Is Jake awek?'

'Yes, Alan, 'e is, 'n' if that means "as 'e told you what 'appened' then yeah, 'e 'as. I'm so sorry, Alan. I'd no idea, but then I wouldn't 'ave 'cos she'd know I'd tell Jake 'n' Jake would've told you. I'm sorry. I don't really know what else to say.'

She left the room to make the promised cup of tea, strong and sweet. Alan had hoped that it was all a nightmare, that he had been drunk out of his head and imagined everything, but Josie knew too so it was real. He couldn't go home and find everything alright.

Josie placed the magic, healing cup of tea in his hands.

'Didn't you 'ave any idea that owt wer wrong, Alan?'

'No, not a clue. She went to work in a factory as far as I knew. I never had no reason to ask or to question. As for 'er seein' somebody else, well obviously I dint 'ave any idea. What about Jack? I don't know if 'e's mine or not. I love the boy. I love all t' kids. 'ow many of 'em are mine 'n' 'ow many am I raisin' for somebody else?'

'Don't be silly, Alan. You know the kids 're yours. Jack could still be yours, y' know. Don't you remember that photo Alice showed everyone of 'er cousin or someone? Jack looks just like 'im, you know 'e does. You're just guessin.'

'Bit of a coincidence, wouldn't you say, she 'as it off wi' a dark man 'n' we 'ave a dark son? Anyroad, t' only person who can answer t' question is Rose.'

'Are you goin' to see 'er, to talk to 'er?'

'I'll 'ave to. I'll 'ave to sort out somewhere to stay first, though. I can't stay wi' 'er right now. I'd only end up killin' 'er. I 'ate 'er that much. 'ow could she do this to me? All I've ever tried to do is to do right by 'er, but it never seems to be enough.'

'That's just Rose all over, Alan. I know that as well as you do, but mebbe that's one o' t' reasons why we stick around, why we carry on lovin' 'er even though she doesn't deserve it.'

'Why do I still want 'er, still love 'er, even as I 'ate 'er? Oh I don't know. I only know I need to get away, think things over. Mebbe I'll leave for good. Mebbe I've 'ad enough o' bein' shit on.'

'You need to talk to 'er though. You need to sort out about t' kids, about money, even if you're only stayin' away for a while. Don't just leave 'er to flounder, for t' kids' sakes.'

'You're right, Josie. I need to sort out somewhere to stay first though. I'll go 'n' see Chris this mornin'. They've got a spare room 'n' I know 'e took today off, same as I did.'

Neither of them knew the right words to say and so the silence was broken only by the ticking of the clock, booming the throwing away of time.

'D'ya want to talk about it?'

'What's there to say? I couldn't believe me eyes when I saw that it wer 'er. I thought I wer drunk, seein' things, but I could tell Jake 'd seen t' same thing as me. That wer bad enough. I don't know what I would've said if it'd just been dancin'. I might've 'andled it, but then when I saw 'er wi' 'im all t' pieces fell into place like a jigsaw where a giant piece 'as bin missin' 'n' suddenly turns up under t' setteee.'

'She won't 'ave done it to 'urt you, Alan. She always 'as a reason for doin' stuff does Rose — usually totally illogical — but none–the–less a reason. She works on impulse. There'll be a reason, 'n' mebbe it'll 'elp you to talk to 'er 'n' find out what.'

'Yeah, I can tell you who'll end up bein' blamed for it, though. Me. She'll find some way to twist it round 'n' mek it all out as if I pushed 'er onto that stage 'n' into 'is arms. You see if I aren't right.'

Josie said nothing. She knew he was right.

The sun shared its rays sympathetically, attempting to warm him, to put its arms around him and raise his spirits. The sky larks chirped overhead, breaking the soothing peace with their chatter. He lay with his eyes closed and talked to his father, hoping for divine intervention, as if by being close to his body he would feel his pain, grief, confusion and come to aid his son. He hadn't really known where else to go to think.

He was surrounded by dead people, forever sleeping beneath their grave-stones bearing their names, a reminder to the world that they once existed. His father's grave was immaculate, well-tended and cared for by his loving wife and children. Other graves lay derelict, overgrown and abused, a sad memoir of a life which left behind nothing and no-one.

Yet the sun shone on them all, warming the dead and the living. Alan drifted off to sleep, his body still prisoner to the alcohol which had overpowered it, nodding intermittently in the pleasant glow.

When he awoke, a feeling had seeped into his body, poured softly into his blood; a feeling of calm acceptance which he couldn't really describe. Maybe it was the sun's warmth, maybe it was his father's presence. He preferred to assume the latter. A control was gaining force, as though decisions had been taken without his knowledge and the matter was now settled. So his father was still there for him.

With a last, loving gaze over his father's grave, he started towards the next path down which he must tread.

Alan's key turned silently in the lock. The house was still and he wondered if perhaps she wasn't at home. Then he heard the excited squeals of Annie and made his way towards the back of the house.

Rose hadn't heard him above the noise. He stood scrutinising her, looking for some outward sign that she had changed. He only saw the woman that he loved, as beautiful as ever, the beguiling appearance deceiving the world as to her innocence. He wished that he didn't love her.

She sensed his presence and turned. Her eyes betrayed nothing. She turned away, unsure of what would come next. She'd never played this part before and didn't know how to act, what he would expect, how he would react, so she waited.

'I think you'd best come inside, Rose. We need to talk.'

'But what about t' kids?'

'They'll be fine. We can see 'em through t' window. Come on. There's no avoidin' this now.'

They sat at the dining table from where they could see the children; two people joined together by years and children now strangers. The table was a defence line between them.

'Why, Rose? Why did you lead this double-life? You know I've tried to do me best for ya. Don't I deserve better 'n' this?'

She stared blankly back at him, deciding which dice to roll. She heaved a sigh and spoke.

'You were never 'ere. I told you. I wanted some fun instead of bein' stuck wi' t' kids, chores, me own company. I didn't think it would do any 'arm, a bit o' dancin'. It's not as if I wer strippin' or owt. I could earn good money wi'out 'avin' to sweat me guts out in some grotty factory wi' all t' low-lifes. I wanted better, 'n' by dancin' I could earn t' money to get better. Surely ya can see that?'

'I'm not talkin' about that 'n' you know it,' he mumbled, straining to maintain his composure, knowing that if he lost his temper then they would be finished.

'I don't know what you mean,' she lied, not daring to look at him. Could she ride this and bluff her way out of it?

'Please don't tek me for a fool, Rose. That's over now. You've bin doin' it for long enough. Now I want t' truth. I deserve that much.'

Her children played innocently on the other side of the window and she knew that whatever she said would affect the rest of their lives, knew that this was her last chance to give this man some respect by giving him the truth if she dare.

'Okay, Alan, you want t' truth, well 'ere it goes. I never meant to meet someone else. Ya know I've tried to love you as a wife should, 'n' I do love ya. You've been good to me. But I couldn't resist t' temptation of Sharif. I don't know what I feel for 'im. It just is. You want to know about Jack?'

Did she have the courage? Did it really matter anyway? In his eagerness to hear the truth, he failed to recognise the moment of hesitation.

'He's your son, Alan. Course 'e's your son. D'ya really think I'd try to pass someone else's child off as yours? What d'ya think I am? Anyroad, would ya love 'im any less if 'e wasn't? Would it change yer feelings for 'im? Ya know you've loved 'im from t' start.'

Alan put his head in his hands. Rose sat silently. She had nothing left to say, nothing left to throw at him. She could only sit and watch as his shoulders heaved with relief. So he still had his son. But how could he ever forgive her for her betrayal?

The children played, oblivious to the devastation which was running through the house and smashing their lives.

'I'm leavin', he whispered, afraid to give voice to what he knew must now happen.

'I know,' was her only reply.

'I'm tekkin Annie.'

She jerked bolt upright with the shock of his words. He continued in explanation.

'I'm tekkin Annie for good reason. I said I'm leavin'. I don't know if I can manage to mek any sense or future out of all this, but I do know if I don't 'ave one o' t' kids wi' me, then t' chances o' me ever comin' back are small. I'm doin' this for your benefit, Rose. If I don't tek 'er, then there's no tie. We don't share owt. The kids are all we've got between us. I can't tek Jack 'cos 'e's a baby, 'n' I can't tek Lydia 'cos you 'n' Alice need 'er. So I'll tek Annie. Then at least there's a small chance I'll come back. A very small chance. If I decide not to come 'ome, then I'll bring Annie back, I promise. D'ya understand? This is the least you can do, to let me at least 'ave one o' me kids for comfort. In one fell swoop you've destroyed me life 'n' me family. Don't dare try to deny me this.'

'Where will you go wi' a child?'

'Chris 'n' Emily 'll put us up, at least til I sort mysen out. Now, go 'n' pack 'er some things so I can get movin'. I don't want to be 'ere when Lydia comes 'ome 'n' 'ave to explain all this to 'er. You can do your own dirty work.'

Rose knew that she was beaten. There was nothing that she could say or do. What Alan had said made sense and it was the only way that this mess might be sorted out. But why did it have to be Annie?

Tears escaped her sad eyes as she packed a small case for her daughter so that her husband could take her away from her. Was the excitement really worth this price? Why couldn't she have been happy to be bored like everyone else?

The battered case was soon full. She dragged it down the stairs and reluctantly handed it over. Now she must steel herself to give away her daughter.

'Annie, come in 'ere, love? Jack 'll be okay for a minute,' beckoned Rose to her daughter.

'Daddy's tekkin you on a li'l 'oliday. Would ya like that?'

'Oh yes!' she shrieked. 'Is Lydi comin' too? Where we goin'?'

'Not very far. Ya can come 'n' see mummy in a little while, 'cos mummy 'as to stay 'ere 'n' look after Jack. Is that okay?'

Rose longed for her to say no.

'Course, mummy. Daddy will look after me, won't you, daddy?'

Alan could only nod. He hated her for reducing him to tears, for wrecking his life. He lifted his child into his arms and set off up the road, suitcase in hand, a lonely, broken figure of a man.

He didn't look back, didn't see his wife on the doorstep bent double in pain, a strangled yell caught in her throat, blood seeping from her hand where her teeth had broken the skin as they fought to kill the agony within, left there by the theft of her child. She was deaf to the sound of her other child crying, abandoned in the back garden.

Lydia had had a brilliant day at school. She was the cleverest in her class and enjoyed the attention which this brought. She found the work which she was given easy and soon completed her lessons. This always meant that she was the first one to finish, so she would then spend her time helping the others who hadn't finished as quickly.

She loved sitting beside her friends and explaining to them how she had finished her work. She had to be careful, though, that Miss didn't see her. She didn't want to get Miss annoyed. The children would secretly take it in turns to find their way to Lydia's desk and she would help them willingly as soon as she had finished her own work. She felt important and felt that everyone liked her because she could help them. At school, she knew everyone liked her.

At school, everybody knew who she was. At home, she was ignored and neglected. She didn't mind, though, because she knew that her mum was busy and didn't have time for her, but it didn't mean that she didn't love her.

Everybody had time for Lydia at school because she could help them. She was important and she was grateful that she had been given the brain with which she was blessed.

Today had been extra special. The other girls had been talking about boyfriends for months now. Lydia didn't really understand what a boyfriend was. Of course, it was a boy who was a friend. Big deal! She didn't understand the interest.

'What's so good about 'avin' a boyfriend?' she'd asked her friend, Trudy.

'What d' ya mean, 'what's so good?' Don't ya know?'

'No.'

'It means they love you 'n' they can kiss ya,' squealed Trudy excitedly.

'ave you got a boyfriend?'

'Course I 'ave. Robin Twemlow. Ya know, the boy wi' t' ginger 'air. 'e's cute, don't ya think?'

Lydia didn't because she didn't know what 'cute' meant, but she smiled anyway. Trudy had an older sister and got all of her information from her.

Today had been different though. A boy called Andrew had been talking to her at break-time. He was a nice boy with black, curly hair and dark-brown eyes and a nice smile. He'd asked her if she would be his girlfriend. She didn't really know if she actually wanted to be anyone's girlfriend, but she had said 'yes' because she wasn't sure if it was allowed to say 'no'. He said thanks and took hold of her hand.

'Ya know, Lydi. I know everyone likes you 'cos you're clever 'n' 'elp 'em 'n' all, but I think you're nice, too.'

Lydia had worn a huge smile on her face for the rest of the day. A boy actually wanted her to be his girlfriend and liked her. Nobody had ever told her that they liked her.

Now as she walked home, the smile still lingered, at least until she passed the brick-works. She hated going past the brick-works. The semi-circular tunnels glowed orange and yellow as the fire inside fought to escape and get her. Her friend Trudy had said that dragons lived in there and that was what all the fire was. Of course, Lydia didn't believe her, but it was better to hurry past just in-case.

She had to come this way home. The only other choice was to go through the old people's housing estate. This was even more full of demons. The tiny flats were all built right next to each other, separated by winding, narrow paths between them. Each building was surrounded by a high, wooden fence which made a maze. Lydia had been lost many times in the maze. She would panic with fear of meeting a boogy-man around the next turn because she couldn't see if anyone was around each corner. Now she chose to take her chances with the dragon rather than risk getting lost with the boogy-man in the maze.

When she reached her house, she found that the door was locked. She tried very hard to pull the handle down, but it wouldn't open the door. She shouted for her mum and knocked hard. She went through the snicket to the back of the house in-case mum was in the garden. There was nobody there, but she didn't worry. She thought that perhaps her mum had gone to the shops and was late getting back. So she sat down on the doorstep to wait. She had plenty to do, anyway, thinking about Andrew, and she had her reading book which she could read. After all, the sun was still warm and she wasn't hungry yet.

Lydia sat for an hour. Then she began to worry. Where was her mum? Where were her sister and her brother? Her head began to fill with swirling clouds of silly thoughts. Perhaps something terrible had happened to everyone and she was left all alone. What was she supposed to do? She could get to her grandad's if she tried very hard to remember the way, but it would take her ages and it would be getting dark before too long. She wasn't sure exactly how long. And she was getting hungry now.

Another hour passed by. Now she was scared. Tears ran down her red cheeks as her bottom began to go numb from sitting for so long. She had to keep smiling at the neighbours as they passed by on their way home because she didn't want to let anyone know that there was nobody there for her. They might think that nobody wanted her.

She tried to wipe her tears away which made her face dirty from the day's grubbiness. She was a sorry sight with her red, swollen eyes and her dirty face. She decided that her mum wasn't coming home. She didn't know where she was, but she obviously wasn't coming home. She must have forgotten about her. She decided that the only thing to do was to go to her grandad's. He'd look after her now that she was abandoned. She grabbed her bag and set off purposefully up the road.

Josie was sat near the window having her tea when a moving figure caught her eye. She turned back to her food and then did a double-take. Quickly she rushed to the door and down the path.

'Lydia. Lydia, where ya goin'?' she shouted.

Lydia was glad that someone had called her name. She retraced her steps back to Josie.

'I'm goin' to me grandad's. Y'see, mum isn't 'ome so I'll 'ave to go to grandad's for tea,' Lydia explained.

'But your grandad's is a good 'our's walk away,' reasoned Josie. She quickly realised what had happened and put her arm around Lydia's shoulders.

'I know what. Jack's 'ere wi' me. Yer mum went shoppin', but she must've missed 'er bus or summat. She wouldn't just forget about ya, would she? Now, you come on in 'n 'ave some tea wi' me til she comes 'ome. 'ow's that sound? We've got chips!'

Lydia smiled and nodded gratefully, her pathetic features tired from her crying. Josie couldn't wait to hear what the explanation for this would be but it had better be good!

Alan explored his new surroundings, the room which was to be his home until he decided what to do. It was more than comfortable and Emily, Chris's wife, had made them very welcome. She'd even gone to the trouble of placing some of her own children's teddy bears across the top of the bed to make Annie feel at home.

His daughter lay fast asleep in the double bed which would provide for them both, cuddled up with a large, yellow bear with an eye missing. She looked so angelic in slumber, her tiny thumb stuffed firmly into her mouth. Was he right to bring her with him? He didn't know if he was being honest with himself about his motives. Had he brought her to entice him back to the family fold, or had he brought her as a bargaining weapon in-case Rose decided that she didn't want him back? He didn't know, but he was certain that it was the only choice that he had.

He was exhausted and needed to sleep, but needed to say thanks to his friend before turning in. Chris and Emily were sat together on the settee, watching television. Alan felt a pang of nostalgia.

'I just wanted to say thanks afore I went to bed. It's really good o' ya both to tek us in like this. It won't be for long, just til I get me 'ead together.'

'Tek as long as ya like,' replied Chris. 'You've got a lot to sort out.'

''n' don't worry about Annie,' continued Emily. 'She'll play fine wi' my two whilst you're at work. One more won't make no difference.'

'Thanks a lot. I'm right grateful. Okay, I'll get off to bed now 'n' let you two 'ave some peace 'n' quiet. Night.'

'Night, Alan. 'ope your room's alright for ya.'

'I'm sure everything'll be fine.'

'Sorry about Lydia, Josie. I did tell 'er to come to you for tea. She must've forgotten. 'Course I wouldn't just forget about 'er,' explained Rose indignantly. Josie smiled affably at her friend, hoping that the disbelief which sat there would not offend her. She did not, however, dispute her explanation.

'That's okay, Rose. They're both really tired now, though. I 'aven't mentioned owt to Lydia about what's 'appened, so she'll no doubt be wonderin' where Annie is. You will explain, won't ya?'

'Come on, Josie. What d'ya tek me for?'

Rose took her children home. Her temper was at boiling point. She couldn't take anything more today. She had tried to see Sharif to gain some comfort, something, she wasn't sure what, but she hadn't been able to trace him although she'd tried since Alan had left.

She recognised the danger signs and knew that she needed to get the children to bed as quickly as possible. Her head was pounding, her breath coming short and quick. She could feel the demon squirming, struggling to escape and take control.

'Where's Annie?' asked Lydia innocently.

'She's gone to stay wi' yer daddy for a little while,' was her feeble explanation.

'What d'ya mean stay wi' daddy'?' She thought for a minute. 'Daddy stays 'ere, doesn't 'e?'

'Me 'n' daddy 'ad a row 'n' 'e's gone to stay somewhere else for a while.'

Lydia didn't understand, and as she concentrated on puzzling out what this meant, she forgot her usual ability to sense her mother's mood and to keep quiet.

'When's 'e comin' back?'

That was it. Rose let go of the reins. She lunged at Lydia with an almighty slap with the back of her hand across her face. Lydia was stunned and fell back against a chair, hurting her back as the chair fell to the floor behind her.

Lydia cried out in pain, but Rose's fury was now beyond control as she reared upon her daughter. She rushed towards her and kicked her fiercely on the leg as she lay on the floor. Lydia could only whimper in response. Rose bent above her, lurching menacingly as though ready to strike again.

'You little bitch. Quit wi' the questions. You've already got people questionin' me, even Josie. Shut it, you 'ear, or I'll really 'urt ya.'

Lydia stayed as still as a chameleon as it hides from its prey, petrified that a single movement could bring on another onslaught. Her mother seemed to lose interest and went off to the kitchen. Then the baby began to cry.

The hairs on the back of Lydia's neck rose in fear as the chill surged down her spine. The baby. She had to get to the baby before her mother did. She closed her mind to the pain and half-dragged, half-walked to where he lay on the settee. As deftly as she could with her injured leg, she carried Jack up the stairs, desperately trying not to make a sound. She pulled herself and the baby onto her bed, took off her shoes and got under the bedclothes fully clothed, still in her school uniform. She cautiously shushed her brother, scared that even this small sound might bring her mother running, until he went to sleep. Then, her face red and sore, her limbs stiff, she let her body be taken by the blessing of sleep.

Lydia opened her eyes. The room was bright and the baby was gone. Panic jumped through her stomach as she crept to the baby's cot. A sigh of relief escaped her cold lips as she saw him lying there, fast asleep, seemingly unharmed.

A noise behind her spun her around, bringing her face to face with her mother, her face betraying her fear. When Rose saw the harsh, red welt on her daughter's face, she recoiled in horror.

'Oh Lydia. I'm so sorry. I didn't mean to 'urt ya.' She took her daughter's bruised face in her hands. 'I'll never do it again, I promise. I was just so angry.'

Lydia put her hand up to her mother's and held it.

'It's alright, mum. I'm okay.' She smiled wanly and was rewarded with a smile from her mother.

'I'll try to keep me temper better, 'onest. It's just that me 'n' your dad've 'ad a fallout 'n' 'e's gone to stay wi' 'is friend for a while. 'e wanted to tek Annie to stay wi' 'im, but everything will be alright soon, I promise.'

Her mother's words hurt her more than her beatings ever could. Why had her father left and taken her sister with him, leaving Jack and her to continue to face the loneliness of life with their mother? How could he do that to her? Surely he knew what happened when he wasn't at home? Why had he taken Annie? Didn't he want them anymore?

Lydia could only return her mother's gaze blankly. She went back to the comparative safety of her room.

Her journey to Godland came fast because she couldn't face the hurt of the answers to her questions.

Chapter Seventeen

The Christmas tree twinkled in the corner of the room, so tall that the top six inches had been unceremoniously lopped. A white fairy guarded the tree, perched with authority at its highest point.

Alan relaxed in the armchair, captivated by the colours which danced kaleidoscopically before him as the lights flashed on and off, on and off. Outside a slow patter of snow fell, the delicate snowflakes disappearing as they hit the floor. He could quite happily have sat there, in the dim light and silence, for the rest of the evening, but there was a job to be done, a conversation to be had. It was Christmas Eve and this was the time. Tomorrow would be too late.

Six months had drifted by in a blur of work. Emily had been a Godsend in caring for Annie for him whilst he was working, and Annie in turn had grown to feel at home with Emily and her children. He could never repay Chris and Emily for the kindness which they had shown to him and his daughter, providing a safe haven where he could begin to make sense of his thoughts and feelings. They had never asked him for money for his keep, although he had tried to give them whatever he could, and for this he was grateful.

He hadn't realised how difficult it would be trying to pay for his home and also to keep Annie and himself too. The money simply hadn't gone far enough over the last six months and the final blow had now been dealt by the Building Society. They were losing their home. He had given the money every month to Rose, but evidently the mortgage had not been paid and now it was too late. There was nothing that he could do about it, and he couldn't say that he was particularly bothered. Where they lived was no longer a priority, never really had been to him as long as they had a roof over their heads. Now decisions had to be made — make or break.

After months of soul-searching Alan had reached his decision. His time alone had helped, along with a couple of dates with obliging 'friends of friends' who felt sorry for him. He had taken them out willingly, grateful to be in female company again. But none of them was Rose, and it was Rose that he wanted, not a substitute.

He knew that his future depended on how Rose would react tonight. He felt drained from the effort of living and was happy to face whatever may come next. He would deal with it.

Rose placed a cup in his hands and sat on the settee opposite him, her demeanour unusually passive.

'Well, Rose. I think it's about time we sorted this thing out once 'n' for all, don't you? We can't go on livin' like this, not knowin' where we both stand,' began Alan, his eyes never leaving her face. Rose said nothing, simply examined the contents of her cup, unsure of what was to come.

'I'll say me piece, 'n' then you can decide what ya want to do. It's up to you, Rose.' He took a sip of his tea, wishing it was brandy, preparing himself to deliver the speech which he had so carefully constructed during the past month, repeating it over and over so that every word was the word that he wanted to say, and now finally had to be voiced.

'I still love ya, Rose. God knows why, but I do. I love me children, too, 'n' want us all to live together as a family. It won't be easy, 'n' I can't forget in 'urry what's gone on, but I'll try.

As for Jack, I believe you that 'e's mine. I 'ave to believe it. I love 'im like me own son, just as I always 'ave. It wouldn't 'ave med a difference who 'is father wer, but I'm glad 'e's mine. I've only two conditions to comin' back, Rose.' He paused, waiting until she looked up, her face still impassive.

'One, you can't go on workin' at that club. I know you're still there 'n' it 'as to stop. Two, you've to stop seeing 'im. You must promise me never to see 'im again. If I ever 'ear you've seen 'im again, then you will be straight out o' t' door, not me.

Don't tek me for a mug, Rose. I'm agreein' to come back 'n' try to start again, not just for our sakes but 'cos I want all t' kids together. If you mess up, then God 'elp me, you won't 'ave any o' t' kids 'cos you'll be t' one who leaves, not me. Understand? Now, I've said me piece. It's up to you. D'ya want me back, Rose?' He sighed and then added as an afterthought. 'Another thing. I've decided to do like ya wanted. If you want me back, I'll give up me shifts so I'll be 'ere more for ya. We won't 'ave as much money, but ya can't 'ave everythin' 'n' at least I won't be stayin' away from 'ome 'n' I'll be 'ere. So what d'ya say?'

Now it was his turn to sit and be silent, to listen, to wait for her reply.

Rose had enjoyed her six months of freedom, because that was how she considered it. She had continued to work at the club and continued to see Sharif. He had never questioned her about that night. He didn't need to know as long as it didn't affect what they had between them.

They'd started meeting during the day, hiding away in his apartment for hours at a time, enjoying long afternoons of pleasure together, their union becoming ever stronger. They neither of them questioned what they felt towards each other; that was one of the unspoken rules. A connection existed which neither of them wanted to break and that was all that mattered.

She had also enjoyed spending and buying the clothes which she craved without having anyone there to continually moan at her, asking where the money had gone. She and Maddy had spent hours scouring the shops, searching for just the right colour, the right length. They had lunched out and tasted freedom from worries. She'd enjoyed a sense of individuality which had been lacking during all these years.

But at what price freedom? What would happen if Sharif tired of her? How would she manage without Alan's income if he left her? What about the children? They needed a father and she didn't relish the prospect of bringing them up alone. But what he asked was more than she could relinquish. Surely there must be a way to solve this? She still wanted Alan, still needed him, and felt that she owed it to him to give things another try since he was doing the hardest part by agreeing to return after what she had done to him. He deserved that, she owed him that, he was due that much respect at least. The one question which she never asked herself, which didn't seem significant to her, was 'did she still love Alan'?

She raised her eyes to look straight into his. No tears, no emotion, nothing to indicate any feelings of either love or remorse.

'Alright, Alan. Course I want ya back. I'm glad you want to after what I've done.' She paused and then finished what she needed to say. 'I agree to your terms. Course, ya could expect nothin' less. It wouldn't be fair. I'll telephone tomorrow 'n' explain I won't be goin' back.'

The relief lit-up Alan's face, the jagged lines of fatigue washed away as he put out his arms to his wife.

'Come 'ere then love,' he smiled, ''n' let's 'ave a cuddle.'

The cuddle turned into something more. After so long apart, Alan was eager to regain his wife's body, eager to feel the silky softness of her skin, take her breasts firmly in his hands in domination and possession. He had forgotten how delicious she tasted, how well she moved against him, what passion her body encapsulated. How could he possibly have believed that he could live his life without her? She was part of him.

Finally spent, they lay entwined in each other's arms, glad that this conflict was to all intents and purposes over, hopeful that they could get their lives back to normal. But Alan had one more bombshell to drop, one final piece to complete the jigsaw.

'I'm sorry to bring this up now, love, but I 'ave to. We

might as well get it all sorted out at t' same time. I got a letter from t' Building Society today.'

The fear slithered frostily up her back and burrowed itself deep inside her neck, as though it knew what would come next.

'Where did t' money go for t' mortgage?' he asked, making the question sound casual, too weary to want a fight.

'I don't know. I thought I'd paid it, but I guess I missed a few months.'

'Well, that's it, Rose. We're losin' t' 'ouse.' A stunned silence rested between them.

'There's no way we can catch up on six months arrears, especially since I won't be earnin' as much on days. I've asked at t' council 'n' we can 'ave an 'ouse on Woodville. We 'ave to let 'em know first week in January.'

'Woodville? I don't want to live on a council estate! I can't live there!'

'No, Rose, I don't want to live there either, but you've not left us wi' much choice. We're so far be'ind wi' t' mortgage on this place now we can't afford another place. We don't 'ave any choice.' He paused. 'It's a nice 'ouse, they said, three bedrooms 'n' gardens front 'n' back. Right next to t' school 'n' all.'

They had both heard such stories of life on the estates that neither of them relished the idea of being forced to live there. It was for people at the bottom of the pile, no-hopers. Is that what they were now?

'Well, as long as we're all back together, then that's all that matters.' Alan stood to leave. 'I won't be long. I'll go get Annie 'n' our things 'n' get Chris to run us back. Then we can get sorted out ready for t' mornin'. It's Christmas Day, after all.'

He took her face in his hands, trying unsuccessfully to read what it hid.

'I love you, Rose. Promise ya won't let me down this time. Please. Because this is our last chance, ya know, 'n' it won't be easy for a while yet. You'll 'ave to bear with it.'

'I promise.'

The best Christmas present that Lydia could have hoped for was there waiting for her when she got up in the morning. Her daddy.

'Daddy! Daddy!' she cried as she ran to throw herself into his arms. 'Oh I've missed you so much. 'ave ya come to stay?' She looked questioningly at him, eager, her head tipped to one side.

'Course I 'ave. We're all back together for good. 'appy Christmas.'

Annie was glued to her mother's knee and had to have her presents passed to her to open them. All of the children had more than their fair share of presents as both parents had bought gifts for them not knowing what the other would have bought. Still, that didn't matter because at least it may go some small way to making up for the last six months of upheaval and for the upheaval which was about to come. After all, this was to be their last Christmas in this house.

In only a short space of time, the room became a rubbish tip with paper everywhere, torn and thrown over their heads in their eagerness to open their presents, and for once Rose didn't complain.

''ere y' are, love. I bought this for you,' murmured Alan softly, brushing her neck with his lips. Rose opened the present to find inside a beautiful gold watch with her name engraved on the back; 'to my precious Rose'. It shone brightly in the light from the Christmas tree behind her, the silver-coloured face a contrast to the gold hands upon it. Tears of gratitude welled in her eyes. She hadn't expected anything like this.

'Thanks, Alan. It's really nice o' ya,' she whispered and kissed him. She shamefully realised that she hadn't bought anything for him, expecting that they would still be apart, and hoped that he wouldn't notice or, if he did, wouldn't mention it.

Christmas dinner was shared with Alice and Bert.

'It's lovely to see ya back, Alan. That's t' best Christmas present we could 'ave 'ad, int it, Alice?' laughed Bert, who knew his son-in-law to be a good man. His daughter had been a fool for risking the loss of him.

'Yes, you two, we're ever so pleased for you both. Let's hope it works out better this time,' added Alice.

They shared a wonderful Christmas day together. The meat was succulent, as one would expect from Rose, and Alan dutifully carved the giant, tender turkey. Annie continued to cling to her mother just as Lydia clung to her grandfather. Then, as was tradition, they all snuggled in front of the television and the fireplace for the Queen's speech and the Christmas Day film.

All in all, a perfectly happy Christmas Day was had by all. None of them knew that it was to be their last together.

Shame and despair threatened to strangle Rose as she hurried inside, eager to disappear. The removal van pulled up outside number three, the second house up. She had an overwhelming desire to pick up her dainty legs and run as fast as she could back down the road, away, anywhere except here, but she couldn't because this would now be her home.

The house was a semi-detached in a row of houses which were all exactly the same; same gardens, same doors and windows all painted the same colour, dark-red. Curtains twitched to either side, which she felt rather than saw, as the neighbours looked to see what the new inmates were like. That was how Rose felt; like an inmate being driven into her new prison house. No matter how poor her parents had been, they had always been able to call their house their own. Now she and Alan were being forced to live in a house where God knows what people had lived before them.

She turned the key in the lock and prayed that it wouldn't turn, that there had been a mistake and this was all a bad dream and they could go back to their nice, safe, comfortable home. The key turned, the door unlocked.

Rose's spirits lifted slightly as she poked her head around the door and found that things were not as bad as she had expected. The kitchen was bigger than the kitchen which she had left in Wykon, although it was bare with not even any units in. A large, white pot sink sat underneath a metal-framed window which looked straight into the window of the kitchen next door. It was, mercifully, clean. She gave a silent word of thanks to the previous occupants and remonstrated with herself for calling them. After all, they could have been people just like themselves.

A contraption which she deduced must be a back-boiler of some sort stood against the wall, its colour best described as sooty, its feet firmly planted where it had stood for years in dutiful service. A door led to a small, concrete-floored room at the back of the house. She wondered what this was for until she lifted the catch to a small, wooden door and was hit by the smell of coal. So this was what they called a 'coal-'ole.'

To the other side of the front door, she found the living room. She was pleased with its size and had to confess that it was bigger than her old living room. Already her horror was fading as she realised that she at least had a clean house with which she could begin to show her talent again at renovation and redecoration; start afresh. Having said that, the decorating wasn't so bad, either. It would certainly do for a while.

Upstairs, she found more of the same; large, clean rooms. There were three bedrooms, exactly as she had before, and they were equally as large. She could have cried with joy that they weren't being thrown into a tiny, little back-to-back house, cockroach and rat-infested with mould on the walls, which was the vision which had burrowed in her head for the past weeks as they had readied themselves for the move. This house, had it been anywhere else except here, would have been as good as her old house.

She retraced her steps back down the stairs to Alan, who hadn't moved from the front step, anxious to see her reaction and waiting with trepidation.

'This'll do fine, love,' she smiled. He smiled back with relief. Now that he had her approval, they could begin unloading the van.

Rose took charge, hurrying the removal men inside. She didn't want the whole neighbourhood to see everything that was going into the house. The transfer was quickly completed and the removal men drove off, pocketing their tip.

'See if there's any coal in that coal–'ole,' directed Rose. 'We need to get t' back–boiler goin' afore we collect t' kids. It might warm things up a bit upstairs. I'll turn t' fire on down 'ere.'

The fire didn't work. As she snapped the stiff switch to 'on' and watched the spark jump, there was nothing, not even the faintest whiff of gas.

'Alan, t' fire's broken,' she shouted so that he would hear her in the kitchen. A scurrying of feet across the floorboards followed.

'I think it might 'ave summat to do wi' this,' he shouted back. She went to investigate what 'this' might be, and came face–to–face with a gas meter, which was being kept company on the wall by an electric meter.

'You need two bob bits to pay for it,' grinned Alan, and they burst into fits of laughter at the ludicrous situation of having to pay for gas and electricity before using them. They would never have thought of that, and laughed at their own naivety.

'Well, at t' same time as searchin' out somewhere to get some coal, you'd best get some change,' laughed Rose. 'You'd best try t' shops we saw on t' way 'ere, just round t' corner, 'cos we don't 'ave much time afore we need to go 'n' collect t' kids.'

'What we doin' 'ere, dad?' asked Lydia, her small face contorted with incomprehension. 'Why aren't we goin' 'ome?'

'This is 'ome now, Lydia. We didn't tell ya before 'cos we didn't want to worry you, but we decided to move 'n' this is where we live now,' replied her father gently.

'But what about me friends? What about me school? 'ow will I get there?'

Dread clouded her features now as she wrung her hands together, desperate to understand.

'You won't be goin' back to that school. You see that school there,' he pointed to the school in the field over the road, 'well, that's where you'll be goin' from now on. It's a real nice school. I'm sure you'll like it. Annie can go there too, 'cos she's five now 'n' can start.'

Lydia said nothing. There was nothing that she could say. Her eyes filled with tears as she turned a look of betrayal upon her parents and trudged up the stairs to the bed which they had told her was now where she would sleep.

Lydia stood at her bedroom window and stared into the windows of the flats which overlooked their house. There were dustbins overturned in the yard which had lots of washing lines in it, and rubbish was hiding in the corners of the yard where the wind had blown it.

She could see a group of children crouched down in a corner. She wondered what they were doing out after dark. She couldn't see what they were playing, but didn't like the thought that they could see straight into her bedroom. She bobbed down and pulled the makeshift curtains together, but they didn't quite meet properly in the middle. She turned out the light so that she was invisible. Closing one eye and peering through the gap, she peeped over at the flats. The walkway which ran along each row of doors was littered with rubbish and she could see a pram. She could hear a baby crying from somewhere, but she couldn't see it. One of the doors opened and a fat woman came out onto the walkway.

'Shut that fuckin' kid up will ya?' At least that's what Lydia thought she said because she had never heard anyone say the swear word before close up. She'd only heard it whispered in corners at school.

The small group cowered further into the corner as the light from the open door flooded the yard. What were they doing?

As the baby became silent and the woman went back in, slamming the door, the yard once again fell into darkness. Small pinpricks of light shone from the corner and Lydia guessed that the boys — she automatically presumed that they were boys — were smoking. She knew that you weren't allowed to smoke unless you were grown-up and was shocked by what she had seen. Shocked yet strangely excited. Excited because she knew that she was watching something that was wrong. She didn't like the feeling, being excited by something which she knew was wrong. Why was she excited then? She watched as the gang moved off to continue their smoking where they were less likely to be disturbed.

Then she remembered. This wasn't some film from the telly about life somewhere else. This was where she lived now. These were the people who lived near her. Why had this happened? What about all her friends at school, the friends who liked her and thought that she was clever? Would she be able to be clever at this school? What about Andrew? He said that he liked her and she couldn't even say goodbye to him? Why couldn't she go home to her nice, cosy bedroom with curtains that closed?

She slid beneath the covers in her icy bedroom, listening to the noises of people, noise which was so alien to her; noise of a television blaring out, a radio in the room next to hers, *somebody shouting, another baby crying, a dog barking. The cacophony assaulted her ears and made her head want to explode.*

Her already battered world was being shattered, everything which was familiar being thrown away and buried. Please take me away to Godland. I can't find my way there. Please take me. Don't take that away too. Please let me in. She closed her eyes as the gentle guardian came to take her hand and lead her to oblivion. A smile crossed her face as she fell asleep, safe for a while.

The next day, Rose was interrupted whilst cleaning by a firm knock on the door. She opened the door and was confronted by a small, buxom woman with short, dark, curly hair and a broad smile fixed to her face.

'Hiya, love. I thought I'd nip 'n' say 'ello. I'm Melanie, but everyone calls me Mel. I live next door,' she informed Rose, indicating the house adjoining her own. Although it was only morning, she carried with her a bottle of brandy.

'You'll like as not need this whilst you get used to livin' 'ere,' she laughed. 'It's not exactly t' Ritz, but it's alright once you've been 'ere a while. I've been 'ere for three years.' She made it sound like a prison sentence.

Rose learnt that Mel had three boys, Kevin, Nigel and Robert. Her husband, she informed Rose, worked nights. Rose simply nodded and smiled. 'Worked nights' covered a multitude of options so she thought it best not to ask. She immediately liked Mel — not backwards at coming forwards — and was appreciative of her efforts to make her feel welcome.

Mel felt it her duty to give Rose all of the relevant information which she would need to survive; not to leave washing out if she left the house and to keep a good eye on it when she was in, who to tell about her comings and goings and who not to tell, where the nosy-parkers lived and which women were good for a laugh and a favour, where to let her husband go and where not to! By the time that Mel left, Rose was half a bottle of brandy worse for wear and had consumed the entire volume according to Mel of 'how to get by in Woodville!' Maybe this wouldn't be such a bad place, after all.

And so life began in their new home. Rose was contented to have a decent roof over her head with a good neighbour, and her husband was at home every night. What more could a woman ask for? Alan didn't need to work so hard to keep his family and had his wife and children at home for him. Things were back to normal, just in a different place.

They soon came to realise that life on Woodville wasn't as bad as they had expected it would be. Different, yes, with a new set of rules, but not that bad. Most people were friendly once you accepted them for who and what they were, just ordinary people. Just people. People just like them.

Chapter Eighteen

A cry escaped her body as it shuddered with the intensity of the orgasm which enslaved it, blood rushing through her veins as their passion reached its climax, pounding in her head. Her hands gripped tightly wherever they could take hold, beckoning, kneading, pleading to stop, pleading to carry on, her body in control where her brain had once been. The urgency of the body inside her own urged her on still further as it pushed and pulsed, burrowing ever deeper, demanding possession. A surge of energy, passion, frustration, then the stillness of satisfaction.

They lay together in the lull which followed the gratification of their bodily needs, their energies spent, their union once more sealed.

The afternoon sun threatened to break through the curtains which had been so carefully drawn against the world. The rest of mankind could disappear for the short, precious time which they shared together. All that mattered was here and now.

She knew that this was wrong, yet it never felt wrong, never felt sordid or dirty. It only felt right. She knew that, no matter what happened, she could never willingly give up the time spent with this man for it bore deep into her soul, her very being, and there was nothing to replace it. Her only sorrow was that they were forced to continue in secret for the sake of their spouses, forced to continue a sham of a life which made them prisoner to themselves, for the sake of propriety, for the sake of their children.

Sharif tenderly stroked her head where it lay on his shoulder and pulled her closer towards him.

'I love you, Bonita,' he murmured. It was the first time. She had longed for him to say those words, yet they filled her with dread now that they were spoken, though she knew not why.

'You know I love you too, Sharif,' was her response.

Lydia was lost in her jumbled-up thoughts, holding her sister's hand tightly as they rushed the short distance to their house from the school. She had just been told that they were moving her to the other class after the big holidays. Why? Why did she have to be moved? She was the only girl being moved, along with a boy called Gary. She knew that he was a trouble-causer, a Scottish boy with a Scottish temper to go with it. They had probably moved him to give him fresh children to bully.

But why had they moved her? What had she done wrong? She couldn't really understand and felt that she must somehow have done something to upset Mrs Jenkins. She liked Mrs Jenkins and wouldn't deliberately do anything to upset her. She was so kind. She must be a bad person, then, Lydia surmised. If she had managed to hurt Mrs Jenkins and needed to be moved, then she must be bad. Her mother was right, then, that she was a bad person. She was always telling her that.

'You're stupid, Lydia, an idiot, 'n' to top it all you're a bad person who tells lies,' her mother would say. She didn't understand why she was bad or what lies she was supposed to have told, but she was told this so many times that it must be true.

She didn't want any of her friends at school to know about her, though, and her fear was that, by being moved to the other class, they would begin to question about her and find out that she was really bad. As long as they only knew that she was clever, as long as she was top, then they wouldn't ask any further, she would simply be the clever girl, not the bad girl or the lying girl. She'd have to make sure that she was top of her new class.

They reached their house, Annie still tightly attached to Lydia's hand, and yet again the door was locked. Lydia sat down on the step with resignation. Not again. She was getting used to coming home and finding that her mum wasn't there. At first, she had cried, but this had upset Annie and she had cried too. When her mum came home and found them both crying, she had been angry and sent them both to bed with no tea.

She didn't like getting Annie into trouble, so she had tried to make up games to keep them amused whilst they sat there. It wasn't too bad when it was sunny like today, but it had been awful in winter when it was freezing cold. They had huddled together to keep warm, playing 'I spy' for sometimes an hour at a time, but they never complained again. They simply went inside once mum returned as though nothing had happened out of the ordinary.

They were used to sitting outside, anyway, for they had to go and sit outside whenever their mother had cleaned the house. They didn't understand why, but she would make them go out and play, even when it was rainy or freezing, whenever she had cleaned, and they weren't allowed back in until their dad came home. He never seemed to question why they were sitting outside in the rain. The girls had got used to it, anyway, and as soon as they saw their mother cleaning, they would start searching out their gloves and scarves.

They had a whole routine of games which they would play under the tiny veranda which stood beside their front door. It was a peculiar contraption with three vertical, dark-red bars which they would play on and they were grateful for its shelter.

Sometimes, when the weather wasn't bad, they would go down to the bus-stop and sit on the wall counting red cars or green cars until their mum appeared or their dad came home. Sometimes they would write down number plates. They spent a lot of their time outside.

Today they were lucky. Mel was just coming home from shopping and she saw them sitting like a couple of orphans.

'You two stuck outside again?' she asked. The two girls smiled politely and nodded.

'Come on in, then. I'll mek ya some beans on toast 'till your mum comes 'ome. 'er bus must be late again, mustn't it?'

'Yeah, right!' Mel thought to herself. She had seen the signs too many times not to know what was going on next door and she hated to see the children neglected as they were. She was taking them in more and more often these days. She didn't mind feeding them, but one time Alan would come home and catch her, and then what would she say. She packed them off upstairs to wash their hands and face.

They were familiar with the house next door now. When they came down, their beans on toast sat piping hot on the table waiting for them. The girls thanked her, smiling gratefully, and guzzled down the orange feast. Mel busied herself in the kitchen whilst they ate, preparing the meal for her three boys and husband.

Lydia ate silently, as she always did. Funny girl, thought Mel not for the first time. She wondered what things the girl had seen in her short life. Annie, on the other hand, was as bright and bubbly as always and chattered constantly between mouthfuls.

'Please don't speak wi' yer mouth full o' food, Annie,' chastised Lydia quietly. Annie answered by sticking out her tongue, but she did as she was told.

Mel couldn't quite weigh up the situation in the house next door, despite getting to know Rose quite well. She played her cards close to her chest did that one, but there was something about her that Mel liked. Maybe they were two of a kind. She knew that Rose acted like lady muck but in actual fact was not what she seemed to be. What she was Mel didn't know, but she was not stuck-up. Mel had seen through the act, but couldn't interpret what she saw there. She'd asked around, but no-one seemed to know anything. Still, that didn't matter. They were friends and right now she was wondering what her friend was up to.

A knock at the door crashed through her pondering. She smiled at the girls.

'Bet that's yer mum now, girls,' she comforted. As she opened the door, she saw that her guess had been correct.

'Sorry, Mel. Are t' girls 'ere?' asked Rose hurriedly.

'Course they are. You don't think I'd leave 'em just sat there, d'ya? They're just finishin' their tea.'

'I'm sorry, Mel. I got tied up wi' summat 'n' couldn't get away.'

Mel pondered, deciding whether she ought to say anything, whether it was her place to say anything. She decided that, having fed her children on more than one occasion then yes, she had a right.

'Look, Rose, I don't quite know 'ow to say this wi'out offendin' ya, but 'ere goes. Listen, love, I'm a bit older than you 'n' I've seen a bit more than you so don't try to kid a kidder. I know what you're up to.'

Rose opened her mouth to speak, her face adopting a harsh expression. Mel raised her hand to stop her.

'No, don't try to deny it. Look, I aren't interested in what you're doin', but put it this way, there's nowt secret round 'ere. There are too many tell–tale signs when you're playin' away from 'ome 'n' you're doin' 'em all, so let's not pretend, eh? If I can see what's goin' on then there'll be others who will too. There are lots o' people about wi' nowt better to do than nosy into other folks' business.'

'Will you say owt to Alan?'

'Don't be silly, love. That's yer one savin' grace, that people notice things but say nowt 'cos they've got plenty 'emselves as they don't want anyone to know. But you'll 'ave problems if ya get anyone who's got their eye on your Alan 'cos they'll tell 'im as soon as look at 'im if they get to know. 'e's not a bad looker your 'ubby, ya know? I 'ope this guy's worth it?'

She immediately realised that she had overstepped the

mark. 'Sorry, love, I didn't mean that. That's your business, but I'm just warnin' ya. As a friend.'

'Thanks, Mel. I appreciate it. I'll tek t' girls now.'

Rose's head hurt, giant fists thumping away at her brain. Her efforts to keep her affair secret had obviously failed dismally. A fearful insecurity swept over her, replacing the feeling of contentment which had so recently filled her. Besides hurting, her head was running the wool on its loom backwards and forwards, backwards and forwards, trying to figure out how she could change things so that they would no longer guess. She had been foolish to presume that her behaviour would go unnoticed. Nothing went unnoticed around here. Why couldn't they just mind their own business and leave her alone?

'Mum, I got my report yesterday. I didn't get chance to tell ya,' started Lydia, cautiously.

'What report? 'ave you bin misbehavin'?'

'No, my school report to say 'ow I've done durin' t' year,' she continued hopefully, her small head nodding.

'Well, put it down there 'n' I'll look when I get chance, okay?' Rose pointed to the kitchen table.

'But mum, I wanted to tell you....'

'Didn't you 'ear what I just said, you idiot,' bellowed Rose. 'Get up to bed now, 'n' tek Annie wi' ya. Go on. Now.'

Lydia scurried out of the kitchen, giving her mother as wide a berth as possible, fearful that a smack might follow. She grabbed her sister from the living room and fled upstairs.

'What's matter?' asked Annie, confused as she had been watching television quietly.

'Nothin', Annie, it's just bedtime now. Come on, let's get ready quick 'n' I'll give you a cuddle to get to sleep. Alright?'

They hurried into their night-dresses and snuggled into the top bunk where Annie slept. Lydia should have been upset by her mum, but she was unable to feel anything very much anymore. She didn't really go to her safe world these days. It was almost as though her safe world had wrapped itself around her like a protective blanket and feelings just didn't matter now. She didn't really understand what they were anymore, how they felt. They all sort of got confused up together somehow, wrapped around each other like barbed wire which couldn't be untangled and you couldn't tell which piece was which. She didn't try to understand anymore. It didn't really matter, did it? Feelings only hurt you anyway. She stroked her sister's head and closed her eyes. She must have been tired, or something, because she fell asleep where she lay.

Lydia awoke to the sound of her brother screaming; not the normal screaming of a baby when it needs something and has no other means of communication. This was a scream which she had heard before, not often, but she had heard it before, and it filled her with terror. This was the scream of a child begging for help.

She half–fell down the ladders as her body had only one aim, one thought, one compulsion; to help her brother. Tears of fright were already streaming down her face and her body heaved with her sobs even before she opened the door. The battle to force her eyes to look into the room was fierce for she didn't want to see what was happening, yet she knew that she must help him. She let out a howl of horror.

'Mum, what're ya doin'? Leave 'im alone! Leave 'im.' Her brother's arms and legs were twisted around his tiny body in his vain effort to protect himself, for he was being systematically kicked around the floor like a football by his mother. With each attack on his tiny form, he would attempt to escape the next with a hurried scuttle, trying like a wild animal to hide behind any piece of furniture, whilst attempting to maintain his protection, such as it was.

'Get off 'im! Get off!' yelled Lydia as she grabbed at her mother. Her pathetic endeavour was thwarted as she caught a fist to her shoulder which knocked her off her feet, but she felt nothing in her bid to free him. She instinctively knew that she could do nothing. Her mother was like a creature possessed, her face snarled and contorted. She hardly seemed to notice that Lydia was even there.

Lydia jumped to her feet and rushed from the house. Banging as hard as she could on the house next door, she yelled for Mel for all that she was worth. Mel was shocked at the sight of this child in her night-dress, screaming for her as she opened the door.

'Quick, it's mum,' was all that Lydia could say before she raced back across the garden into her house. Mel asked no questions but followed barefoot, spurred by the intuitive knowledge that something was terribly wrong.

She couldn't believe what she saw and lunged to grab hold of Rose. She escaped her grasp and went to throw a punch at Mel. Rose was no match for Mel, even in this state. Mel dodged the punch and slapped Rose hard across the face.

'Give up, you silly cow! Stop it! You'll kill 'im!' bawled Mel as she took hold of Rose yet again, shaking her roughly.

This time she didn't let go. As Mel stood with her arms tightly encircling Rose, Lydia threw herself at Jack where he lay shaking on the floor. 'Thank God,' Mel thought, 'if he's shaking, he's alive.'

Lydia carefully put her arms around him, slowly, so that he wouldn't be afraid. He flinched and tried to pull away, but relaxed his body when he realised that it was his sister. His feeble arms reached out and clung so tightly to her, trusting that she would somehow protect him. They entwined their arms around each other, waiting to be rescued. All Lydia could do was shush, shush.

'What the hell's goin' on 'ere!' someone shouted.

Mel turned around to see Alan standing in the doorway, a look of incredulity stamped upon his face. She threw Rose bodily at him and turned towards the children.

'Tek 'er out of 'ere, will ya? Now!' she commanded, leaving him in no doubt that her instructions should be obeyed.

Mel crouched over the children.

'It's alright, Lydia. Ya can let 'im go now, love. Yer mum's gone. Let 'im go so I can 'ave a look at 'im, will ya, love? Then we can see if 'e needs 'elp. Alright?' she asked gently. Lydia's eyes betrayed the hunted fear which lived there. The boy had the same look and Mel knew that this was not the first time for either of them.

Mel knew that this went on all the time in umpteen families on the estate, but this was the first time that she had seen it up close, and it made her flesh crawl. She had to force herself to put her feelings to one side for now, to give her full attention to the boy.

She examined him gently and carefully, not moving anything sharply in-case it was damaged, and was surprised to find that, despite his severe punishment, there was no blood to be seen. His face was untouched.

The thought sprang to her mind that this was a well-practiced instinct so that no-one could see the evidence. Well, she'd succeeded. Apart from the redness from his tears, his face remained unblemished.

She cautiously took one arm from Lydia and opened it out straight. Nothing. No screams. She gave it back to Lydia. She followed the same procedure with his other arm and his legs. Once she was certain that nothing was broken, she cautiously prodded about on his tiny body. He winced a little, which she presumed and hoped was due only to bruising, but there were no major outbursts.

Satisfied that he didn't need to go to hospital, though God only knew how, she turned to Lydia.

'If I carry 'im upstairs for ya, d'ya think you can get 'im into bed?' asked Mel. Lydia nodded. He was already in his pyjamas, so would not need to be moved much.

Mel carried the fragile piece of humanity upstairs and placed him gently into his bed. She said goodnight and left him with Lydia. Lydia sat beside him on the floor, scared that she might hurt him if she sat on the bed, and stroked his head as she had done for her sister earlier. It wasn't long before sleep descended to deliver him from his fear and pain.

Lydia was exhausted. As she headed at last for the comfort of her own bed, she became aware of the whimpers from the top bunk. It suddenly struck her that Annie must have heard most of what had been going on.

'Are y' alright, Annie?' she whispered.

'What's 'appened, Lydi? What's up? What wer all t' screamin' 'n' shoutin' for?'

'I would've thought you'd be used to screamin' 'n' shoutin' in this 'ouse by now,' she tried to joke.

'Will ya sleep wi' me?' Annie murmured, her whimpers threatening to increase in intensity once again.

Lydia hesitated, desperately tired and knowing that she couldn't get much sleep in the tiny bed, but knew what she must do.

'Course I will, if ya like. Budge over.'

Alan had taken Rose next door, well away from the children. As Mel walked through the door, Alan immediately asked,

'Where are t' kids? Are they all alright?'

'I've checked Jack as best I could. As far as I can see, 'e'll be okay, but 'e'll be black 'n' blue. Unless owt drastic 'appens 'n' 'e teks a turn for t' worse, I'd try to deal wi' this yoursens. If you tek 'im to t' 'ospital you'll never see 'im again, t' state 'e's in. They'll 'ave 'im in care afore you can say a word. She hung her head and shook it.

'What are you on, woman? 'ow could ya do that? What 'appened?'

Rose seemed to struggle to understand what Mel was

saying. She stared blankly forward, not seeing anything.

'I told 'im to stop cryin'. I couldn't think. 'e wouldn't stop cryin'. 'e wer tired but 'e wouldn't stop cryin'. 'e wouldn't stop cryin',' was all that they could get out of her.

Then she stopped talking. Her eyes glazed over, her face turned death white, her eyes slowly closed and she slid limply to the floor.

Rose didn't know where she was. Her head wobbled on her shoulders as she struggled to gain its control and failed miserably. Falling back heavily onto the pillow, she lay with her eyes open and stared unblinkingly at the ceiling, her mind devoid of thought.

A voice broke into her head, a stranger's voice, a man's voice.

'How long has she been like this?' she heard him ask. She didn't really care. It felt nice and peaceful and she wanted him to leave her alone, to let her lie there, forever.

A short examination of her bodily functions ensued, and then the verdict.

'Well, there's nothing wrong with her physically, but it looks to me like a meltdown; a breakdown. She's well and truly lost it. So we need to get it back for her.'

Somewhere in her head Rose heard a laugh. Lost it. How very astute of him. She knew that already. She knew that she had lost it. She had lost the fight with herself, lost the fight between the person that she wanted to be and the person that she had to be. Lost the fight to keep sane living with a man that she had tried so hard to love and couldn't, lost the battle to live between the times when she saw her lover, lost her fight to control the demon inside, lost her pathetic attempt to be a mother.

She wasn't really too sure how hard she had tried at the last one. Probably not hard enough. But she never asked for it. She could never defeat the resentment inside her at being forced to live a life which she didn't want.

And now the fight was over. She could happily just lie here forever. Great. She needed loving, she needed attention, she needed tenderness and without them she couldn't survive.

Why couldn't Alan see that? Where were the loves, the kisses, which she needed as much as she needed the breath of life itself? She was so confused, so frustrated, so angry, so desperate. Her body ached with the fatigue of fighting, the fatigue of fighting to be who she wanted to be.

Now she could stop fighting. Now she could just lie here. She felt a needle enter her body and a stillness descend once again as she gratefully drifted back into oblivion.

'What do we do now, doctor?' asked Alan, wearily.

'Well, it's up to your wife. I can't force her to go to Lynfield — more of a sanctuary for her to get herself together than a psychiatric hospital — but that is where I would suggest that she goes. She's not a danger to herself or anyone else, so the decision has to be hers.' They hadn't told him about Jack for fear of repercussions. 'All that you can do for her now is to let her rest. I'll give you a prescription to take home for her, just to keep her calm for a few days, and then once she's rested the decision must be hers, but I know that she would benefit from it. You know where I am if you need me.'

Alan thanked the doctor and waited for Rose to wake up so that he could take her to Alice's house where she could rest quietly.

But what then? For he knew that Rose would never agree to go to Lynfield.

A few days later, Alan sat waiting patiently for his wife to be brought home by her father. The children sat patiently too, the atmosphere tense. Jack sat on Lydia's knee with Annie close beside her father.

'Mummy's all better now, kids. It'll be nice to 'ave 'er 'ome, won't it?' They all smiled at their father and nodded.

The familiar red Vauxhall Viva drew up outside and their mother stepped out. The apprehension dissipated as their frowns were replaced by smiles of sunlight glowing from their faces.

He should not have worried. He should have known that the children would easily and quickly forget what had happened. Children were like that.

Rose had a peculiar smile on her face, placed there by the medication which she took to prevent her from thinking. She gratefully accepted the shows of affection from her children and sat amongst them on the settee. They didn't notice that her limbs were slow in moving. Why should they? They were simply glad to have their mother home.

Later, when the children were safely tucked up in bed, Alan and Rose hugged with the comfort that years together brings.

'Why won't ya go, Rose? Ya know it'd do ya good.'

'I don't need to. As long as I've got these tablets I'll be fine.'

'But you're like a zombie, love. Ya can't stay like this forever. Ya need 'elp.'

She gently placed a hand on his face and tried to reassure him.

'I've got all the 'elp I need right 'ere,' she smiled. He accepted that his attempts were falling on deaf ears.

'We'll be alright now, love. I promise,' she slurred.

Alan had no choice but, once again, to believe her and hope.

Chapter Nineteen

'You are my sunshine, my only sunshine
You make me happy when skies are grey
You'll never know dears how much I love you
Please don't take my sunshine away.'

Happiness swirled around their heads like a drug, invisibly filling their nostrils with the scent of contentment as the girls sang along with their mum. Lydia hadn't heard mum sing her song since Annie was little and it was so good to hear her voice raised in song rather than anger. Lydia remembered her mum like this, knew that she lay hidden, ready to say hello when the time was right. It was a mum which she did not often see these days, but she was glad that she was here today.

Alan had decided that a day out by the sea might help Rose to recover, so they were going to their favourite sea-side resort. The sun was already high in the sky, although it wasn't yet ten o'clock. The windows in the car which Chris had loaned them were part-way down and a cooling breeze chased away the sweaty vapours which would otherwise have stifled them. A perfect day.

The children scrunched in the back, Jack in the middle, breathing steadily as he slept. Alan had come to accept over the last few weeks since 'the incident' that this was how Jack was going to be for a while; a little bit quiet and sleepy. Everybody had noticed, but nobody dare mention it as to do so would be to stir up the events for Rose. They had no wish to remind her.

She had been unusually calm since that night. Alan knew that the latent monster which had become his wife over the years was being tethered by the vast number of drugs which she swallowed each morning. For now, he liked her the way that she was. They were enjoying a time of normal family life. He couldn't remember things being normal, but presumed that this was it, or as near as you could get.

The drive was trouble-free, apart from the expected tailbacks in two of the small villages along the way. The narrow, winding roads had not been built with the intention of coping with the large flows of traffic which daily fought their way along them to allow their passengers to have a glimpse of the sea. Annie's chattering was incessant as they slowly crawled along in the caterpillar in which they were trapped, but today nobody seemed to mind. Jack still slept but a sickly, sweet smell slyly permeated the car now that the breeze was not running so freely.

Poor Jack. He had had dreadful diarrhoea and sickness for the past few days. It was questionable as to whether it was a good idea to bring him along, but Alan had decided that he would be alright as he would sleep most of the time anyway. Now they needed to stop at the next public house or café which they passed so that Jack could have his nappy changed, which Lydia did. She was used to having to change Jack and didn't want anything to snatch her mum from her good mood, and if anything could do that she was convinced that the sight of Jack's insides so graphically displayed would do it.

As they neared Flintby Bay, Lydia and Annie were literally on the edge of their seats, both eager to be the first to spot the sea galloping over the horizon. They drove down the ravine towards the seafront, the trees hovering protectively above and sheltering them from the sun which was now scorching. They had stood like this forever and, at the end of the day, they would shade sun-weary holidaymakers as they made their way back up the ravine to their holiday homes. The steepness of the ravine was God intended, Lydia was sure, for footsteps were carried quickly down to the sea yet were impeded by the effort of the uphill struggle when it was time to leave it, just as people would descend with eagerness to the sea and leave it at the end of the day with a heart heavy at saying goodbye.

Now, as they neared the bottom where it levelled out onto the promenade, squeals of delight signalled the emergence of the untamed beauty of this most fascinating of nature's gifts. The tide was quite high and the small waves gently curled themselves into balls and then twirled over as the foam escaped from inside. The whooshing sound lulled, like the long-forgotten sound which begins life in the womb.

As soon as the car was parked, right on the sea-front, the girls jumped out and went to hang over the horizontal, blue rails which marked the drop down to the sea and the beach.

As Alan put Jack warily into the pushchair, an unconscious fear tugged at his stomach, though he couldn't quite work out why. Yes, he needed changing again and yes, he did look flushed, but then they were all flushed with the heat. He was still sleepy, but heat did that to babies, didn't it? He dismissed the feeling as paranoia and they set off to walk along the promenade with Jack asleep in his pushchair.

Rose and Alan, for once arm in arm, laughed at the girls skipping and running ahead, thrilled by the sensation of freedom and abandon, butterflies fluttering with excitement in their stomachs as their joy threatened to spill out of their small bodies. Seagulls squawked overhead as they dipped and dived, ever vigilant for scraps of food left behind by picnickers. There was a background hum of noise as passing conversations were muffled by the density of the hot air, which joined with the whoosh of the sea to perform a symphony of relaxation ballads.

Everything was perfect. Alan was well aware that this wasn't his wife but some drug-induced replica, but he didn't care because he knew that this was once how his wife had been without drugs. Or had she? He couldn't really remember. Today it didn't matter. Today everything was perfect.

They hungrily ate fish and chips out of the paper as they sat on the top part of the beach which had yet to be eaten by the advancing waves. The sea air brought out the flavour and their mouths watered as they filled their stomachs.

Alan carried Jack as they stumbled across the pebbles towards the brig. The boy was still unusually hot, despite having almost every item of clothing removed, and Alan hoped that the cold air on the brig would bring him round a little.

The brig was the favourite place in the whole world for all of them, Rose included. As they cautiously inched their feet over the holes and crevices which lay underfoot — where the sea had slowly, inch by inch, worn away each small indentation with hundreds of years of angry battering — a sense of discovery and exploration carried them forward.

It always felt the same, as though time could have no effect, as though it had stood still since the last time that they were there. The sounds of the beach began to die away, a stillness fell as they ventured ever further, away from the world, out towards the sea.

The brig stretched out at the end of the beach, copying the contours of the cliffs beside it, except that when the cliffs stopped, the brig didn't. It journeyed onwards, making a large niche of savage, desolate land which jutted and poked itself towards the horizon until it fell, starkly, suddenly, into the jaws of the huge waves.

The most remote rocks, where gigantic chunks lay scattered like dice, forgotten forever where they had been thrown, were where Lydia would throw her arms out and feel something that she didn't quite know how to name, like she was in a place where nobody and no-one could hurt her, where she didn't have to be scared, where she didn't have to look after someone else, where she didn't feel bad. Here she felt that she belonged, like God could see her. Her outstretched arms reached

*for Him, reached for safety, reached for freedom for her spirit —
and she found them. The sea held the power to hypnotise people
and make them feel .... nice, because that's what it did to her.*

The sight and sound of this mighty creation stirred
some latent, long-forgotten primeval yearnings, jolting them
awake after thousands of years lying dormant.

Alan felt it too and breathed deeply, the strong breeze
running through his head like an opiate, casting out the
worries and strife of the past months. He remembered the
many times that he had been here, both as a boy and a man,
and was staggered to realise that the benevolent glory of this
place never failed in its labour of mercy to free his very soul.
He wore the smile of a person set free, contented — beside
him sat his wife with a smile, blank and calm. Yes, a perfect
day.

He was jolted back to reality by the wriggling of his son
in his arms. He gently lifted him upright, his tiny body held
aloft in Alan's massive hands, and tried to get his attention.
Jack smiled weakly in acknowledgment. Alan again felt an
ominous fear as he was hit by the sickly smell which had
followed them for days now. It was time to go.

Lydia and Annie had dragged their weary bodies to bed
as soon as their feet touched the carpet inside the house. Lydia
had hesitated as she said goodnight to her mum, longing to
give her a kiss goodnight, feeling that she might receive a
response with the way that she was, but she restrained herself,
the fear of rejection greater than the desperation for a kiss.
Rose had attended to Jack whilst Alan had taken the car back
to Chris, becoming slightly more alert as the need for the
renewal of her medication neared.

Perhaps if she had undressed Jack earlier during the day
she might not have noticed that he was boiling hot; not just
hot with the warmth of the day, but fever hot. Grabbing the
thermometer from the bathroom cabinet, she slid it under his

armpit and lowered his arm. Jack never moved, just lay there, inert. Rose placed a cold flannel on his forehead, but the only response was a tiny wriggle, nothing more.

The reading on the thermometer threw her into panic, now fully alert. She didn't need to be a doctor to know that the temperature was way, way too high. What should she do? Without thinking, she ran next door to Mel's.

'Mel, can I use yer phone?' she blurted out as Mel answered the banging on her front door. She took one look at Jack, limply dangling in Rose's arms, and pulled her inside.

'I'll ring for ya. Robert, get some more cold water on that flannel,' she instructed as she pulled it from Jack's head, alarmed by the warmth of it. Rose perched on the edge of a chair as Mel rang for the ambulance.

'Don't worry. It'll be here soon,' she comforted. 'Where's Alan?'

'He's just tekken t' car back. We've bin out for t' day, to Flintby,' she answered, as though it mattered. ''e'll be back soon. Will you stay wi' t' girls until he gets back?' Without waiting for an answer, she continued. 'I should've noticed sooner. I should've noticed summat wer wrong. 'e's almost unconscious. 'e's 'ad diarrhoea for days, 'n' today 'e's 'ardly bin awake, but I've been so drugged up I didn't notice. I should've noticed 'n' I didn't.'

Mel wished that the ambulance would hurry up. This time, when the flannel was placed back upon Jack's forehead, it brought no reaction. After what seemed like an eternity, blue flashing lights blinked through the window. Mel helped Rose into the ambulance together with her son.

'Where you tekkin 'em?' she asked the ambulance men as they were climbing back inside.

'To t' fever 'ospital up Leeds Road,' was the reply.

'Listen, she's on medication for 'er nerves 'n' it's wearin' off. Keep an eye on 'er an' all, will you? I'll get 'er 'usband there as soon as I can.' They nodded, and were just about to drive off when a bang on the door stopped them. It was Alan. He quickly jumped inside, having been reassured by Mel that she would watch the girls. The ambulance left, its blue lights flashing the emergency.

The distinct, disinfectant–clean, nauseating smell filled the grey–walled waiting–room where Rose and Alan sat, both remembering the last time that they had been forced to wait like this; Rose for her daughter and Alan for his father.

A distance of three chairs separated them physically. A distance far wider separated them in reality. Rose, deep down, was blaming Alan for not recognising the signs earlier. Alan, deep down, was blaming Rose for placing his son in such a weakened condition and for being too drugged up to notice what was happening. They both attempted to deal with the blame, both tried to denounce it so that they could provide comfort to each other, but the blame kept rising like bile and refused to be driven away.

And so they sat, each lost in their own feelings of disappointment with the other, both fighting the urge to voice their anger, both knowing that this was not the time or the place, that the only thing that was important right now was Jack. Neither dare speak to offer any conversation for fear that the suppressed volcano of anger might erupt. So they sat in silence, scared that their son had been so feverish, so helpless, so small, so ill. His face had wrinkled in torment at his discomfort even as he slept. What if he died?

The opening of the door brought them both to their feet.

'ow is 'e, doctor?' begged Alan heatedly, unable to wait another moment to know the truth.

'Yes, doctor, 'ow is 'e?' interrupted Rose, delaying the answers to their questions.

'As you will obviously be aware, he is not well at all. He has a condition known as gastroenteritis. In itself, this is not life–threatening, but in someone so young and in an already debilitated condition, the situation is very grave. We've placed him on a drip and we're starting him immediately on a course of antibiotics. There's really nothing more that we can do for him, except to keep him isolated in order to prevent him from being weakened further by any stray germs or viruses, so we're keeping him in the isolation ward. You can go and see him now, if you wish. I'll just warn you though, so that you're not alarmed, that he has several monitors on him, and then with the drip as well, it does all look very severe, but please don't worry too much. We are doing everything that we possibly can, and we are confident that he will pull through, but it's largely up to him, I'm afraid. He needs to have the will to live.'

Hatred for Rose thumped hard on Alan's heart, for the only chance that his son had of survival was his will to live, which, he now knew, she had unremittingly attempted to quell during his short life.

He moved away from her, afraid that his hatred might escape. He prayed that Jack would survive for he feared for his actions if he didn't.

They put on the gowns and face-masks which they were handed before entering the isolation ward. Surely it must be very serious for them to have to wear these things?

They barely recognised Jack. As the doctor had warned them, he resembled a physics experiment rather than a child, still unconscious and so small. They weren't allowed to touch him, only to watch him. Alan would have done anything to take away the hurt and pain from his son, anything, but he was left stranded and useless.

The next three weeks were fraught with dealing with the plight of their son and attempting to keep a life going at home for their daughters. Lydia and Annie couldn't understand why they weren't allowed to see their brother. They were both well aware that people in hospital had visitors, so why couldn't Jack? Rose and Alan had tried to explain how ill Jack was, but the girls' understanding seemed impervious to this information.

Jack, thankfully, began to recover, slowly but surely. He was painfully thin, his emaciated arms and legs barely more than bones on which flesh hung, but his gentle smile had returned.

Alan and Rose were grateful, but the recovery of Jack had not brought them closer together, for neither of them had dealt with their negatives feelings for each other and, therefore, continued to avoid them, building them up inside and building their own internal walls. Still, they had managed to get through it, mainly thanks to Rose's medication.

Alan and Rose had taken it in turns to visit Jack, deciding that more hours could be filled by them taking different shifts and they could also share the task of dealing with the girls. The unmentioned and unacknowledged reason was that it also meant that they would not have to deal with their feelings for each other if they were together less often.

This particular night it was Alan's turn to visit and he was waiting for Jack to drift off to sleep. He stood beside the metal cot, leaning over and gently stroking the child's head as he often did.

He was being entertained by a young nurse who, he thought, had taken quite a shine to him and he certainly wasn't going to complain at the attention. Karen, she was called; a friendly girl, tall and pretty, but just missed being beautiful.

Alan had been under the impression that she was Irish for she displayed the characteristic pale–blue eyes to compliment her long, dark hair and milk–white complexion, but he had been forcibly advised that this was not the case.

"ow could ya? I'm Yorkshire born 'n' bred, me. Me dad came from down South somewhere, 'n' we lived down there for a while, so that's why I don't talk as broad as p'rhaps I should, but I'm Yorkshire through 'n' through, ya cheeky monkey. Don't ya know that's biggest insult you can throw at a girl, not recognisin' a true Tyke?'

Alan laughed at her mock indignation and settled down to listen to her five-minute account of her past few days with her boyfriend. She would talk for no more than five minutes at a time, aware that she would be severely reprimanded if sister found her not doing her work, so after her five minutes was up, she stood and left. But she had cheered him up.

'See ya later,' she whispered conspiratorially. 'I'll be back soon. Don't miss me too much!'

And she was gone, leaving Alan to his chuckle with his boosted ego. The numbness which was spreading over his bottom told him it must be almost time to leave. He couldn't understand why they felt it necessary to torture visitors with these wooden, ramshackle chairs when they had to spend so long with their posteriors locked onto them. Still, it would only be a few more days now.

As he stole a last glance at his son, curiosity led his hand to the notes on the end of the cot, neatly attached by the huge metal clip to a board. He took them off, feeling criminal, reassuring himself that he wouldn't actually look at them. Funny, but he'd never bothered to look at them before, probably because he hadn't thought to. Now, checking quickly over his shoulder, his eyes devoured the information before him.

There was every piece of information which he could possibly need to know about Jack; every illness that he had ever had, every injection, every painkiller, every antibiotic. There were more general notes: his weight, his height, his skin colour, his hair colour, eye colour, blood group. His blood group.

Alan had never really thought about blood groups before and was interested to see what his son's might be. He knew that he was 'O' Positive because he had been given blood tests for something or other when he was young, and he also knew that Rose was 'O' Positive from when she was pregnant. As he read further, he saw that Jack's group was AB. AB. What did that mean? He had thought that children had the same blood group as their parents and was rather intrigued to see that it wasn't even the same as Rose's.

As if answering an unbidden request, Karen sneaked through the door, checking that no-one had seen her coming in again.

'Just the person,' smiled Alan. 'I've a question 'n' you're just the person I need to answer it.'

'Fire away!' she laughed, 'as long as it's not rude or personal!'

'D'you know owt about blood groups?'

'Yes, quite a bit, actually. I took a special interest in blood — haematology you know — when I wer studyin'. Why?'

'Is it strange for a child to 'ave a different blood group to its parents?'

'No, not at all. It's very complex 'ow it all works out, but if ya think about it, it's not often that both parents 'ave t' same blood group, so each time that a different combination mixes together, a different result 'appens when they 'ave a child.'

'I wer just wonderin', that's all, 'cos both me 'n' Rose are 'O' Positive 'n' Jack's blood group is AB.'

'No, you must be mistaken. That's not possible. Ya see, there are certain blood groups which, when they're matched together, mek different blood groups, a bit like maths really, 'n' if 'O' Positive and 'O' Positive are added together then it's virtually impossible for there to be a child produced which is of the blood group AB. Yes, virtually impossible.'

With her last words, she realised the enormity of what she was saying, saw it reflected in the murderous look of hatred which spread over Alan's face.

'Oh, Mr Knowles, I'm so sorry if I've spoken out o' turn. I'm so sorry.'

He turned to look at Jack and accepted that he had, after all, lost his son almost as surely as if he had died. The pain in his chest threatened to overpower him. He headed purposefully for the door.

'Don't worry yoursen, love. It's not you who should be sorry.'

A dusty, brown suitcase sat by the living room door. Alan stared at it as though it was a giant bug, transfixed, trying to recapture in his mind all the times that he had filled this suitcase and now it had been filled again. He needed to concentrate or he knew that he would lose everything with the loss of his temper, because he would kill her, barehanded. He was quite sure about that.

He had asked Mel to come round and take the girls home with her for a while, if she wouldn't mind. She had seen the case as soon as she walked into the room.

'So you've found out then?' she asked innocently, sympathetically.

'Yes,' was his only reply.

'T' whole estate knew about 'er fancy man, love, but no-one wanted to be t' one to tell ya. I'm glad ya found out. 'ow did ya find out?'

He closed his eyes, a sole tear escaping as yet another sword of deceit stabbed into his back.

'It doesn't matter now, Mel. It doesn't matter. Please, just tek t' girls for me. You'll know when you can bring 'em back.'

And so he sat and waited and counted the suitcase-packings. And the promises. And the lies.

Rose knew that something was wrong when she saw the suitcase. Alan sat in an armchair, turned around to face the door instead of the television. The hairs on the back of her neck rose in preparation for what was to come. Fear put its fingers around her throat and she knew that she wasn't going to talk her way out of this one. The look of hatred, betrayal, hurt on Alan's face told her that. He knew something.

'You lyin', cheatin' slut. You selfish, disgustin' slag. 'ave ya no morals, no principles, no conscience.' She froze, not daring to reply, afraid by the venomous delivery of his words.

'You knew Jack wasn't mine. You knew, 'n' yet ya let me go on believin' 'e wer my son, when all t' time I wer carin' for 'im, feedin' 'im, lovin' 'im for ya fancy man. 'ow could ya do it? Please don't deny it,' he said, raising his hand, 'please don't insult me further, ya schemin' cow, 'cos I've got proof. I 'ad a very interestin' discussion about blood groups today 'n', d'ya know what? Surprise, surprise? Either I'm not Jack's father or you're not 'is mother. Now which d'ya think it is?'

Again she went to speak, and Alan raised his hand again, this time moving closer to Rose

'Don't even think about sayin' it, you whore, 'cos that's not all. 'ow long've ya bin seein' yer dark boyfriend be'ind me back, then?' The look of surprise on Rose's face immediately gave the game away, caught off guard as she was.

'Oh, yes, you whorin' bitch. I know that too. 'ow long? Did y'ever stop seein' 'im? I bet ya didn't. Couldn't bear to be away from 'is dick, could ya? Well, good, 'cos 'e can bloody well 'ave ya. I don't want ya no more. Anythin' I felt for you 'as just been shot to pieces, never to rear its ugly 'ead again. Go on, ya slag, piss off 'n' shack up wi' 'im, 'n' I'll tell ya summat else. You can tek 'is bastard son wi' ya, 'cos I'm not feedin' 'im no more.'

She finally found the courage to speak.

'What about t' girls?'

'Don't you even begin to think about tekkin 'em. D'ya 'onestly think I'd let a low-life like you bring up me daughters? You must be jokin'. I warned you afore, Rose. You go, t' kids stay. That wer t' deal if ya fouled up, 'n' from where I'm sittin' it looks pretty much like you've fouled up. Now, if I wer you, I'd pick up that suitcase 'n' get the hell out of 'ere afore I forget I'm a gentleman 'n' beat seven bells o' shit out o' ya 'cos, believe me, right now nowt would give me greater pleasure.'

And so Rose picked up her suitcase and prepared to leave her home.

'I never meant to 'urt you, Alan. You're a good man. I'm sorry.' She turned and walked out of their lives forever, for she would never return to their home.

Alan hunched, his head in his hands, and finally broke down. It was done and his strength had ceased. In the house next door, an inhuman cry could be heard, and Mel knew that Rose was gone.

Chapter Twenty

Lydia and Annie sat close together on the settee in their night-clothes, their thin legs neatly pressed together. Alan stood before them. He didn't know what to say. Dear God, when would this all stop?

'I'm really, really sorry but I've summat to tell ya. I want ya to be brave and I want ya to try to understand. Is that okay?' They nodded solemnly. 'Ya know mummy's bin poorly?' Again, understanding nods. 'Well t' doctors think she needs to live somewhere else now so she can get better, so it means she can't live with us no more. It won't be very nice for us, and we'll miss 'er, but it 'as to be this way.'

'So won't we see mummy ever again?' Annie asked, her bottom lip quivering.

'No chicken, you won't. She can't look after ya no more. But I'm 'ere. I aren't going nowhere 'n' I'll alas look after you 'n' keep you safe.'

'What about Jack? When's Jack comin 'ome?' asked Lydia, fear staring back at him.

'Well, 'cos Jack's a baby 'e 'as to stay wi' 'is mum, so 'e won't be coming back neither.'

Silent tears slid down all three faces. Lydia put her hand to her father's cheek.

'It's okay, dad. Don't worry, it'll be okay. Can we go to bed now 'cos Annie's tired?' whispered Lydia.

They kissed him goodnight. His eyes followed them as they disappeared through the door. He felt lost, alone, out of his depth. How would he look after them? How would he keep them safe? He didn't know how, but he knew that he would.

'Go to sleep now Annie. It's real late 'n' ya won't be beautiful if ya don't get lots o' sleep.'

'Will ya sleep wi' me? I'm scared. I want mummy.'

Although every fibre in Lydia's body burned to rest in

her bed, she snuggled up to her sister, listening for the sound of the heavy breathing which told of her sleep.

Lydia didn't understand. Why had her mum gone away? Was it because she was bad like mum said? Was it because she didn't like her? Why had her brother gone too? Mum couldn't look after him — only Lydia could. Who would cook the tea, do the washing, clean the house, take care of Annie — and dad? What if anything happened to dad — where would they go?

As these questions ran through the trees towards her like an army of wolves, Lydia slowly crept into the cold, rocky cave and snuggled up under a thick, pink blanket and put her head inside. The questions couldn't get her there because they wouldn't find her. Something inside her was pushing, kneading, punching, trying to get out, something terrible which would, she knew, kill her.

She took the feeling and put it in a box. She took all of the questions and put them in a box. She put her mum in a box. She placed everything that she could find in a box, including every emotion except the love for her brother and sister, for her dad and her grandparents. They had to stay out or she would die.

She piled the boxes neatly in a corner of the cave and covered them up with an old, dirty sheet. And there they would stay forever. Because now she had to be a grown-up — because she knew who would have to do the chores and help her dad. She closed her eyes, the blanket warm and soothing, shielding her from the boxes, and as she drifted into the merciful arms of sleep she said goodbye to her childhood.

''ere I am agen dad,' Alan laughed, his can waving unsteadily in the air. The grass was damp and his trousers were getting wet, but he didn't notice.

'What am I gunna do dad? I can't let t' bairns go into an 'ome, but 'ow can I look after 'em? Who'll look after 'em whilst I work?' He took a long, hard swig from the can and burped loudly.

'I suppose Lydia could if no-one knew. 'n' Bert or Alice 'll be there durin' school 'olidays. Could I really do this dad, keep me girls, keep 'em together 'n' safe? Well I can't do owt else 'cos I'm not gunna let 'em down. Please 'elp me though, won't ya, 'cos ya know I'm no good at this stuff? Dad, can y' 'ear me? Will you 'elp me?'

'Don't worry son, it'll all be alright, I promise.' A large, firm, reassuring hand fell firmly onto his shoulder. He turned to find Bert standing silently behind him, the promise of hope shining through his smile.

Chapter Twenty-One

Her nightmare always began as soon as she closed her eyes. It started when Alan threw her out with nowhere to go. She didn't dare go to her parents. They would hate her for what she had done, she was sure, even her dad couldn't forgive her this. So she had slept at the hospital with her son, not daring to leave him in case he was taken away too. He was all that she had left in the world.

She relived the day that she had taken Jack from the hospital alone, not knowing what to do, where to go. She had Sharif, though, didn't she? He had told her that he loved her. Perhaps he would take her in? Perhaps he would leave his wife and look after her and Jack? Yes, that's what she would do — she would go to Sharif, because Sharif loved her.

She sneaked into the club through the hidden staff door and quietly slid her way towards Sharif's office. She held Jack close — proud and eager for people to see her son, the son of Sharif — but the place was deserted at this time of day.

Without knocking she slowly opened the solid door of his office. She stood shock-still at what she saw in front of her. A pert, pink bottom was bobbing frantically upon the familiar brown lower limbs of a body impaled beneath it on the leather settee. She didn't need to see the face to know the man. The bobbing continued for a second longer until something distracted the woman who swung her head around. Dayna.

The couple hastily disentangled themselves and Dayna, grabbing her clothes, slunk into the bathroom beside the office. She smiled an apologetic smile over her shoulder.

'Rose, where've you been? I haven't seen you for weeks honey', his desire to avoid a scene evident.

'I can see you're distraught, Sharif.'

'Come on, Rose, you know how it is?'

'No, Sharif, I thought I did.' She sighed, no choice but to

continue. 'Look, Sharif, I came for ya to 'elp me. Alan kicked me out.'

Sharif didn't reply but stared quizzically at the boy holding her hand.

'Who is this?'

'I'd say that wer rather a dumb question wouldn't you? Look at 'im. 'e's your son.'

'You mean you've had my son all this time and never even bothered to tell me? I thought the child was Alan's. How could you do such a thing? How could you have a child, Rose? You knew the rules. No ties. No connections. I'm a respected married man, married to a rich woman. I cannot afford for there to be any scandals. You know that. You know the rules.'

He was becoming agitated, remembering how Dayna had treated Barney and the years that he suffered before his wife had forgiven him. Sharif didn't like complications.

'But you said ya loved me. I never expected owt till ya said ya loved me. Didn't ya mean it then?'

'We all say things we don't mean because we know that they are expected to be said.'

They remained trapped in a stare, in a moment, neither of them knowing what to say next. Sharif decided to take control.

'I suggest that you leave Rose. I can't let rumours get around about the child. No-one must see him.'

'But I've no-where to go. Won't you 'elp yer own son?'

'He is no son of mine. If Alan hadn't found out would you even have told me? I never asked for a son and you had no right to take one from me. Now please go Rose, and I think it best if you don't come here again. Ever. Goodbye.'

His final words obviously spoken, he turned his back to Rose, no longer able to look at her. She had no choice but to turn and leave.

'Goodbye, Sharif. 'n' just for t' record, I said I loved you 'cos I meant it, ya know. What a fool I wer to believe ya felt t' same.'

Sharif's dark features twisted into a frown of despair. She could never know how much he hurt, how this was tearing him apart. She would never know and would hate him forever for doing his duty to his family. He could never again tell her that he loved her — because he loved her in every way, in every part of his body, mind and soul. And he always would.

As Rose dragged herself away, a shout came from the dark, empty corridor behind her.

'Wait. Wait, Rose.' It was Dayna, Maddy, whatever her name was. Rose didn't care anymore.

'Listen Rose, I'm real sorry. But you didn't come back so I thought you'd left him. You know I wouldn't cheat on you. Please don't blame me.'

'Don't worry, Maddy. I don't. If 'adn't bin you it would've bin someone else, 'n' if 'e's gonna get laid 'e might as well 'ave t' best lay in t' place, don't ya think?' She smirked at her friend's mock horror and, despite the severity of the situation, they laughed together.

'I don't know what I'm laughin at. I've nowhere to go. Alan found out about Sharif 'n' 'e's kicked me out wi' Jack. 'e wouldn't let me tek t' girls. I'm in such a state, Maddy. I've nowhere to go.'

'I know a place, but it's a bit of a dump. It might just tide you over till you get yersen sorted though.'

And there the nightmare would end — or begin.

So Rose had taken up residence at Trilby Gardens. What a joke? Gardens? More like Dump City. She couldn't believe that she had been there a year, a year which had zoomed by in a blur of tranquilisers and alcohol, occasionally shattered with the demanding cries of a child seeking some seed of human tenderness and attention.

She had tried to get work, but she had no qualifications,

she who should have been in university couldn't even get a job as a cleaner! The only jobs paid so little that they weren't worth having by the time she would have paid for Jack to be cared for. She could easily have found work on the streets, but somehow she just couldn't do it. Maybe she did still have some pride, or maybe it was the memory of girls at the Jojoba Club, left unable to work from beatings and rapes, their faces haggard from years of self-persecution. It wasn't worth the risk, or more to the point the effort.

So she had joined the ranks of the permanently desperate in the dole queue. As she stood weekly in line in the dismal, smokey, overcrowded room she laughed inwardly at the irony of finding herself here. She had once derided these people, called them beggars, scroungers, no-hopers. Why couldn't they get a job like everyone else? Why did they stand like sheep, dirty and unkempt? Why didn't they have some self-respect? Why did they have children when they couldn't feed themselves? Well, now she was one of them.

She wondered what people saw when they looked at her now, standing in line with the sheep, her hair greasy, straggly and limp, the once voluptuous body now a shapeless frame hidden beneath a once-expensive, shabby dress, a snotty-nosed boy in worn-out denim trousers which were a year too small for him clinging to her leg? Where was her self-respect? It had tumbled away, like the petals of a rose, like so many bags of self-respect taken from this room, taken away by the twists and turns of life.

Nobody made eye contact, just stole glances, eager to find a face that they knew, eager to be able to say 'oh good it's not just me who ended up here'. It wasn't their fault. It wasn't her fault. It was life.

She collected her cheque and walked the short distance to her flat, her room, her hovel. The nightmare which she had expected to be realised in Woodville had finally come to life.

She and Jack existed in one room, overrun by damp, visited by cockroaches, thankfully not too often. She had tried to make it clean, make it better, but she never seemed to have enough energy. Her head hurt too much from the tablets to think about anything except sleeping so she stayed.

She knew that she had to take the tablets or she would die because her head would explode. They told her that the tablets would keep her stable. Stable? She wasn't sure about that but she couldn't think so that was good. She could survive not thinking. She didn't feel either, again the tablets and not a bad thing, but she wasn't sure that she had ever been able to feel. A vague niggle reminded her of someone who lived inside her soul but she couldn't find him anymore — or even remember properly.

She sat alone watching life go by on the black and white television in the corner. Madge, the woman next door, had given it to her when she had been given a colour set because she felt sorry for the boy, the boy who knew only life inside these grotty four walls, the child who knew life through small, moving people on a television screen, who never spoke because no-one spoke to him, who didn't know what it was to be hugged or feel love. Madge would listen on Friday nights as his sobs crept through the paper-thin walls as he cried himself to sleep alone, his mother to be found in the 'Dog and Gun.'

Rose always went to the pub on Friday night after she had cashed her giro, buying a bottle of whisky and a bar of chocolate for Jack on the way home. No-one could say that she didn't love her son, could they, or she wouldn't buy him chocolate would she? At eight o'clock she would put a drink of juice in Jack's cot, smile at him and leave the flat, leaving him to wonder why she left him alone and if she would be coming back.

She hadn't gone out much for the first six months —

depressed by the divorce which Alan had thrown at her, depressed at losing Sharif — but eventually she had decided that she deserved not to be lonely and so Friday night was the one thing in her life which she could bear. She had felt scared going into a pub alone at first — nice girls didn't do that — but she soon realised that nice girls didn't live around here and there were many lone females in the pub.

It hadn't been long before an attractive young man had offered to buy her a drink. She had gratefully accepted. Then she had accepted another and another. She didn't remember him coming home with her. She didn't understand what demon had possessed her to so totally disregard any morals which she once might have had — maybe that was the tablets? She didn't remember what they did. She didn't even know his name and he had left before daybreak. So much for company.

And so another step along the road to self–destruction had been trod. She soon became a Friday night regular, part of the gang who got their money and drank it away, drank away the misery. She had thought of asking for money from the random men who came back with her, but she was always too drunk to think to ask.

She hoped as she worked her way through the pile that she might meet a man who would want her for more than one night, but she was losing hope of ending her loneliness.

Chapter Twenty-Two

A blinding sliver of light sneaked through the gap in the curtains, stabbing at her eyelids. Her limbs hung, dead weights dragging her body deeper into the lumpy mass beneath her. She told her arm to lift but there was no response. Her body shivered as the swirling draughts floated across her skin, cold despite the sun outside, spider-like fingers creeping down her naked body.

Careful not to lift her head, she manoeuvred her slight frame underneath the covers, struggling to pull them around her as though they were stuck. The only reality was the thumping in her head, the result of the alcoholic cocktail which she had thrown down her neck the night before.

She couldn't remember anything following her tenth gin and tonic; everything was blurred — no, blank. She must go back to sleep before her head exploded. Just as she could feel the fluffy cloud beneath her carrying her off, a cry dragged her from it. A child's cry, demanding attention.

She must get up, she knew that, but she couldn't. The child would just have to cry until it stopped. It always did. She started her flight back to her cloud.

'Oy ya lazy cow,' came a raucous bellow accompanied by a thump from the other side of the cardboard wall, 'are ya gunna shut that kid up or what?'

The dulcet tones of Madge boomed, all thirty stone of her projecting the noise, and she knew that she would get no peace until she had dealt with Jack, or else Madge would add more thumping to the cacophony attacking her head.

'I'll stuff some cornflakes in front of 'im. That'll keep 'im quiet for a while, especially wi'out a spoon,' she told the wall. She only had to move, but still she couldn't.

'Yeah, you gunna shut the kid up or what, Rose?' slurred a voice beside her, a voice that she didn't recognise. Oh no, who the hell this time. Yet another kind, young gentleman who, out of the goodness of his heart, had bought her drinks and then, as if by some miracle, appeared the next morning in her bed.

She forced one eyelid to life and found that it was the same apparition that had appeared a few weeks ago. That was lucky! She had her reputation to think of after all, hadn't she?! With lead in her bones, she hoisted her slender frame sort of upright.

Unfamiliar clothes strewn on the floor glared accusingly of lust satisfied. She wished she could remember — it must have been exciting! She draped her now–too–thin legs over the edge of the bed, gripping her feet against the flea–ridden, dark–red rug which disguised the rough, dirty floorboards.

Her head hung limply, eyeing the sad apples which had replaced the ripe melons upon her chest. Her body told the tale of ravage over the last year; too much drinking, too many pills, not enough food.

Stand up, stand up, stand up. She gave the order and nothing happened. Her head swirled, her nose wrinkled as mould, sick and male sweat assailed it. Sick? Whose sick? Her eyes traced the source to the new pebble–dashing on the red rug. Who was crying? Then she remembered the baby who was no longer a baby but still slept in a cot.

Robotically she lifted one leg after the other — the focus of her concentration the avoidance of the rug — aiming for the oak chest of drawers with the wonky leg and the missing drawer. If she could just reach it she would be halfway there. The cries were more insistent, the thumping on the wall louder. The old bag had brought out the broomstick.

An age later, she reached the wooden bars which held her son. The cup of juice which she had left last night lay abandoned on the floor, its contents splattered. She was too tired to be angry, too tired to care.

The ramshackle cupboards held little. Rose threw a few mouthfuls of cornflakes into a bowl which had lain unwashed for a while. There was no milk. She placed the dish carefully inside the cot in front of Jack. Carefully. She didn't want to spill. She did care. She was good. She smiled weakly in his direction, avoiding the pleading in the dark, sad eyes which followed her movements. She grovelled her way back to the bed. One more thing to do before sleep.

'Time ya left don't ya think?'

No argument. He staggered around the room, collecting his clothes. She peeped from beneath the sheets. His long hair had seen cleaner days, but apart from his lack of personal hygiene he was quite attractive in a peasant sort of way, his sharp chin hidden under a ragged beard. The puny body was disappearing inside the baggy clothes.

'Oh shit!' His bare feet found the rug. Rose didn't care. By the time that the door banged shut she was swimming in a sea of slumber.

Rose lay staring at the ceiling, awake, her head slightly clearer. Jack had curled up beside her and gone to sleep.

The putrid smell of vomit stung the air. Rose staggered to the sash bay window and struggled to raise it further up. There was only a gentle movement of air as the outside swirled inside. It would have to do.

She stood over her son, taking in the life for which she was responsible. She kept forgetting to change his nappy and he must have pulled it off for his scrawny bottom, bright-red and blemished from the urine which clung to it, smiled at her. She should have potty-trained him by now, but she had forgotten how and didn't have the energy.

A trickle ran down her face at the guilt which was hers. What sort of a mother was she? How had she ended up like this? What had happened to the little girl, so loved by her parents, so well brought-up and respectable? Or the young woman who had so much to live for, to look forward to. The siren, who was so pretty and charming, so full of life and eager to grasp all that it had to offer.

Could this pathetic creature really be her? No, she had

died a long time ago, replaced by this monster who had taken her over.

As she smiled lovingly on her frail, tiny son, for the first time in her life she knew what she must do.

Chapter Twenty-Three

Rose stepped off of the bus onto familiar soil. The sweet pangs of homesickness yanked and twisted her heart, the pain physical.

In that brief moment, as she saw her house again, she realised the full enormity of what she had lost, what she had let slip through her fingers.

She tiptoed to the door of the house next to hers, checking that no-one was around to see her. She smiled lovingly at the sleeping child in her arms, struggling to decide if she could do this, if it was what she should do. But she knew that it was the only thing left to do. He was all that she had left in the world, and she couldn't even care for him properly. She didn't have the energy.

So she was doing the only thing that she could do to show her son how much she loved him. She was giving him a better future than she ever could, giving him a life worth living.

Nervously she tapped on the door, half-hoping that nobody would come, half-scared at what they would say if they did. She needn't have worried.

'Rosie love. Come in. It's so good to see ya. It's bin so long, a year almost isn't it? I wer so worried about you 'n' t' li'l one.' Mel thought that by the look of them both she had been right to worry. The woman before her was stick thin and the child no heavier than a feather.

Rose sat gratefully on the settee whilst Mel went to make the magic cup of tea.

'Nobody knew where you'd gone? Did ya find a place to stay?'

'Yeah but it's 'ardly t' Ritz. I've only got me dole money.'

'I could've found ya summat, love. There's alas summat.' Rose hadn't wanted 'summat'. She could have got that by herself.

'Mel, I've come for a reason. Is Alan in?'

'No love. Didn't you know 'e's....... no, 'e's out all day today.'

'Good. I don't want 'im to see me. You can see for yersen what state I'm in, don't pretend you can't. alf o' t' time I'm drugged up, 'alf o' t' time I'm drunk. I've no money 'n' I can't even feed mysen, never mind Jack. 'e gets left alone when I don't know what I'm doin' 'n' 'e can't even talk prop'ly yet. What I'm tryin' to say is that 'e's better off wi'out me.'

Mel started to say something but Rose stopped her.

'No, don't. No discussion. I've thought about nowt else 'n' I'm too tired to think any more. Jack's all I've got left in t' world, but I'm just no good for 'im. You know that Mel. I never 'ave bin any good for 'im. I suppose I've always resented 'im for bein' Sharif's 'cos I knew Sharif would never want 'im, 'n' every time I look at 'im it reminds me I can't 'ave Sharif, just like I resented Lydia for bein' born 'n' ruinin' me life. I'm just not meant to be a mother, that's all. Look at you. You're so good at it. I'm not.

So listen, will you give 'im to Alan for me? I can't bear to give 'im to some stranger, to t' Social. 'e'll 'ave to struggle all 'is life if I do that, but I know Alan loves 'im 'n' at least this way I'm givin' 'im a chance. If Alan doesn't want to keep 'im then that's 'is decision. 'e must do what 'e thinks is best. Please will ya do it? You don't know what could 'appen to 'im if I tek 'im, 'onest ya don't. I'm scared for 'im. Please don't mek me tek 'im. I'm not right in t' 'ead most o' t' time, ya know that.'

Tears ran unchecked down Rose's ghostly face, her emotions straining to be free as she clung to her child. She muttered over and over again into his tiny head that she loved him, she loved him, and that was why she must leave him. Then, as if the feel of him burnt her body, she thrust him into Mel's arms and turned towards the door.

'I 'ave to go quick Mel afore I change me mind. Thank you. Thank you so much. You're a good woman.'

She surged towards Jack, took his delicate face in both of her hands and sealed a kiss on his mouth, a mother's kiss which would have to last a lifetime.

'Please forgive me. Please don't 'ate me.' The only reply was a pair of sad, tired, black eyes.

And then Rose was gone, leaving her son to the mercy of an unknown destiny.

As Rose opened the door to her shabby room, she smiled the smile of the beaten, the smile that meant that she need fight no more. She reached for the bottle of whisky from the cupboard with no door and grabbed the bottle of white tablets from the floor. Déjà-vu.

There had been another night, so long ago, when she had a hand full of white tablets, when she laid on her bed and prayed for them to give her back her life.

How different would her life have been if they had worked? If just that one moment in time was changed. Would she still have instilled such pain and torment on her own children had her life taken another road? Would she still have become a heartless, selfish bitch had she been allowed to have a life of her own, one which she had planned, one which she could have worked for? Might she have been able to love Alan, who deserved so much more, if she hadn't been forced to marry him? Might she have loved him as she had loved Sharif, as she still loved Sharif.

Well, she would never know and she no longer cared. Fate, God, whatever you wanted to call it, had had its last laugh at her expense. The fight was over.

She opened the bottle of whisky, opened the bottle of tablets. As she finally lost consciousness, both bottles lay empty beside the once-vibrant, once-beautiful woman with a smile on her face at last.

Chapter Twenty-Four

'How do you plead, guilty or not guilty?'

'Your Honour, she pleads not guilty on the grounds of diminished responsibility.'

Rose frowned in bewilderment. She turned her head to see the people sat in rows, all staring at her, all staring as though they wanted to kill her. Why was she awake? Shouldn't she be dead? Obviously history had repeated itself and the pills hadn't worked again. But why was she in jail — she hadn't done anything? Was it a crime to kill yourself? She didn't think it was.

Rose decided to just sit there and wait for someone to tell her what to do. She would think about all this later when she could think. What on earth were they going on about, pointing at her? Why was Madge here and the guy with the beard? As she struggled to turn towards the angry pack, she made out the face of her father. She smiled, but he was part of the pack.

Oh my God what was that? Why would anyone want to see that — was the judge mad? The child in the photograph looked as though he had been in a car crash. His tiny leg was bent in a way that wasn't physically possible, his hands were clamped tightly together, but he was red — all that you could see was red. She must be hallucinating, because the photograph showed a tiny boy, bleeding and battered, but he looked just like Jack.

It couldn't be Jack. She knew that it couldn't be her child because her child was safe at Mel's. She had taken him, freed him, saved him.

She turned again to the crowd and felt, rather than saw,

Alan's frozen glare. As she tried to understand, unable to look away, the frozen glare gave her a key for a box. She didn't want to take it but the frozen glare insisted.

She put the key in the box and slowly it turned in the lock. She lifted the lid.

She was on the bus with Jack beside her. She felt calm because she knew that she was doing something good. She smiled down at him, and he smiled back. They were looking out of the bus window as they went down Manor Row. There was a wedding, a woman all in white and a groom. There was a groom. There was a groom.

The cold hand of fear crept up her back as the panic of confusion smothered her. She tried to put the lid back on the box, but it would no longer fit.

She remembered dragging Jack from the bus. Yes, she remembered that. Jack had noticed first because the bus had stopped outside the registry office — the registry office on Manor Row — and he pointed shouting 'daddy, daddy'.

She must have caught a bus back to Trilby Gardens because she was home, like Alice through the looking-glass.

She downed the whisky, each burning mouthful fuelling her anger. She wanted to stop the anger, stop the demon, but she needed the whisky. She wanted to kill the monster before it could escape.

'Daddy, daddy?'

These were the last words spoken by the beautiful being that was Jack, for the demon which had stolen his mother took him from this world.

Madge heard his screams and battered down the door, but not before the screams had stopped.

Something which was once a child lay jumbled and red on the floor.

Rose dragged herself up on the bed where she had fallen, unconscious, aroused by the noise, the empty bottle of tablets falling from her hand. Madge punched her in the face, the pent-up anger and frustrations of so long listening and not being able to do anything at last released.

Madge frantically tried to save the boy, to breathe new life into him, but it was too late. She held him in her arms, tears washing the blood away from his peaceful face, and she knew that he was better where he was — he was safe now.

The End